# Finding Forever

## Pacific Coast Romance, Book 2

•♥•♥•♥•♥•♥•

Kate Pelczar

Finding Forever (Pacific Coast Romance, Book 2)

Copyright © 2024 by Kate Pelczar

All rights reserved.

No part of this publication may be reproduced, distributed, or transmitted in any form or by any means, including photocopying, recording, or other electronic or mechanical methods, without the prior written permission of the publisher except for the use of brief quotations in a book review.

This book is a work of fiction. Any references to historical events, real people, or real places are used fictitiously. Other names, characters, place, and events are products of the author's imagination, and any resemblance to actual events or places or persons living or dead is entirely coincidental.

Published by Pelczar Publications, LLC

Edited by Nancy Sieck

Cover Designed by Shey Kolee

ISBN 979-8-9899662-1-9

*To Mike, the pirate to my poppet.*

Finding Forever *contains themes of explicit sex, sexual assault (historical, off-page), and mental health (PTSD, depression).*

·♥·♥·♥·♥·♥·

*Dear friends and family, at this point I'd ask that we don't discuss any of those scenes, but... how well did that work with book 1?*

# Contents

1. Summer Break — 1
2. Catching Up — 9
3. Beaches and Bonfires — 23
4. Failing at Being an Adult — 43
5. Trees and Snowpiles — 55
6. Hotel Hot Tubs — 71
7. Maple Drive Apartments — 83
8. Graduation — 97
9. Final Goodbyes — 119
10. We're Off! — 135
11. Our. Own. Apartment! — 147
12. Missing Furniture — 161
13. Actually Adulting — 169
14. A Cure for Loneliness — 181
15. Toph — 191
16. Friendships and Expectations — 197
17. Lying to Yourself — 207

| | | |
|---|---|---|
| 18. | Haunting Wakefullness | 215 |
| 19. | Heavy Breathing | 221 |
| 20. | Strawberry Lemonade and Burgers | 233 |
| 21. | Selective Amnesia | 245 |
| 22. | Road Trip | 253 |
| 23. | Finding Forever | 267 |
| Author's Note | | 279 |
| Acknowledgements | | 281 |
| About the Author | | 283 |

# One

# Summer Break

"Ow! What did you do that for?" Will shrieks into the cold morning air.

I look up with a fiendish grin from behind his ass. "Whatever do you mean, babe?" I ask in my best southern belle falsetto.

He twists to face me and raises his eyebrow demanding an answer. I don't relent in my mischievous ways. I settle on the bed and scooch slowly back from the monster I've awakened until I'm scrunched up against the headboard with nowhere left to flee.

Will stalks my path across the bed on all fours. As he reaches me he pins me between his strong arms and demands, "Veronica Welch, did you just bite my ass?"

I bite my lip and shake my head. "Me? I would never! Not to you," I taunt him.

Will leans in and takes my breath away with a kiss. His corded arms pull me closer and my body moulds to his. His hands roam my sides as his lips nip and pull at my own. I wrap my arms around his neck and deepen our kiss.

Will only entertains me topping from the bottom for a few seconds before taking this scene into his own hands.

He flips me over and presses me into the bed. I can feel the evidence of his desire pushing against my ass cheek. *How does he not hurt himself doing that?* He's so hard it feels like he's stabbing me with it. As I'm about to protest he angle his cock differently when he starts biting at my neck. It's light enough not to bruise but hard enough to have my toes curling.

I moan into the pillow beneath me and wriggle my ass against his erection, begging him to hurry his foreplay up but enjoying his teasing tactics.

Will chuckles in my ear and blows a soft, warm breath into it. That has me losing all control and he knows it.

I move to wriggle underneath him and take back some of the power but before I can get my arms braced to aid in the position shift, Will grabs my wrists and pins them above my head. He's only using one hand! Will's domineering strength only arouses me further as his other hand snakes its way down my side and dips below my underwear.

He lifts off of my back and uses his hand placement to pull me up into a kneeling position while keeping my hands pinned and useless.

"If I let go, will you behave?" His husky voice whispers into my ear.

I moan out, "Yes." Waiting to see what he'll do next.

His hands work together to lazily pull my underwear down my thighs. He leaves them bunched at my knees and rests a hand on my now bare ass, giving it a light squeeze. The sheets have been pushed off us and in the chill of the cold cabin air, my skin starts to prickle.

Will tsks at me. "This won't do. This absolutely will not do."

I move to twist and see what he's looking at but he stops me with a verbal reprimand. "That's not behaving Nikki."

I let out a frustrated whimper and wait impatiently for him to decide he's ready to continue.

After an agonizing few seconds of feeling my heartbeat below my waistline, he starts moving again. His hand snakes under my stomach and slithers up between my breasts wrapping firmly around my neck.

He squeezes lightly reducing blood flow but not cutting off any oxygen.

His free hand slides across the curve of my ass and slips to the apex of my thighs. He dips one finger into my core followed immediately by a second, just the way he knows I like it. I moan into the hold he has around my neck.

With a heavy breath he asks, "You like that Nikki?" against the shell of my ear.

All coherent thoughts have left my mind. The only response I can come up with is a nod of my head.

He chuckles and continues to play with me.

I pant into the pillows below me as I grow ever closer to my release. Will's learned to play my body like it's his favorite musical instrument. I bite my lip as his thumb finds my clit. He rubs it so perfectly. His deft fingers remind me why he's first chair in my own personal symphony.

I moan a warning, "I'm going to..."

Will pulls his hand away from my body.

"What?" I demand of him in anger, "I was so fucking close!"

He doesn't deign to respond. Instead, he removes his hand from my neck, slaps my ass with a ferocity that feels like revenge, but only excites me more, and kneels behind me.

I'm about to yell at him again when I feel his tip slide through my juices.

I whimper in anticipation of what I know comes next.

Will notches his dick at my entrance and buries himself inside me with one quick thrust. We both moan into the cold morning air.

"Fuck Nikki, you feel so amazing!" He growls before biting my shoulder blade.

I arch beneath him and the change has him hitting the perfect spot inside me. I let out an appreciative groan and push my hips back, begging him to fuck me.

Will starts slowly. His hips rocking back and forth rhythmically behind me.

I drop my hand from above my head and move it toward my clit. I just need a little more friction. Before I can make contact, Will swats me away and takes control. His hand cups me as he continues thrusting from behind. His fingertips curl just the way I like around my waist, and I have to grip the bed sheets to keep from slamming into the headboard in front of me. One of his hands moves to circle my clit and I mewl pathetically.

His dick fills me so perfectly. I basque in his ministrations and let my instincts take over. My hips rock back into his and together we near our crescendo.

I know Will is getting closer because his thrusts are growing harder for me to brace against. I relish how his arms cord around my body. One hand grips the back of my neck, helping to keep me in place. With the other, his fingers push down on my clit.

"Yes, Will! Right there!" I cry in encouragement right before his talented fingers cause stars to fly across my eyes.

He prolongs my orgasm as he keeps pounding into me. Every push of his dick causes sparks of ecstasy to spread throughout my body. His hands move to my hips and they hold me just right for him to find his release. Will roars into the cabin as he spills deep inside me.

He calms behind me and slowly withdraws.

I feel our combined juices spill out and grin at the proof of our fun spreading across my inner thighs.

Will pushes to my side and lays down on the bed.

I roll over and rest my head on Will's chest. He's breathing as heavily as I am. I enjoy his warmth as I look around our home-away-from-home for the weekend. Nana lets anyone in the family use her cabin whenever we want. It's about a two-hour drive from San Diego and the perfect end-of-summer break getaway.

I feel Will's breath start to even out beneath me but I don't want either of us to move. Being wrapped up in his arms, buried under multiple comforters, in the crisp morning air is replenishing my soul by the second. We left the windows open last night and now there's a soft breeze blowing through them. Now that our breathing has calmed, I can hear the chirping of birds in the distance mingling with the rhythmic beating of Will's heart. I wish we could stay like this forever.

Will squeezes me lightly. I've come to learn that this means he wants to move when I'm draped across him like this. I whine in protest, "No."

He chuckles softly and kisses my hair. He doesn't say anything and lets me have a few more moments enjoying this calm before our day begins and we head back down the mountain to reality.

Unfortunately, my relaxed mind has officially been awoken. Somehow his hug has started my mind racing about all the things we need to get done before classes begin next week. I start my mental checklist of what we need to do before we leave: take all the trash down the hill with us, wash all the linens, pick up any crumbs on the counters, wash dishes, write in the guest book, remake—

"Will you stop stressing babe?"

Will's question interrupts the creation of my to-do list. "Stop what?"

He gently pushes me off of his chest and rolls us so we're lying facing one another on our sides. Will kisses my nose, "You stopped relaxing and your brain started thinking too hard."

I push out my bottom lip in a pouty face. "You can't know that."

With another kiss to my nose, Will rolls over to get out of bed. "Stay here, relax. That means no thinking," He chastises as he pulls on his discarded pair of boxers. "I'll make us some breakfast." He walks past the foot of the bed and I enjoy my view of this beautiful shirtless man until he disappears through the bedroom door. I hear the patter of his feet across the wooden floor of the cabin and try my best to snuggle deeper under the covers and try this mysterious *relaxing* Will spoke of.

I close my eyes and imagine what he looks like in the kitchen. Nana's cabin is open concept. The kitchen cupboards are a little lighter wood stain than the boards that comprise the walls. The kitchen has a giant window facing the forest beyond. I imagine Will standing there, still only dressed in boxers, sipping his cup of coffee and watching a squirrel scurrying past. That visual is so picturesque it's something I'd rather experience than lie here imagining.

I let out a small groan as I commit to getting out of this cozy bed. Once I whisk the bedding away I immediately regret it. The cabin is so cold I have no idea how Will is walking around casually, clad in only his boxers. I pull on my underwear and find my pajamas set in a heap across the room. I finish off the look with a pair of fuzzy slippers and a messy bun that holds back my reckless red waves.

I open the bedroom door and approach Will on silent feet. I look around the cabin, assessing what chores need to be done before we leave. Two recliners are bracketing a wooden ladder that leads to the loft overlooking the living space. Will stands beyond them in the kitchen area. It's a modest space with a full fridge, sink, stove, and barely enough counter space to prep a meal. To my disappointment, Will has more clothes on than when he left the bedroom.

"Where did those come from?" I ask him as I wrap my arms around his waist from behind.

Will rubs my forearms with his calloused hands as he replies, "It's way too cold in here for only boxers. Once I put the coffee on I grabbed my clothes out of my suitcase." He twists his arms toward me and pulls me around to his front for a proper hug. We stand in the kitchen wrapped in each other's embrace for a few minutes.

I listen to the bacon sizzling and savor how peaceful it is up here with him. I pull back, tilt my chin up so I can look him in the eyes, and ask Will out of the blue. "Do you think this is what the Gods feel like on Mount Olympus?"

He looks down at me and his lips crinkle into a half smile as he replies, "What?"

I return his earnest interest in my random thought with a full smile. "It's so calm and secluded up here. All we have to worry about is what we're going to eat, and whether or not we should have sex again. The stresses of the real world are so far removed. Do you think that's how the Gods at Mount Olympus feel?"

Will separates us and gets a cup from the cabinet. He pours my coffee as he replies. "I can't say I've ever thought about that before, Nikki."

I take the drink he offers and slurp a delicious sip. There's nothing like a fresh cup of coffee with a view. I internally chuckle at that. I can't decide if the better view is the man cooking in front of me or the forest beyond the window of this kitchen. "Well, regardless of Mount Olympus' feelings, we've got to reset the cabin before we head back. How long until breakfast is finished?"

Will evaluates the state of the bacon and says, "Eggs and toast should probably be done in about 20 minutes."

"Okay, I'll get dressed and start the wash then." I perch on my tip toes and give him a peck. I love how such a simple task, tidying the cabin, feels so right with this man. Like something I could see us doing together for the rest of our lives.

# Two

# *Catching Up*

THE NEXT DAY I lay on the beach listening to the surf crash into the shore in soothing swells. It's a sound that I could hear for the rest of my life and never tire of. Seagulls flying by give the occasional squawk, reminding me that we're not entirely safe from their target practice. I dig my toes into the sand at the foot of my towel. Today is the perfect combination of sunny with enough breeze that it's not stiflingly hot like it is further inland. Combine that with high tide happening before noon today and it's the perfect setup for a relaxing time at the beach.

Tipp's dark brown hair won't cooperate with the wind at the beach. It keeps escaping from her ponytail and I silently wonder how long until she'll submit to its wild nature. It is her hair, after all; makes sense that it's as untamable and free as she is.

Tipp and I lay out sunbathing and reading. Well, that was our plan when we decided to join in the boys' beach fun. I was going to sink my teeth into the next book in Kathy Haan's *Bedlam Moon* series, but Tipp's presence has been distracting me from that goal. I haven't even managed to pull my book from my bag yet.

She finally gives up on taming her hair as she asks, "Okay other than the mind-blowing sex, how has the summer been for you?"

I scoff. "I didn't tell you any details about our sex life thank you very much."

Tipp gives me a knowing grin and jabs back. "If the sex wasn't at least satisfactory, you'd be complaining to me about it. That smile plastered on your face? Tells me it was better than baseline."

I bite my lip thinking about Will and our weekend at the cabin. Tipp's not wrong, the sex is sensational. Those days contained many, many, orgasms. For both of us. Instead of granting Tipp an answer about the details of my sex life, I look out to the coast and find where Stefan and Will have drifted to. The current has been steadily pulling them further and further to the right as I look out over the water. The sunlight glinting off the ocean makes it hard to recognize the dots floating on the horizon but I think I spot the guys. Will's white rash guard makes him easier to see than Stefan's more sensible dark blue wet suit.

Tipp interrupts my spectating by declaring, "You don't have to fear that you're making me jealous."

Her words puzzle me. "What is that supposed to mean?" I ask as I tear my attention from the surf and look her in the eyes.

Tipp lowers her oversized sunglasses and pulls her phone out of her bag. Her white bikini is covered in watermelons. Its reflection in the bright sunlight makes it impossible to see what she's doing on her phone. I watch her motions enough to piece together that she's unlocking the screen and scrolling through something on the phone. She turns the phone toward me and I lean in. On it, I see a picture of a man I've never met before.

"His name is Ryan," Tipp says as she scrolls through various images of him, "He's cuter in person."

He's not the type I thought she'd go for but maybe that's a good thing. He's only an inch or two taller than her, thickly built, with dark brown hair shaved so close it looks like he's at boot camp. "Going for tallish, dark, and handsome then?" I tease her.

Tipp elbows me in the ribs before standing up for him. "He may be under six foot, but his presence is so dominating I forget that every time I'm near him." I watch her literally swoon thinking about this Ryan. Tipp has never swooned over a male before in her life!

I move to place a hand on her forehead before noticing it's covered in sand. I wipe it on the edge of my towel and finally perform my theatrics. As the back of my hand rests and meets her forehead Tipp glares up at me. "What are you doing?"

"Just checking to make sure that you're not feverish."

"Oh, you bitch!" Tipp scolds me. "I'm allowed to kinda like a guy, maybe."

I narrow my eyes at her. They're covered by my sunglasses but I think Tipp will get the message.

Her phone screen blacks out and I hear the telltale click of it locking down. Tipp gently places her phone into her bag before saying anything else. She takes a breath and pivots her whole body so our shoulders are squarely facing each other. "We met at that bar where I love to go dancing."

I nod my head, afraid that if I speak I'll frighten her out of telling me any more.

"It was nothing at first. Light flirting, 'let me buy you a drink' bullshit. Then he took me onto the dance floor. Nikki I..."

Her hesitation has my brows draw together with concern. What the fuck did he do to my best friend?

"I've never felt that way when I danced with someone before. He is a literal God on the dance floor. Night one he had me doing flips and spins that I've only dreamt about before."

I'm giving her a full-blown grin now. My bestie is in like with a guy! My body feels like it's vibrating with joy for her, but if I show it she might startle like a deer in headlights.

Tipp's shoulders rise and fall with a deep inhale. "We've been exclusive since June."

I can't hold back my commentary any longer. "What! You've been dating this guy since June and I'm just learning about him now!"

Tipp uncharacteristically tucks some free flying hair behind her ear as she looks anywhere except at me.

I don't let her off the hook that easily. "You do know it's the end of August now right?"

She whips her head back to me. "Of course, I know what month it is. You were busy galavanting into the sunset with Will all summer long. I was waiting to tell you when it was just the two of us."

I purse my lips together. "Oh."

"Yeah, so don't get on me about this."

I hold my hands up accepting my partial responsibility for this lapse in communication. I reach out and grab her hands in mine. "Hey, I'm glad you've found someone who whisks you off your feet. But there has to be more to him than his incredible dance moves. What else drew you to him?"

Tipp's shoulders roll back and her face morphs back into that confident, kick-ass woman I'm more accustomed to. "Well, he's originally from Texas and is stationed out here."

My mind does a fist pump. Fucking called it that he looked military. "So," I draw out. "A military man?" I lick my top row of teeth as I bait her.

Tipp's cheeks flush bright pink.

"Okay, dancer, military, what else does Superman do?"

She pulls her hands out of my grasp and pops her knuckles. The action builds my suspense for whatever is about to come. She quickly mumbles, "He rides a motorcycle."

The words leave her mouth so fast it takes me a minute to process them. I dip my chin and swivel my neck as I look back at her, purely for dramatic effect. "Tristan Powell, you mean to tell me you found a cowboy, who can dance, that's also in the military, AND rides a bike? You're not late are you?"

Her eyes bug out. "What?"

I shake my head. "You know, immaculate conception upon all those details wrapped up in one man for you?"

"Bitch," she laughs as she smacks my bicep. "That is why I have an IUD and you know it."

"All I'm saying is don't let Booktok know."

She gives me a conspiratorial grin. "Oh I know, I can't even take him out in public. We—"

"Someone you can't take in public? You're not talking about me, are you Tipp?" Stefan interrupts.

We both whip our heads up and see the guys a few steps away. The saltwater glistening on their skin gives them a faint glow in the sunlight. I smile at Will as our eyes meet.

"For once no. You're not the man I'm obsessing over, oh glorious Stefan." Tipp jibes with a saccharine smile.

Stefan clutches at his heart, pretending to be hit by an arrow. He pants out, "My heart, it can't take..." and falls into the sand at his feet in a mock death.

Will leaves his surfboard impaled in the sand behind Tipp and walks around our towels until he's behind me. He leans down and kisses me on the head, he's still sopping wet. Droplets of salt water pepper my skin and hair with his movements. He stands again and looks at Tipp. "Good to see you Tipp," he greets. "Having fun catching up?"

I watch the claws Tipp uses to interact with Stefan slide into their metaphorical sheath as she turns her attention to Will. "Of course, you took my girl away for too much fun this summer."

Stefan has miraculously recovered from his previously fatal wound and is kicking up sand as he closes the distance between their boards and our towels. "Nice melons Tipp," Stefan says, reintegrating himself into our conversation.

Will and I freeze.

Will finds his voice first, "Dude what the fu—"

"Thanks. I like how small they are, makes me feel even cuter." Tipp offers to Stefan sweetly.

My mouth drops open. Stefan just commented on Tipp's boobs and she's fine with it? Okay, one of the guys' surfboards must have hit me and given me a concussion or something. I'm in an alternate universe where this is somehow okay, right?

Tipp turns her gaze back to Will and me. She must register the shock on our faces because she breaks into a laugh.

Stefan follows suit. Then he clarifies, "Her swimsuit, it's covered in melons? Get your heads out of the gutter you two."

I let out a sigh of relief and see Will shake his head. I never know what is going to come out of Stefan's mouth. One of these days Tipp's going to beat the shit out of him!

"Shall we?" I ask the collective group. Everyone nods or murmurs their assent and we start packing up the towels. Stefan and Will put all of their valuables in my bag for safekeeping while they surfed. It's bulging with the weight of their keys, wallets, and phones but I shoulder it and move to pick up my towel. As Tipp and I grab our stuff, the boys start a show all their own.

Stefan always wears a wetsuit surfing which means once he's out of the waves the show gets a little less exciting. His over six-foot frame is squeezed into a skin-tight suit that's designed to suction and contour his body. I watched the spectacle of Stefan undressing the first time I came to the beach with the guys and vowed never again. I can still hear the squelching of the wetsuit as it protested its separation from his flesh. His facial expressions were even worse as he had to fight the suctioning power that had adhered the suit to his skin and try not to rip out all of his body hair at the same time.

No, Will is a much better source of entertainment. In the summer months, he wears his board shorts and a rash guard surfing. The duo works very nicely together on his frame. I unashamedly watch as he strips off the long-sleeved white rash guard to reveal his sculpted torso. His abs are revealed first as he moves to pull it over his head, followed by his pecks and broad shoulders. Last, his defined arms are revealed. Will's muscled arms always reduce me to a simpering puddle. When you add his summer tan, and his skin glistening from the sun, I lose control of my face. I stare at my man as he shakes out his salt water wavy hair and I may have let out an audible appreciation of the sight.

I feel a finger beneath my chin lightly exerting pressure to push my mouth closed. Only then do I realize that Stefan and Tipp are watching me as I stare hungrily at Will.

"Hey Tipp, think I can get a ride back into town with you?" Stefan asks. "I don't think Nikki's gonna be able to wait to jump Will's bones until after I'm gone."

Tipp chuckles, "While you're probably right, I can't. I'm meeting up with a friend at Coronado."

"What friend? We're your only friends." Stefan challenges her.

Tipp rolls her eyes at him. "I do know more people than the three of you."

"Oh yeah, name ten other..." I hear Stefan begin to argue with Tipp just as I notice Will's eyes zero in on me.

I feel his gaze start at my face and slowly, appraisingly, he takes in my body in my suit. I've never been comfortable showing off my stomach in a two-piece swimsuit. Luckily for me, size inclusivity has become a thing in the last few years, and clothing companies actually make cute one-piece suits now. I notice Will's eyes pause a little longer at my chest and silently thank the designers of my pink, purple, and blue suit for remembering that a lot of curvy women are well-endowed. The girls are definitely on display in this suit, but I think Will is actively appreciating that.

He shakes his head before continuing to peruse the rest of my body, then looks away from me to interject in Tipp and Stefan's conversation, "Now that she's proven you wrong let's get to the showers man."

"At least one of them has a brain," I hear Tipp murmur as the boys go get their boards.

I quietly laugh at her sentiment as we turn and lead the trek through the sand to the showers. Once we get there I realize I have two options. I can ogle Will as he showers off in public, and deeply regret carpooling with Stefan today. Or, I can force myself to turn around and avoid being horny and unsatisfied for at least eight more hours. Stefan leans his board against a bench and starts peeling his bottom half out of the rest of his wet suit. Fate must have been listening in because that sight immediately sobers up my sex-crazed mind.

"Can you watch our stuff while I wash off my feet?" I ask Will.

Still holding his board he smiles down at me, "Of course, I'll find your shoes."

The showers are surprisingly empty for it being a weekend. I don't have to wait any time to step up and use the lowest button to wash off my feet. The water shooting out shocks my system with how harsh it is pelting against my skin. I know the force is necessary to dislodge any dried-on sand, but damn that's aggressive. Once I'm satisfied with the cleanliness of my feet, I tip-toe back to where our group stands in various states of undress.

I approach my friends with a smile. Tipp is pulling on her jean shorts over her bikini bottoms, Stefan is finally free of his wet suit revealing a Speedo, and Will is clad only in his board shorts. He offers a seat for me on the bench. With a glance, I notice he's laid out my shoes on the ground before it. "Thanks," I say as I accept Will's silent offering.

He kisses my head once I'm seated and we trade places. He takes his board with him and I work extra hard with the proffered towel to get every piece of sand out from between my toes before sliding into my sandals. Watching Will take off that rash guard was enough foreplay. I do not need to watch him shower.

I've run out of distractions... I try to sneak a peek. I twist my neck slightly toward the showers, and the decision is made for me. Instead of glimpsing Will rinsing off, I see Tipp crossing her arms and staring down at me accusingly.

"You horny bitch."

I swallow, having obviously been caught trying to drool over my man again. "I have no idea what you're talking about," I innocently reply.

She rolls her eyes at me. "Do I need to stay and chaperone or will the sight of Stefan's one-man show be enough to dull your appetite?" She steps to the right and I can see him making a ridiculous scene in the shower. His hands are running through his hair, which is too short to need that much effort, and his hips are dancing unnecessarily to the tune of the music playing inside his mind. My nose wrinkles as I watch Stefan be his ridiculous self and turn my attention back to Tipp.

"Nope, that did it."

She picks up her bag and puts her phone in her shorts pocket. "Okay, I gotta go then. Just try to keep it in your pants until Stefan is gone alright?"

My lips pull into a smile. "But only until he's gone. Then, no promises." I stand and pull her in for a hug. "Tell Ryan I say hi. I want to meet him soon okay?" I whisper in her ear.

Tipp breaks our hug and gives me a shy smile. The movement is so out of place on her usually confident face. "Will do." She says as she heads out. I see her give a wave to Will and Stefan as they come back my way. While my mood has simmered, I can still appreciate the sight of two sculpted men walking my way, speckled in shower spray and carrying their surfboards. I suddenly get the appeal of *Baywatch*, even if it was technically before my time.

The guys slide into their flip-flops and we head to Stefan's truck. It's a mini truck from the nineties, but it gets the job done. They slide their boards carefully into the bed and finish their changing. Both of them wrap their towels tightly around their waists and begin the awkward surfer's scramble of pulling off their wet bottoms. Stefan appears to have an easier time of this since all he is wearing is a skimpy Speedo. Will has to lean against the side of the truck to make sure he doesn't fall as he shimmies out of his trunks. I stand a ways back and watch the two of them. Both of their sopping bottoms hit the pavement with a wet smack. It's then that I realize I'm standing there with two men who are naked beneath towels that are barely clinging on. I turn from Stefan and grab Will's suit from the ground as he reaches for the dry boxers he'd draped across the side of the truck bed. With my eyes focused on folding Will's trunks, I let the guys finish dressing in peace. This also ensures I won't get an eyeful of Stefan's junk. I wouldn't mind so much if that happened while I was watching Will.

When Will's trunks are folded, I place them below the surfboards and hop onto the tailgate. I stare over the rows of cars in the parking lot and watch the surf break along the shore. I hear a towel slap onto the side of the bed, signifying Stefan is now publicly decent. Shortly after the same sound comes from Will's side of the truck. I watch some girls walk by in the lot and notice that their eyes linger on the guys. A smug sense of satisfaction settles in me knowing that one of these gorgeous men is mine, and the other is basically his brother. I'd be jealous of me too.

Will comes around the truck and spreads my thighs so he can settle face-to-face between them. The truck is small enough that Will is still taller than me as I sit here. He leans in and gives me a tight squeeze. We stay there for a few moments, wrapped up in each other. I savor the warmth of his skin and the salty smell of his hair in the light coastal breeze.

Stefan's voice startles me from Will's cuddles. "Ready to get some lunch?"

Will pulls back to answer but keeps his hands on my hips. "I'm starved, where ya thinking?"

"No clue, any preferences Nikki?"

I tilt my head to the side and pucker my lips. My mind wanders through the choices, in Southern California the options truly are endless. My tongue tastes all the options as they flicker through my brain but it settles on my favorite. "Mexican, please."

Stefan claps his hands together once as a grin spreads across his face. "Perfect! There's this new taco shop that opened up in Santee that I'm dying to try."

"Let's do it," Will confirms as he picks me up and places me on my feet. I watch them both strap down the boards and throw their other items into a bag in the bed of the truck. When the tailgate snaps up we all head for the cab.

This is the tricky part of going surfing with them. I look in the cab and remember how cramped the drive to the coast was—forty minutes stuck on a bench seat tucked between two huge men. At five foot seven, I'm not exactly small either, but when compared to these two I guess I am. I open the passenger door and hesitate.

Will's arm wraps around my waist as he asks, "What's up, babe?"

I let out a heavy sigh and admit, "I know it's not intentional, but every time Stefan shifts the gears he grazes my ass with his arm. Just not looking forward to another half hour of that. Well, longer because we're going to stop for food."

Will says nothing as he kisses my cheek and moves from behind me into the truck. "Okay, he can fondle my ass this time."

I start laughing, "What?"

He slides across the bench seat and plants his ass firmly in the middle. Rather his hip is bunched up against Stefan's and they've left about six inches for me to squeeze into, but his ass will indeed be the one in the way of the gear shift this time. Will pats the open space to his right, come on in.

I shake my head as I clamber into the cab. I close the door and the three of us sit in silence. "You going to turn her on?" I ask Stefan.

"I can't."

"What?" Will asks.

"Yeah, your giant body is in the way of everything. I have to have more room if we're going to drive back to my house safely."

I let out a resigned sigh knowing I'm going to need to change seats with Will. "It's fine, we can switch. I'm bendier than you are."

"No." Will challenges. "You may be bendy in all the right places," he gives me a wink, "but we can figure this out. Stefan's ass fondling needs to be spread equally among friends."

Before I can deign a response, a humongous hairy leg is shoved into my face. I pull back in shock. "What are you doing?"

Will inserts his foot between my thighs and slithers it down so he's the one draped across my lap. Then he leans into Stefan and does the same with his other leg. My boyfriend drapes an arm around my headrest and for a man that has over six inches on me, he has also managed to drape himself into my lap.

"Satisfied?" He asks Stefan.

"Absolutely." He replies as he turns the truck over.

That's how we ride down the I-5 back to town; Stefan making conversation about various work and summer antics, and my giant boyfriend cuddled into my lap. I think he was a fan of this new seating arrangement from the way he kept nuzzling into my neck and hugging me close. It definitely beat the drive to the beach when Will and my positions were opposite.

We pull up to the taco shop soon enough. Stefan, Will, and I enjoy our meal in good company and travel back to Stefan's house without delay. When we arrive, Stefan immediately heads up the front steps of his house. Will pulls me aside and we linger behind.

I look up at Will as he asks, "Do you want to hang out for a while? Or would you rather head back to my place?"

My internal beast from earlier must have settled back into its slumber during lunch because to my shock I reply, "We can hang out for a while. I was too busy catching up with Tipp to even open my book so I've got plenty to keep me occupied."

Will's face blossoms into a striking smile and I grin back at him instinctually. He bends over and gives me a quick kiss. "Best girlfriend ever," he states as if there's no doubt what he says is fact. Then he takes my hand and leads the way up to Stefan's house.

As I follow behind I notice the newfound pep in his step and my smile grows. I adore the friendship these two have. I also appreciate that they gave up on teaching me how to play video games months ago and let me read in peace while they're nerding out. Surfing, good food, and hanging out with friends. This is the perfect ending to a wonderful summer.

# Three

# *Beaches and Bonfires*

## Fall Term

A FEW WEEKS LATER, I lay on Will's bed petting Aurora as I hear Will's sister, Meghan, tinkering around in the kitchen. I think Aurora likes me best. Whenever I come over to Will's she immediately runs up to me. I know that's typical for dogs, but she also likes snuggling with me while I do homework. I love watching her circle three times before plopping down on the bed. Aurora may be solely responsible for my good grades this term. Her affections make me look forward to studying.

I hear Meghan's cooking utensil gently scraping the edge of the pot as she cooks dinner for all of us. Will's at his computer chair across the room and I'm lounging on his bed doing homework.

With Fall term underway, we have settled into a familiar routine.

Go to classes.

Do the learning.

Work our shifts.

Finish our homework.

Somehow in between all of that, we fit in time to learn more about one another and build the foundation of our relationship. This semester is different because our schedules don't allow for a mutual meal break as the Spring term had. It's also changed because Tipp is at San

Diego State University now. It's amazing that she got in, their program is highly competitive. I'm proud of her, but I miss her too. Being at different schools has changed the dynamic of our friendship. So, instead of hanging out with everyone on campus, we're having to work harder at hanging out on the weekends. I pet Aurora absentmindedly as I think about how easy it's been to adapt to weekend hangouts with Stefan and Will. If they're off we're hanging out. It's a given. Unfortunately, Tipp has been a lot harder to stay connected with.

I'm over so often that Will has cleaned out a drawer for me at his sister's condo. I don't keep much here. Just a spare outfit and the necessities in case I stay over unexpectedly. Sitting on Will's dresser is my overnight bag. Its become a rather permanent fixture in his bedroom considering I've been staying over about four nights a week all summer.

"Dinner's ready!" Meghan calls from the kitchen.

I close my books and slide off the bed. Will hasn't made to move from his desk yet. I walk over and notice that he's listening to a recording of one of his textbooks. I tap him on the shoulder and he jumps.

Will pulls one of his over-ear headphones to rest on the side of his head and looks up at me. "What's up?" His arm slides down the side of his chair and wraps around the back of my leg, with his hand resting solidly between my thighs. It's intimate without being intrusive and I love how natural it feels having him touch me like this.

I grin down at him and lean in for a kiss. When I stand again I say, "Dinner's ready, you didn't hear through your headphones."

He smiles back. "Thanks, head on in. Let Meghan know that I need to finish this section? Should be less than five minutes."

"Sure," I chirp to him.

A cacophony of food being plated mixed with staccato shooting noises hits my ears as I leave the peaceful environment of Will's bedroom. I head down the hallway and emerge into the open concept living space of Thomas and Meghan's condo. It's a two bedroom one bathroom and is the perfect size for two people. Maybe three if one of them was a baby. When you throw Will into the mix and then sprinkle me in fifty percent of the time it feels small. That's why I try my best to stick to Will's room, I don't want to cramp their space.

"Hey," Meghan greets as I sit in my usual spot at their wooden circular dining table. My back is facing the front door which is my least favorite spot at a table, but I'm their guest so I comply with their desires.

"Will doesn't want to lose his train of thought. He'll be out soon." I offer in greeting.

I pivot in my chair to watch Thomas. He's sitting on their aquamarine couch playing a video game on the T.V. "Same!" He calls out while his fingers click on the controller at a furious pace. I see streak marks of bullets flying across the screen as his body weaves and dodges on the couch making it seem like he's part of the action.

My gaze drifts to Meghan in the kitchen. Over the summer we've grown to mutually respect one another. I don't think Meghan and I would be friends in the natural world, but she likes seeing her brother happy... and well, apparently I'm the cause of that lately. I stand and take the two steps needed to be on the edge of her workspace. I learned early on, don't cross the threshold of the kitchen when Meghan is in it. You will be in her way, no matter how hard you try not to be. While I know this is an unspoken rule of their household, I still want to help her. I hold out my hands offering, "How can I help?"

She gives me a crooked grin as she plates the last of our stew for the evening. It smells decadent. Honestly, it's a miracle that I still fit into the same sized pants that I was wearing at the beginning of summer. Meghan's cooking makes you forget about healthy portion sizes and reminds one how food can solve all your problems. "Is it still considered plating if you're putting the food into a bowl?" I ask as her ladle dips back into the chunky meat and vegetable filled stew.

Meghan softly laughs, "Do you want the answer to that in technical terms, or simplistically?"

I shake my head at her. She places a bowl in my hands. "Will's," she instructs.

I turn toward the table and place the bowl at Will's spot as I mull over my options. "How about a combination of both? I'd love to know the real reasons, just in terms I can understand."

She's facing the stove again when I head back to the kitchen. I hear her begin, "Technically plating isn't the act of putting food on a plate. It means so much more than that." She puts another bowl in my hands. "Thomas."

I turn and place it on the table accordingly as she expands her original statement. "Plating is the term for the overall presentation of a meal. It encompasses all the elements of a dish. Varying from how the food looks on the plate, to the design of the particular plate, or bowl chosen. Even the placement of garnishes like this green onion." Her head tilts toward the chopped green onion that she is currently sprinkling on top of the next bowl of food.

"Yours." She instructs placing it in my hands.

"Plating can also include the decorations on a table and the place settings if you want to get technical. The casino has a different department for those elements though. At work, I'm in charge of the plating options that pertain directly to the food and dishes it's served on."

My head tilts to the side as I take in all her words. "I had no idea there were that many components involved in making a meal," I say in astonishment.

Meghan's face breaks into a full smile, "That's just how it looks, Nikki. Don't get me started on how to balance acidity and make sure that all the flavors are interacting in a complimentary way. And that's really just the tip of the iceberg."

"Oh, I believe it." I agree nodding my head. I'm a menace in the kitchen, everyone here knows it. Luckily they took me at my word and haven't asked me to cook anything.

As Meghan and I sit down, the boys finally gather in the dining area. They head to the kitchen and start getting everyone drinks. Glasses clink onto the marble counter as they fulfill their end of the bargain. Meghan says if she does all the cooking they can get the beverages and do all the cleaning. I'm still navigating how I fit into that equation. Thomas tops off Meghan's preferred drink, a glass of red wine, before getting himself a beverage.

Will grabs drinks for us. His milk glugs into his glass as he asks, "Water babe?"

"Yes please," I respond as I pull out my chair and sit at the table. I wait for them to join us before digging into our dinner. "What are we eating tonight?" I ask Meghan. The closest thing I can compare it to would be stew, but the consistency is thicker than the kind that Nana usually makes.

Meghan sips her wine before answering. "Jambalaya."

"Oh yum, babe!" Thomas says. He kisses the side of her head before taking his seat next to her.

Will joins us quickly after.

"Dig in!" Meghan exclaims once we're all seated.

I do as instructed and the first two bites are delicious. I learn that it's a shrimp and sausage jambalaya that Thomas and Meghan had talked about a few weeks ago. She wanted to make it for him then but hadn't had the time to get to the store and get the correct ingredients until today.

I keep eating the jambalaya and notice my nose starts running. I sniffle not wanting to blow my nose at the table. I put my spoon down and take a sip of water. It's starting to feel hot in here too. I think there's even sweat beading on my forehead.

I swallow the water but it does nothing to abate the heat permeating from my chest.

Will's gaze is focused on me. Concern laces the drawn lines of his face. "You okay, Nikki?"

I pull at the collar of my shirt and clear my throat. "Yeah, I think so. I just got super hot."

Meghan and Thomas are focused on me now too. "You look flushed Nikki." Meghan comments with concern in her tone.

I shake my head, "Eh, it's probably just a little warm in here. My Irish coloring always makes how I'm feeling appear in my cheeks."

Then I hear Will cough lightly into his napkin.

I take another drink of my ice water and start to feel a little better. I pick up a dinner roll and rip off part of it. I dip it into the sauce of the Jambalaya and take a bite.

My taste buds ignite into an inferno as soon as the Jambalaya makes contact. I swallow it down and stare into my bowl.

It's the Jambalaya.

It must be a slow burn that builds on itself with every bite.

I start to feel clammy and know my body is incapable of finishing this dish.

Someone coughs. When I look toward the noise I see Will downing half of his milk at once. He places the glass down and wipes his mouth with his napkin. "Did you—" he begins before breaking into a coughing fit. When he's recovered he tries again his voice coming out raspy, "Did you maybe go a little heavy-handed with the spices?"

My head jerks to watch Meghan's reaction. You don't insult Meghan's cooking. *Ever.*

It's then that I notice she hasn't eaten much of her dinner either. There are crumbs from a roll on a small plate next to her Jambalaya, and her glass of wine is drained. She likes her wine, but that's fast, even for her.

Then she sniffles and wipes her nose. "It's possible this dish is spicier than I intended."

"What are you talking about? It's perfect. First time I've tasted real spice in a long time." Thomas says excitedly between bites of his meal.

I look between Meghan and Will. I'm not getting in the middle of this, but I have to figure out an excuse to not eat anymore without hurting her feelings.

Picking up my spoon I decided with resignation that if I can eat half my bowl Meghan's feelings will be saved. As I'm about to take another bite Will puts his hand on my arm. "Nikki, you don't have to eat this."

I lower my spoon and bow my head. "I know I don't have to, but I think the spice has passed."

Will gives me an apologetic look. "We both know it's too spicy for you."

*Way to put me on the spot with his sister.* I guess the best way out of this is the truth. My hands withdraw to my lap and I fidget with my fingers under the table. I nervously tell Meghan, "I'm sorry. From what I can taste I think it's delicious, but Will's right. I can barely handle regular spicy foods. I think this Jambalaya is a bit too much for me."

Will then decides to back me up. "Meghan, you know how much I love spicy food. I don't think I can handle a full bowl of this either."

Her face is starting to redden. I don't know if it's from anger or embarrassment. I also don't know how to help in this situation. I start to worry my bottom lip in anticipation of where the conversation will head next.

Thomas has devoured his meal and decides now is the time to save Meghan. Or is he saving us from her? Thomas puts his hand on Meghans' shoulder, "Babe, this might be the best meal you've ever made for me. Who cares if these two don't like it? Just means more leftovers for me."

Her face softens at his words.

"Just think how jealous my coworkers are going to be this week when I bring leftover Jambalaya in every day. The lunch room is going to smell good just from reheating it. Best yet, it's all mine."

I chance a glance at Will and he jerks his head toward the kitchen. We both get up from the table and clear our dishes. Will turns on the sink when Thomas calls out, "Just leave them there. I've got clean up tonight."

Will shrugs in response and grabs my hand. "Thanks for dinner," I offer to Meghan as we walk down the hall to Will's room.

Once inside, he closes the door behind us. I sit on the edge of his bed, unsure of how to proceed.

"I think we should probably get lost for the rest of the night," Will whispers out. He goes to the closet and pulls out a pair of shoes and a jacket.

I nod my head in agreement and find my shoes. "Good thing we've got the bonfire tonight then."

Once we're dressed and ready for an Autumn evening on the beach, we head back into the living space. Thomas is in the kitchen cleaning up and Meghan is nowhere to be found.

"Thanks," Will says to his brother-in-law.

"No worries," he replies. "Probably a good idea that you two stay out until we're in bed though. I'll text you when it's safe to return," he says with a wink.

Will shakes his head with a soft chuckle and ushers me to the door. "Yup, we definitely don't want to be anywhere near here tonight." He reaches the door and opens it for me. The chilly dusk air brushes against my skin and we descend the stairs to the walkway that leads to Will's car.

"Do we need anything?" I ask as we get into his car and Will starts driving to Mission Beach.

"Nah, bonfires are Stefan's thing. He prides himself on bringing all the supplies."

I grin at that and take over DJing. I will never trust Will's music choices. He's lucky to have me as his copilot. I plug the auxiliary cord into my phone and press play on the playlist I've compiled for tonight. *I'm Like A Lawyer With The Way I'm Always Trying To Get You Off* by Fall Out Boy plays through the car's stereo system.

I settle in for the drive and enjoy watching the sunset over the greater San Diego area as Will takes us to the beach.

When we arrive at Mission Beach the parking lot is nearly empty. Will pulls into a spot next to a truck that I recognize as Stefan's. On the other side of it is Tipp's Jeep.

We get out of the car, kick off our shoes, and head over to the bonfire that's already blazing a couple hundred feet away. Our group of friends are spread out on various towels and blankets socializing while roasting marshmallows and enjoying the fire. I see a man I don't know next to Tipp. Stefan's brother and his girlfriend, Chuck and Brittney, are here too.

I start heading over to Tipp to meet this Ryan when my eyes snag on someone else. Next to Stefan, I see a slender figure. There's long dark hair blowing in the beach breeze and then she turns and faces me. I immediately recognize those pouty lips and her naturally surreal beauty. "Mia's in town?" I call out as I awkwardly run through the sand to their blanket. She stands as I approach and wraps me in a giant hug.

"Good to see you too, Nikki." She says into my hair with a smile in her voice.

I pull back and grasp her elbows taking her in fully. She looks good. In the flickering of the firelight, I can see more definition in her arms and a harsher cut to her cheekbones. It only adds to the severity of her beauty and I find myself wondering how Stefan convinced such a lovely woman to date his pompous ass.

"How long are you in town?" I ask her eagerly.

She glances back at Stefan before answering me. We haven't known one another long, or well, but something feels off. "I leave in two days." She admits to me quietly.

"What!" I shriek into the quiet evening air. I quickly turn my indignation on Stefan. I point at him accusingly as I stalk toward him. "You've been hiding her from us? How long has she been here?"

Will intercepts my path and wraps me up in his arms. "Geeze babe, she's his girlfriend, not yours."

I roll my eyes at him, not that he can see, as he hauls me over to where he's set up a blanket for us. I plop down and cross my arms pinning him with a pouty look. "I know that," I start, "But I like her more than him. And I'm stuck seeing Stefan a lot more than Mia."

Will laughs at my justification and pulls me in for a kiss. I don't want to let him distract me but there's something about his lips. They do things to me. Make me feel some things, and forget others. As his hand tenderly weaves into my hair, perfectly angling my head to grant him access, I hear a throat clear from nearby.

I don't want to acknowledge whoever is trying to interrupt us. I'm inclined to think Will feels the same as he parts my lips with his tongue and deepens our kiss.

Then I feel a smack on my calf.

I break our contact and shout, "Ow!" in surprise.

Will's hand is still twisted in my hair as I pull away to see who dares to interrupt our fun. Tipp is standing behind Will with her arms crossed and her hip popped. I see her head tilt and the fire, flickers perfectly lighting up her eyebrow as it arches at me.

Will sighs into my neck. His hand leaves my hair and lands on my cheek. He pulls my face back to his and gives me a kiss that promises all the things I can expect from him when we're alone. "Until later," he whispers into my ear, nipping at my lobe.

I feel goosebumps prickle over half of my body and my core heats up. It has nothing to do with my proximity to the fire.

Will stands at the edge of our blanket and offers me his hands. I take them and he pulls me up. I'm now standing mere feet from Tipp and her new beaux.

She's smiling while softly tisking at me. "Can't keep it in your pants for one evening?" She taunts as she pulls me in for a hug. I don't remember her being this affectionate before; I guess Ryan is changing her. My eyebrows dart together as I worry if this change is for the better or not. When I feel her loosen her grip, I fix my face into a neutral expression and mentally prepare to meet the new love interest in Tipp's life.

She turns and beckons him to step forward. Ryan reaches out his hand to formally shake mine. I smile at him hoping it's coming off as a mixture of welcoming and intimidating. "If you're dating my bestie you better get used to hugs," I warn him as I stretch out my arms and hug him hello.

He's broader than Will is, but he's also barely an inch or two taller than me. I don't want to judge a book by its cover but this man is wearing cowboy boots on the beach. *That has to be a red flag right?* I mentally ask myself. But Tipp seems happy. I scold myself internally and grin at him. "Nice to meet you. I hope you know what you've gotten yourself into." I joke winking at him.

Ryan seems to soften at the jest and wraps his arm around Tipp's shoulders. She leans into him comfortably and pats his chest while smirking up at him. "Oh, he knows exactly what he's gotten himself into."

He looks down at her and uses his free hand to tap the tip of her nose. I hear him quietly reply to her, "Enough to want you to move back to Texas with me next Summer."

She doesn't respond to him but pushes him back to their blanket and snuggles into him once they're lying down.

That's what I love about bonfire nights. We're all here. We're happy to hang out. However, when we're on our own blankets we can have private conversations hidden between the crashing of the waves down the shore and the popping of the fire we're circled around.

I crawl across our giant blanket and choose the best spot for roasting marshmallows as Will gets s'mores supplies for us from Stefan. We sit on the edge of the blanket with our skewer sticks hovering near the fire enjoying the warmth but not filling the silence with idle chit-chat.

I stare mesmerized into the flames as they dance across the sky. The reds, oranges, and yellows blur together before my eyes and I watch transfixed. The gentle popping of logs serenades the flames as they twirl and spark their movements. My eyes wander to the embers dying at the base of the fire and how they desperately cling to the oxygen in the air around them trying to ignite again. I feel my neck lolling to either side as the fire ebbs and flows depending on the strength of the breeze surrounding us.

I'm only removed from my trance when Will interrupts it. His voice sounds like it is coming from a tunnel, "Babe, I think your marshmallow is done."

I'm jarred back to reality. My eyes are burning from staring so intently at the fire. I blink them a few times and then focus on the end of my skewer stick. Not only is my marshmallow done, it's well done. It has been burned to a black charcoal lump. I sigh, "Yeah, that's not going to taste good." I lower my metal stick to the logs fueling the fire and wipe off the black marshmallow. It starts to boil on the logs and I watch as the once deliciously gooey consistency melts to a liquid and becomes unrecognizable in the base of the fire.

When the show is done I reign in the skewer stick and prick another marshmallow onto the end. This time I focus on the sizzling of its edges and roast it to perfection. It catches on fire twice and Will blows it out for me quickly. When all sides have been browned enough I remove it from the stick and squeeze it off between the rest of my preassembled s'more pieces. I put my stick down and pick up my plate. The chocolate below the marshmallow has already started melting down the sides and I know this will be a sticky mess.

I smile with anticipation. I can't wait.

I pick up my s'more and lick my lips before taking a bite. I practically unhinge my jaw as I open up to devour it. With a huge bite and the satisfying crunch of the graham cracker mixed with the molten chocolate and squishy marshmallow, I'm transported to a state of nirvana.

My eyes roll into the back of my head and I let out a satisfied moan as I enjoy my first bite.

When it's gone, I smack my lips together and open my eyes, preparing to take another bite.

I'm surprised at the sight in front of me though.

Instead of focusing on my plate and the remaining dessert, I see Will. His eyes are dripping with desire. He's staring at my lips. He looks like he can barely contain himself.

I force a nervous swallow down my throat. I squeak out, "Hi?"

He takes my plate out of my hands and puts it on the blanket behind me. "We're gonna need to leave that here."

My jaw drops open and I'm about to protest when he takes my hands. Then he quickly pulls me to standing, and immediately throws me over his shoulder in a fireman's carry.

"What!" I yell in surprise into the calm evening air.

Will, holding me by my arm and leg, stalks away from the fire with me slung across his shoulders. I look back at our friends and see Stefan shaking his head at us. Tipp shouts at our retreating forms, "Don't do anything I wouldn't do!"

I shake my head and let Will walk away with me. I hope that he's planning on acting on the look of desire that was plastered on his face as I was devouring my s'more. I hear the noise of the crashing waves grow as he continues to walk.

"You can put me down," I say as I smack his ass.

He doesn't break his stride. "We're almost there."

After a few more steps I feel him crouch beneath me and then my foot hits the ground. It's not solid because we're still on sand, but it's ground nonetheless. Will loosens his grip on my arm and steadies me by grasping my hips.

I lick my lips as I look into his eyes. His chest is heaving as he steadies his breathing. Carrying my five foot seven ass across the beach like that was hot. I'm amazed he didn't collapse halfway here. I turn to see our friends' fire flickering faintly in the distance but I can't make out any distinct shapes around it.

I turn my focus back on his frame and bite my lip seductively. "Why ever would you take me so far away from the warmth of that fire?" I ask with an innocence that contradicts what my core is hoping for.

Will growls at me. He takes a step forward until our bodies are flush against each other and then pivots me to stand against the wooden post that was just at his back. Before I have time to fully register our position change he crushes me against the pole and devours my mouth in a passionate kiss. I lace my hands around his neck like I have a million times before and enjoy the closeness of his body.

Will moans deep in his chest and I twist to the perfect angle so we're both getting what we want from this kiss.

Then I hear it. Voices from somewhere above us. I place my hands on his chest and push him back from me just a fraction. I feel his body want to fight my silent request but he heeds my non-verbal directions. When he comes up for air, I'm given a moment to look around.

It's then I notice- we're under the pier. He has me pushed up against a pillar that gets submerged in ocean water during high tide. Mere feet above us is the bottom of the pier's boardwalk with tourists who have no idea about what's going on below their feet. I scan our surroundings and note we're the only people down here. The closest humans to us are back at the bonfire.

We're effectively alone.

I feel Will's erection grind into my pubic bone. My breathing turns ragged. "Yeah?" I huskily ask him.

He nods at me. "Think you can be quiet enough?"

I take in an unsteady breath and bite my bottom lip. Keeping with the theme I nod my head instead of speaking.

"Thank fuck." Will moans as he closes the distance between us again.

My hands instinctually knead into his hair and I start pulling just enough to make his scalp tingle without hurting.

Will greets my encouragement by zeroing in on the zipper of my jeans. He undoes the button and slides them down my legs without breaking our kiss.

I find his zipper and pull it down. The harsh scraping of the teeth of his zipper separating brings the concern of being discovered flooding into my veins.

Will eviscerates that thought when he slides his fingers along my core. His lips move to my neck and he lets out a warm exhale along the shell of my ear. "Do you have any idea what you do to me when you eat like that?"

I tilt my head to give him even more access to my neck. I whisper back, "I'm guessing it has something to do with this," as I slide my hand into his boxers and grip his erection.

Thirty seconds of making out with this man against a pier pillar and we're both panting like horny teenagers.

His hips thrust into my hand encouraging me to stroke him. I do as I'm bid and he rewards me by inserting one finger inside me.

My back arches off the pillar and my mouth parts in a silent moan. Will's finger pumps steadily in and out of me. It takes no time before I feel my core weeping for more of him. I squeeze his cock harder in my hand while picking up the pace of my pumping. My free hand grabs hold of his head and I pull his ear down to my lips. "Are we going to stand here and jerk each other off like we're afraid to get caught at prom or are you going to fuck me, Will?" I finish off my question by biting down on his neck with a little more force than necessary.

Will's cock twitches in time to my teeth grazing along his neck. I feel him growl into my breasts and then the unhinged man that I've learned to love to fuck comes to the surface. I softly exhale into his ear, taunting him into action.

"Have it your way." He warns before removing his hand and gripping the back of my thighs. He picks me up, legs spread open in front of his hips, my pants dangling around one ankle. I whip my hands out to steady myself by gripping his biceps. They flex even harder under my touch and I'm bewildered by how much natural muscle is in his body. Will gives me a devilish smirk as he pins me against the pillar and waits for me to assist.

I dig back into his jeans and free his throbbing member. His tip glistens with pre-cum in the moon light and I salivate in anticipation at how good it will feel sliding inside me. I align his cock with my entrance and wait for Will to take over.

With agonizing control he slowly inserts himself. Both of our mouths are opened in silent ecstasy. He starts to pick up pace and all I can do is hold on. Will's thrusting picks up speed and I'm internally grateful for the waves that have broken against this pillar so many times that its surface is smooth. It would suck to get splinters in my ass from a fucking this wonderful. As I'm about to giggle at the thought, Will adjusts his grip on my legs and his cock starts hitting that perfect spot inside of me.

I feel my eyes cross in agonizing appreciation for the wonders that are this man's penis.

"Rub your clit," he quietly instructs between labored inhales.

I obey without hesitation and feel myself inch closer to the edge.

"Fuck, Nikki," he groans as I clench around his girth.

With every thrust, I'm shoved closer to my climax. I bite down on my free hand to keep from crying out. One more circling of my clit provides the perfect friction and pressure for my body, fireworks spread across all my nerve endings. I shake against Will's hold.

He's close, I can tell by the change in pace of his thrusting. He's morphed from rhythmic to jagged and needy. His continued thrusting inside me causes my first orgasm to blossom into a second one. With my inner walls clenching, I feel Will twitch against me. His head tilts back in a silent roar as his orgasm tears through his body.

Will pulls my back from the pillar and he gently drops down to his knees while remaining inside me. I wrap my arms around his neck and we stay entwined until both of our chests find a slow and steady rhythm again.

"Wow," Will whispers to our surroundings.

I nod my head in agreement. I've never been an exhibitionist before. *Guess I can't say that anymore...*

"We better get dressed before someone thinks to look down here," I suggest while pressing down on his shoulders to help myself stand. He slides out of my body easily and I immediately miss being connected to him in such a carnal way.

Will assists in getting my foot back into the pant leg that was previously discarded. Only when I'm decent again does he look down and notice that he needs to put his cock away. With a swift tuck and a quick zip, Will looks as though nothing has happened.

In a hushed tone, I ask, "How can you look so put together after fucking me so incredibly? I feel like an absolute mess."

He wraps a hand around my waist and pulls me away from the base of the pier. He angles us toward our friends' bonfire and replies, "You look beautiful. Thoroughly kissed, but beautiful."

I'm glad it's dark so he can't see me blush. I know he means what he says, but sometimes it's still hard to believe that this wonderful, kind, and honorable man wants to be with me.

Once we get back to the bonfire I notice there's a blanket missing. Chuck and Brittney are still secluded, doing their own thing. Stefan and Mia are cuddled together chatting. Our blanket is left barren.

"Tipp needed to leave?" I ask Stefan.

He nods. "Said something about wanting to go dancing with her new man I think."

I shrug. *We did wander off but it wasn't for that long was it? Oh well, I'll just call her tomorrow.*

"So," Mia draws out. "Did you two have fun?"

I bury my face into Will's arm. He started it, he can explain it to his friends too.

"I haven't the faintest idea what you're talking about, Mia," he says with a straight face. He picks up our skewers and goes back to roasting marshmallows like he wasn't just interrupted by a very public fuck fest of his own creation.

Stefan takes his cue and changes the topic. "So, what do you two plan on doing when you go to Oregon in December?"

# Four

# *Failing at Being an Adult*

## Winter Break

FALL SEMESTER PASSES IN a whirlwind. When Will and I talked last summer about visiting Oregon over Winter Break it had felt so far away. Now, as we're standing in line at the airport, I'm excited December has come so quickly. A grin pulls at my lips as I start daydreaming about our future together. Will pulls out his ID and I catch a glimpse of his full name. I can't believe we haven't had this conversation before...

"That's your last name?" I ask Will as we're waiting to go through TSA.

He takes a step forward to close the gap between us and the party ahead. "Wait, you don't know my last name?"

I squeeze his hand. "No! I would remember a last name that different." I say still staring at his boarding pass. "How do you say it?"

He looks over his shoulder at me, we're next in line now. "Zu-"

"Next!" The TSA agent interrupts our conversation.

*Do I follow him up to the podium or wait like I'm a separate party?* I've never traveled with someone who wasn't related to me before. Will keeps my hand in his so I guess I'm following behind him.

We reach the agent and Will goes first. Once the woman clad in royal blue is satisfied with his documentation, she ushers him through and puts her hand out for my paperwork. She scans my boarding pass and with a beep and bright green light, I'm cleared to continue traveling. The TSA agent motions for me to follow Will and moves on to whoever is in line behind us.

We start taking off our shoes and jackets and putting them in the grey bins to make sure we're not smuggling weapons on board. I try to pick up our conversation again, "Your last name literally starts with the word zoo?"

He grins at me as he undoes his belt and adds it to the bin. "Yeah, three syllables. But we can go over them once we're through all of this." He gestures to the conveyor belt our luggage has been thrust onto and the large machines beyond them. "This is my first time flying in a decade, so I feel like I need to focus on how the agents direct us."

"Fair," I say and smile at him. I don't need to put anything else in our bins so I wait with my luggage and push it forward as space opens up. I glance around the area and it's rather strange to see this many adults standing around in socks. The agents bark at people to take off their belts and remove any laptops from their bags. Will's backpack has a special pocket where he can leave his laptop in the backpack but the whole thing unzips to make it TSA-friendly.

"Ma'am, is your water bottle emptied?" I hear a man's voice ask.

I snap out of my thoughts. "Yes," I offer quickly not wanting to waste his time.

"Thank you, you two can go." He motions to the full body scan machine's line. We walk over to it and wait. Will puts his hands on my hips and guides me to wait in front of him. To others looking in we might seem like an adorable couple who are excited to go on vacation. While that's true, I get the feeling that he wants me to go first so he can see how it's done and then copy me.

The line passes quickly without us speaking and I break from his light hold when another agent beckons me forward. They all wear the same royal blue shirts with yellow lettering and black pants. The only individuality they're allowed is from the neck up.

I step into the machine and place my sock-clad feet on the scuffed yellow footmarks on the ground. When I look up I see an image that has their arms raised above their head. There's a slight bend to the elbows and the hands lock together. I copy suit and wait for the scanner to do its job. While I'm standing there like a statue I take a moment to appreciate that the silhouette is androgynous. It's nice to not have to conform to another thing that's male centered in this world.

"Come on out." The agent in charge of the scanner calls to me.

I comply and wait on a mat while a woman looks at my body scan. *My hair will make it go off, always does.* I think as I wait.

"I need to pat down your hair," the female agent informs me.

I nod my permission. "Every time," I say in a neutral tone as her hands lightly check for any paraphernalia hidden in my luscious red locks.

With a final pat of her hands, the TSA agent says, "You're good."

I turn to her and smile, "Thank you." Then I'm off to the scanning line that our luggage is due out of at any second. There are people littered along it, putting their shoes on and blocking the path of egress to take care of themselves. My mother taught me differently in all of our travels. Will's backpack clears screening first so I grab it and zip up the laptop safety pocket. Next, his bin of shoes and other miscellaneous items pops out.

I feel a hand on my lower back and startle before I recognize that it's Will. He moves to take his shoes out of his bin. I block his hands with my arm, "Not yet."

Will looks at me quizzically but doesn't argue. When the rest of our bins and carryons pop out of the machine, we shoulder our backpacks, grab our suitcases, and I lead the way, carrying my bin of belongings to a table that's out of the way.

"Why do you want us to put away our belongings over here?" Will asks as he puts on a shoe.

I'm pocketing my phone into my leggings as I explain, "Whenever I traveled with my mom she always made my brother and I get our stuff and take it away from the scanning area. I didn't understand it then, but I think it's out of respect for other travelers."

He looks up at me, "So it's what you're used to doing?"

I nod. "That's not what's important though. How do you say your name?"

"Will."

I scoff, "Not that and you know it."

"William."

I grab his head between my hands and pretend to shake it violently. "How do you say your last name, William?"

He wraps his large hands around both of my wrists and pulls my hands from his head. "Zoo-kaus-kiss," he sounds out for me.

I try it out for myself. "William Zukauskas. I like how that feels on my tongue."

Will's eyes immediately darken upon hearing his full name on my lips. He stands, reminding me of how much larger of a person he is. I have to take a step back to maintain eye contact without straining my neck. "I'm going to need you not to say that again in public."

"I can't say your full name anymore?" I ask with a confused tilt of my head.

"Exactly," he bends down and wraps his arms around my waist before continuing. Then I hear his voice whisper, "Because when you do, all I can think about is how much I want those pretty lips wrapping around something other than my name." He pulls back to his full height and shoulders his backpack as if he hadn't just declared such a filthy thought in public.

I feel my eyes bugging out and realize my jaw has also dropped a little. I scratch my neck and finish tucking away my belongings.

As we walk hand-in-hand toward our gate, my mind has wandered on its own accord. I hear myself mentally trying out *Veronica Zukauskas*. It's got a nice ring to it, I think.

· ♥ · ♥ · ♥ · ♥ · ♥ ·

When we land in Portland it hits me.

We're here.

We're traveling together.

We are the adults on this trip.

Which also means if anything goes wrong, we have to figure out how to solve it. Before my brain can start to spiral, I remind myself of the facts. I'm here with Will, the most level-headed person I've ever met. We didn't check our bags so our clothing can't go missing. All we need to do now is get to the rental car place and find our hotel.

Two things. Anything is achievable when you break it into small, manageable chunks.

I grip Will's hand a little tighter as he reads the airport signs that direct us to the car rental area. He leads us through the busy airport with confidence. I notice that his size helps with the parting of the sea as well. No one wants to get run over by a man as tall as he is.

We go down the escalators and find ourselves in an area littered with various rental car companies. I pull up our reservation on my phone and look for the red and yellow logo.

"There," I point to an area halfway down the ominous corridor. It's at the end of the hallway and gives me an eerie feeling. I'm glad Will is here, I wouldn't want to walk down there by myself. When we get to the counter there's no one in line ahead of us and a sweet little old lady beckons us forward.

"What name is the reservation under dearies?" She asks with a chipper attitude.

"Welch," I answer. I booked the car, but Will is going to be the main driver.

She pushes up the glasses that have been sliding down her nose as she looks at the computer screen. I notice her name badge says Gertrude, *what an adorable little old lady's name.* "Ah, there it is, Veronica?"

"Yes, ma'am," I reply cordially. Will is standing just behind me with his hand on the small of my back. I'm so ready to be alone with him after such a long day of travel.

"Okay, I need the I.D. of the driver and their credit card please," Gertrude tells us.

I get out my card and Will gets out his license. Gertrude's lips purse as she sees us both giving her pieces of plastic. She takes them and examines them. When she looks at us again she shakes her head. "This won't do, dearies. The license needs to be in the same name as the credit card."

I look at Will, he stares back at me. I did not notice that stipulation when booking our rental car. "But I'm not twenty-one yet, and he's twenty-three. Can't I put the car on my credit card as long as we make sure he's the only driver?"

Gertrude gives us back our cards. "I'm sorry kids, but the credit card has to be in the driver's name."

Will steps in. "I don't have a credit card, would a debit card work?"

She clasps her hands together giving us a patient look. "No, but since," she glances back at the computer screen, "Mrs. Welch here has a credit card she can rent the car. We will have to add a Young Driver Surcharge, but you can still use the vehicle."

I swallow nervously. My palms have started to turn clammy holding onto my wallet as well. "How much will that be?" I ask Gertrude.

"If you were twenty-one it would be thirty dollars a day. However you're only twenty, so that bumps it up to one hundred and twenty-five dollars additional per day."

My brows arch in shock. I'm speechless.

"An additional hundred dollars a day because she's not twenty-one yet?" Will asks incredulously.

"I'm afraid so, dearies. I can see you need some time to think about this so I'm going to help the next man in line while you make up your mind." She dismisses us and welcomes up the next customer.

I glare at him. He's definitely over twenty-one. *Asshole.*

Will pulls our suitcases behind him as we step away from the counter to talk through our options.

"I'm so sorry. I didn't see the fine print about the cardholder having to be the same person as the driver. I can't believe I failed at being an adult."

He holds my shoulders. "We both know you're not a failure." Will lovingly scolds me before moving on to reassure, "Babe, you don't need to be sorry about that. It's a silly rule. Who cares where the money is coming from as long as the company is getting paid? I don't have an extra hundred a day for this trip though."

My shoulders shrug dejectedly as I stare at the floor. I've ruined our vacation before it even began. "I don't either."

Will's hands begin rubbing my arms comfortingly. "Let me call my parents and see if they can loan us the money."

I want to object to his suggestion, but I also don't see any other options.

Will leaves me with the baggage as he steps away to make the call.

I watch Gertrude help another customer in the meantime. The lights are bright and harsh. They make me feel like a spotlight is illuminating me, this poor girl who can't even rent a car correctly. My breathing is getting choppy. My heart is pounding too loudly in my ears. Bile is beginning to coat the back of my throat. I recognize the signs of a panic attack and my eyes start searching for the nearest trash can frantically. If I can't get control of my emotions fast enough, I better have somewhere to puke other than the shiny tiled floor.

In an effort to calm down, I take out my water bottle and take a deep drink. The water helps release the bile in my throat. I turn and face the wall instead of watching the car rental company's counter. I fixate on the texture and divots on its surface from where people have run into it with their baggage.

With my mind distracted I start taking in deeper breaths. I grip my reusable water bottle tightly in my hands and hope an answer to this problem is discovered quickly.

"Sorry about that, service wasn't strong enough in here." Will's voice greets me when he returns.

I rotate so that I'm facing him.

Will's face is a picture of concern. He pockets his ridiculous flip phone and hugs me close. "Nikki, it's fine. We'll figure this out. Are you okay?"

I welcome his safe embrace and nod into his chest. My mind clings to his familiar scent of bergamot and citrus mixed with an underlying woodsy note.

Will doesn't loosen his embrace until I initiate the end of our hug. I tilt my head back and look up at him. "What did your parents say?"

His face breaks into an ear-to-ear smile, "Even better."

He takes my hand and leads me away from the dreary rental car hallway. I follow him blindly wondering what could have him so excited.

After going up an escalator, and trudging across half of the terminal, Will takes us outside. I'm startled by how chilly the Portland air is against my skin. I'm wearing a sweatshirt, but this chill needs multiple layers and my heavy jacket is packed away in my suitcase.

"What are we doing out here?" I ask Will as we come to a halt.

"My parents called my aunt while I was on the phone with them. I guess she has a second car that she uses for fun. They asked if we could borrow one of her vehicles since we're stranded here without a responsible way to pay for a ride and she said yes. Her name is Julie and she only lives fifteen minutes away from the airport so she should be here any second."

Just then a Toyota Corolla pulls up in front of us and a chipper driver hops out. "Will, is that you?" She calls across the hood of her vehicle.

"Aunt Julie?" he replies.

She stretches her arms out for a hug as she approaches him. She has shoulder length brown hair that flares out the last inch or so. She's a few inches shorter than me and is bundled up in a large puffer jacket, scarf, jeans, and thick boots. "I haven't seen you since you were at least a foot shorter. Bring it in."

Will hugs her without hesitation and I stand awkwardly to the side, watching their reunion.

Julie's eyes drift toward me as she frees Will from her embrace. He picks up our bags and walks them to the trunk. "And you must be Veronica, my brother has told me all about you!" Then I'm wrapped in a surprisingly strong hug from someone so short. "Come on kiddo, you must be freezing out here, get in the back, I'll take you home."

Like that, I'm in the backseat of a stranger's vehicle, Will's in front, and we're speeding away from the airport. I sit quietly in the back as Will and Aunt Julie catch up in the front seat.

I know we've arrived when Julie pulls the Corolla into the driveway next to a 4Runner. "It gets horrible mileage which is why I prefer commuting in this baby," she says as she pats the dash of her car. "But I can make that sacrifice for my nephew. Just bring it back in one piece, please. When do you need a ride back to the airport?" She asks as we all step out of the vehicle.

"Two days, at eleven I think." Will answers.

"Wow, quick trip! Okay, text me the details when you figure them out. I'm sure you still have my number. You kids have fun." Then she tosses Will the keys across the roof of her car and she walks into her house.

Will catches them and ushers for me to get into the passenger seat. He hasn't even closed the door from just getting out of the car. I hop in and he rounds the hood to the driver's seat. I buckle up robotically still processing meeting Aunt Julie.

"She's not one for drawing out interactions is she?"

Will turns over the car and reverses out of the driveway. "No, Aunt Julie has always been a little socially awkward, but she's family. I think she was getting ready to go somewhere when my parents called her too."

"Oh, okay," I say, getting comfortable in the seat now that it's just the two of us. "Where are you going?"

"No idea," he admits while turning onto a crowded street. "Figured it was best to find a parking lot so we can decide our next destination instead of lingering in Aunt Julie's driveway."

So that's what we do. Will pulls into a large parking lot and tucks the car into a spot in the back, withdrawn from the hustle and bustle of shoppers. We look up directions on how to get to the hotel. It's about an hour from wherever we're parked right now. Along the drive South, we find some fast food and eat it in the car. By the time we arrive at our hotel, I'm beat.

We have to get up early tomorrow to make it to the University of Oregon for our morning tour. So, instead of ravishing each other like I'd been daydreaming about all day, we shower off the travel germs and snuggle into bed. I know the morning will come faster than I want it to. Always does when I'm wrapped up in Will's arms.

# Five

## Trees and Snowpiles

I ENJOY TAKING IN the scenery as Will drives South on the I-5. Last night, I was too wrapped up in worry over our misstep with adulting to take in the beauty we were driving past. In the bright morning light, I'm making up for that and admiring Oregon for all of its natural opulence.

The freeway is lined with trees on either side. There are large grassy fields interspersed with what I'm guessing are crops as well. It's like a completely different world than Southern California. Down there, everything is a shade of beige. Either the hills are covered in dead bushes, or the freeways are lined with shopping centers and houses. They're all varying shades of brown and beige; the only difference is whether it's naturally occurring or man-made.

Here in Oregon, everything is a different shade of earthy green.

The trees are evergreen.

The fields are clover green.

The shrubs are a mixture of Kelly, olive, and hunter, greens.

Best of all, nothing is beige!

As Will drives further South, the freeway merges down to a two-lane road. It feels a little claustrophobic, especially when he needs to pass a semi. I'm more accustomed to large four and five-lane freeways. Passing such a large vehicle with only a few feet between us and certain death feels alarming. I find myself closing my eyes whenever Will needs to maneuver around them the further we get along the freeway.

His hand is resting in its spot on my thigh as the miles pass by. I've put on a random playlist that's connected through Aunt Julie's Bluetooth system.

Before long, Will is pulling off the I-5 and merging onto another freeway that cuts Eastward toward downtown. I see a city sprawling on either side of the road as Will listens to the GPS and takes the offramp. As the roadway opens up, we're greeted by massive trees barren of their leaves lining the street. We follow the road through part of Eugene and then stumble upon the University of Oregon.

The buildings sprawl across multiple city blocks. In the middle of the road, there is an additional street that says Bus Only on the pavement. There is bright green grass everywhere I look, and too many trees to count. Will makes a right turn after the campus sign and we enter a calmer area. It's the middle of our community college's winter break right now, so I assume that the University of Oregon is on break as well. There aren't many people walking around, and those that are have a rushed pace to their steps.

The buildings are a mixture of architectural design. The older structures have external walls of red bricks and the newer ones are made with a combination of brick and glass. Every building I see is a minimum of two stories tall. There are walking paths around all of them. Everything is adorned with the University of Oregon's signature yellow O. My attention is drawn to some larger piles of white that are spread out along the walkways. Come to think of it, the whole campus appears to have a damp blanket spread across it.

"Are those snow piles?" Will asks from the driver's seat.

"I think so," choke out. I've seen snow before, but not lying in a pile on the side of the road. I've never seen enough to warrant needing to clean up after it falls. "Will, does it snow in Eugene?" I ask in shock.

He's grinning as he steers the car around one of the piles that's on the edge of the road. "It must, because those are piles of muddy snow."

"That makes me even more excited to move here." I bounce in my seat, clapping my hands like an excited kid. Will shakes his head as he pulls into the underground parking structure the GPS is directing us to.

He circles down and finds a spot to leave the car while we head off to get a tour of the campus. I already came here at the beginning of summer break with Mom so I know what to expect on our tour but this is Will's first time.

Mom and I spent the second week of summer break driving to all the different campuses that I was interested in in Oregon. I honestly thought the University of Oregon was out of my price range because of the tuition costs of the University system in California. One night, Mom was searching for information about Oregon State University, which I thought was my first choice, and found U of O instead. We changed our original plans, came here, and I fell in love. The campus is the perfect combination of architecture nestled into nature. There is a smaller town fifteen minutes down the road named Springfield. U of O has a top ranked education program. The only thing missing is Will and me attending it together.

A small grin is pulling at the corners of my mouth as Will and I exit the parking structure. I lead the way toward the tour meeting spot. We're fifteen minutes early, which is perfect because I was always taught if you arrive early you're on time, and if you arrive on time you're late. I also need the bathroom.

Will and I are the only two signed up for this tour so the guide clad in a bright yellow rain jacket informs us we can head out a few minutes early.

When the heavy glass doors open and the winter breeze accosts my face, I realize we didn't have to walk outside when we traveled from the car to the building. It feels like someone is stabbing daggers into every part of my skin that is exposed to the freezing cold. I feel Will tense next to me when his body crosses the threshold into what feels like a sub-zero zone. We clasp hands and follow the guide into a true winter environment.

Our guide is kind and chooses spots to stop that are in alcoves that serve as protection from the harshest of the winter winds.

After the first stop in the tour, Will pulls me in close and whispers, "I can't hold your hand babe, I'm losing feeling in my fingers."

I perch on my tip toes and give him a peck on the nose. "No worries, you can make it up to me later." I give him a seductive grin behind the back of our tour guide but Will doesn't return any excited sentiment. Instead, he gives me a miserable grin and follows the guide.

Our next stop is in front of the business complex. The piles of snow are larger in this area probably due to the tall building's prolonged shade from the sun. It's a massive five-story building with two other structures attached to it. The three combined are so large that they all have their own names. There isn't anywhere outside these buildings to hide from the elements so our yellow-clad guide ushers us into the building. "Normally we wouldn't enter, but with most everybody being on break and it being so cold outside I figured we could break the rules." He tells us the history of the giant O on the business complex glass wall. "When sports channels did their broadcasts from U of O campus this was the building that they had in the background, but no one knew which campus they were at. So after a few years of not being recognized by the public, the administration decided to add the O so that anyone watching would be able to identify our campus. Now, it's one of the most iconic locations at the university." Then he gestures behind him, "Also, all those tiny panels take in the brightness and adjust the lights accordingly on the inside of the building. This is the first green building that was built at the University of Oregon."

Now that my gaze has been drawn to the hundreds of square sparkling silver panes that span across the large windows of the business building, I notice them reflecting the light. This building drew my attention when I toured with Mom earlier in the year. I can see myself doing homework on one of the upper floors once I'm enrolled here.

I internally beg for the rest of our tour to wrap up quickly. The chill of the December air has pierced my core and my toes are starting to feel tingly in my slip-on shoes. Will doesn't look like he's feeling much better than I am. He's pulled up the hood to his sweatshirt and tied the head hole just big enough for his eyes to see out of. His hands are cradled in his kangaroo pouch. I told him before we left that he'd want more than one jacket, but I don't think he believed that Oregon could actually get cold.

I want to pay attention to what the guide is saying, but I care more that all of my phalanges are intact when we get back home to California tomorrow. I'm about to ask the guide if we can skip whatever is remaining in the tour when he announces, "One more stop guys, then we can head back and thaw out in front of the fire."

I sigh in relief and muster the courage to push through the last location of the tour. I pull out my hand from my pockets and wrap it around Will's arm. He looks down at me and I see a crinkle at the corners of his eyes but I can't discern his feelings beyond that because his face is hidden so thoroughly from the wind.

"The education department." Our guide calls over his shoulder. I break gaze with Will and look at the modest building in front of me. It's two stories and a beautiful combination of metal, glass, and bricks. The entryway is a set of double glass doors with large metal handles that are four feet long. The yellow clad guide opens the one on the right and holds it for us to enter. I walk into the atrium and look around in awe.

To my left, there is a massive fireplace blazing with heat, welcoming us in. I see the entrance to a quiet study hall beyond the fireplace. There is a large sitting area where I can visualize hanging out with future friends I don't even know yet. To the right is a concrete stairwell with clear glass walls that leads to the second story.

My hand drops from Will's arm and I walk forward into the depths of the building. I take in the wall on my left that is made entirely of windows that showcase a small field surrounded by garden beds. There is covered outdoor seating as well. Across from the windows, there are booths with large tables for groups of four or six friends to gather between classes. The space is completed with a perpendicular hallway that leads to multiple classrooms at the back of the building.

I turn to Will in the middle of the large hallway and stretch my arms out in excitement. "It's perfect!" I say a little too loudly as I stride back to his side.

He's pulled the hood away from his face and asks with a furrowed brow. "I thought you came here with your mother already?"

I loop my arm in his again. "I did. But this building was locked when we came by the first time. It's so much better on the inside!"

"You sound like you're buying a house babe." Will chuckles at me.

I pull out my phone and snap a selfie with the building in the background. I send it off to Tipp to show her my favorite part of campus. "I think this might feel better than buying a house."

Will shakes his head and hugs me. He doesn't say anything and his smile hasn't reached his eyes since our tour started. It has me feeling uneasy about his opinion of Oregon. We stand by the fire for a moment appreciating its warmth before the guide calls out from the doorway. "Ready to get back? Should be about a fifteen-minute walk. I probably won't stop unless you need a break."

Will pulls his hood up in response and I pocket my phone so I won't drop it in a melted puddle of snow. Then I ask, "Is it always this cold in winter?"

Our guide pauses with a pondering look on his face, "Not usually. We had a huge snowstorm blow in about a week ago, and it's expected to storm again in three days. You're just here between two cold fronts I think."

"Does it snow every year here?" Will's muffled voice asks through his hooded protective layer.

"No, I think it snows about once or twice every four years or so. Enough that you enjoy it, but not enough to make you miserable." He turns and takes us back to the building where our walking tour originated.

I grip Will's arm and can't wait to talk with him about this breathtaking campus when we're out of earshot of the tour guide.

As soon as we get in the car, we blast the heater as high and hot as it will go. It's been ten minutes. I've been feeling thawed for a while now but when I asked Will if he was okay with turning it down he said not yet. Will doesn't say much as he follows the GPS directions to the burger spot we choose for lunch. I look at the directions and gnaw on my bottom lip as I weigh whether or not I'm hot enough to take my sweatshirt off only to immediately put it on again in five minutes when we arrive.

I decide to wait it out. I'm sweating enough that I thank past tense me for putting on deodorant this morning. Will pulls into the parking lot and kills the engine. I immediately open my door and let the fresh cold air alleviate the sweltering heat I was bearing for Will.

Once we're seated in the restaurant I wait for Will to open up about how he thinks this morning went. He remains silent as I look at the menu. I choose my lunch and he still hasn't said a word. I catch his eyes and he averts his gaze.

*That's enough patience.* I close my menu and place it on the table. I stretch out my arm and take his hand in mine. When Will looks at me I press, "Will, what's wrong?"

He looks away from me but lets me keep holding his hand. "I don't think I can do this Nikki." He says without meeting my eyes.

I immediately yank my hand from his grasp. Pain must flash across my face because Will looks panicked. He holds his hands up in a bracing motion. "No, no, Nikki. Not that I can't do this," he motions between our bodies. "I can't do this," then he waves a hand to the air around him.

I take half a breath, "More words Will, less this's."

He flashes a charming smile. "Nikki, give me your hand back please," and places his on the table expectantly.

I comply and wait for him to continue.

"I love us. You're mine." He cracks his neck before proceeding. "Nikki, I don't think I can do Oregon."

That has me feeling elated and devastated simultaneously. "Why?" I ask barely loud enough for him to hear.

He squeezes my hand. "Babe it's in the twenties outside. I don't mean to be crass, but I'm a little worried my balls froze off during that tour of campus."

I laugh lightly at him.

"Don't laugh, they could be petrified and frozen to the walkways of the University of Oregon. No one will know what they are until everything thaws out. By then they could have hardened into diamonds." He bows his head seeming to mourn the metaphorical loss of his junk.

"But in all seriousness, why?" I demand from him.

His shoulders rise with a deep inhale. "I'm a surfer dude. I brought this sweatshirt," he plucks at the thin material he's wearing by way of explanation, "And that's it. How am I supposed to not freeze to death up here in winter?"

I feel a weight lift from my chest at his reasoning. "That's it? We can buy you better clothes to wear in winter weather. You're dressed like a San Diegan for winter. Oregon is a much different state with much different weather. If we buy you thicker jackets and probably a pair of gloves do you think you could try it out for me?"

Will nods his head at me and his lips pull to a lopsided smirk. "I guess, but you have to be my doctor later and make sure I still have two balls. I swear they've shot so far up they may never be warm enough to be found again."

I roll my eyes at his dramatics. I'm about to help warm him up with my promises of what this evening holds when our waitress arrives and effectively pours a bucket of snow on both of us.

After we finish our meals, we decide to go to a shopping center that was recommended to us by the waitress. As we walk the interior I find all the stores my fashionista self could need to keep a relevant wardrobe. At the back of the mall is a theater and Will and I decide to make an afternoon of it.

By the time the movie is finished, the sun has set. "It's only five-thirty," I inform Will as we walk to the car.

"Must be our distance from the equator." He comments as he gets the door for me.

We drive back to the hotel, listening to the same playlist from before and I'm surprised to find I feel tired when we arrive. I shower first and have intentions of following through with the role playing discussed over lunch but I must have drifted off while Will was showering.

With my mind in the middle state between wakefulness and oblivion, I feel him cover me with the blanket up to my chin and the kiss that he rests on my hair, but I can't convince myself to stir.

• ♥ • ♥ • ♥ • ♥ • ♥ •

I roll over and squint my eyes at the light coming through a crack in the curtains. My alarm hasn't gone off yet so I know it can't be too late in the day. Will is lying just behind me. I hear the steady rhythm of his breathing and know he's still asleep. I didn't mean to fall asleep on him last night, so I decide to wake him up in the best way possible.

Slowly, I roll over until I'm facing him. He's always adorable when he's sleeping. This morning both his arms are pulled over his head. One of them is resting against his forehead and it looks like he's frozen in the middle of dramatically swishing his hair back.

I take my sleep shirt and underwear off under the covers and slide them to the edge of the bed. The sheets at this hotel aren't as soft as Will's are at the condo, but that's okay. I'll only care about that for a few more seconds.

I've read about waking up a man with a blow job before, but I've never done it. *This is going to be tricky.*

I wonder if it would be best to stroke him until he's hard and then get my mouth involved or if I should start with my tongue. What would feel best for him?

I hear Will's assuring voice from earlier in our relationship, *"You can never do it wrong as long as you don't stop."*

That memory emboldens me to take action. At this angle, I think the best strategy is to use my hand. I fiddle around under the sheets until I find his side. Slowly I glide my hand down his torso, past his belly button, and to his thigh.

I look back at his face to see if anything has registered yet. He hasn't moved.

My hand wanders to his crotch and I find it. He's flaccid, of course, because he's sleeping. I make a face and feel a little excited as I realize I've never had the chance to play with him while he's been soft before.

I begin exploring this new version of him with my hand.

The skin is much more malleable than when he's hard. I gently tug and stroke his girth hoping this will be a pleasant way for him to wake up.

I'm mesmerized by how velvety soft his penis is as I continue to caress it.

Suddenly, I feel it thickening beneath my fingers. I feel relief as his body reacts to my touch and gives me the confidence to continue my ministrations.

After a few more pumps of his member I hear Will groan, "Having fun there Nikki?" His voice is husky with disuse this early in the morning. The effect goes straight to my core and I feel myself getting wet.

I crane my neck and look up at him through hooded eyes. "You asked me to make sure you still have all your parts." I give his cock a slightly rougher stroke as I begin to count, "This makes one." Then I let go of it and find his balls I cup each individually and confirm, "There's members two and three. Looks like your check-up is all good." My hand goes back to his penis and picks up where it left off.

"Well thank you for such an intense exam, Nikki. I don't know what I would do without you confirming my balls didn't freeze off yesterday." He growls at me through clenched teeth. "That feels great, but if you don't let me near your pussy soon I'm going to take over."

I place my free hand on his chest to keep him flat on the bed. I pump him mercilessly with a slight edge of roughness I know he likes. Will's hips buck beneath me signifying how much he's enjoying this.

"Nikki," he growls this time putting strength behind his efforts to sit up and take control.

Instead of granting him what he wants, I push his head back into the pillows.

I hear a gushing of air leave the pillow as Will starts to protest, "What the—"

He's cut off by my body twisting over his. I let go of his dick for just long enough to brace myself next to his body. I hook my leg over his head and move to straddle his torso. In a matter of seconds, I've gone from lying next to Will to having my face directly next to his junk.

I waste no time in opening my mouth and taking him as deep as my gag reflex will allow.

I hear Will moan out, "Fuck." Then his hands are grabbing my ass and yanking me down, closer to his mouth.

With his first lick, I'm undone. I lay across his body savoring the ferocity with which he eats me out. His rough calloused hands grip and knead at my ass and thighs, constantly roaming and gripping me in just the right places.

I continue working his dick with my hands and mouth. I lick and suck him as deep as I can. My hands make up the length that my mouth can't handle, pumping him firmly and bringing him closer and closer to the edge.

All rational thinking is lost to the sensation of how well he plucks the strings of my body while I reward him with equal fervor.

I feel the precipice of my release growing nearer when Will interrupts the building tension in my body and lifts me off of his face.

"Babe," he pants out. "If you don't stop soon I'm going to come down your throat."

With that, I lift my mouth from his dick and give it a final loving lick and a peck on the tip. I turn and look back at him with a devilish grin plastered on my face. Then I slowly drag my body down his until we're aligned for reverse cowgirl.

"Bend your knees and plant your feet," I instruct him. When Will's legs are in position I use them for balance and angle myself above his dick.

Will seamlessly reaches down and guides me onto his penis. "Fuck yes, impale yourself on me," Will growls as he starts thrusting from below.

We find our rhythm quickly and the combined efforts of my body working with his has me climbing toward release again.

He grips my ass and drives into me mercilessly. At this angle, he reaches deeper than he ever has before. I feel my neck loll back, savoring how full I am every time he's sheathed fully inside of me.

Will's hand finds my hair and pulls it to the side, forcing me to look at him. His eyes have darkened with desire. I swallow excitedly, waiting for him to tell me what he wants.

"Play with yourself, baby. Come over the edge with me."

I don't need more directions. I immediately do as I'm told and Will unleashes his control beneath me. His grip on my hips is the only thing holding me here as my focus changes to chasing my climax.

With a few more of Will's determined thrusts and my own ministrations, I moan out, "So close."

"Almost there," Will answers with a husky growl.

I know it's time to take the leap. I apply more pressure to my clit and find the release my body has been begging for since our flight from California.

Will lets out a roar as my inner walls contract from my orgasm. He rides his climax out inside of me which causes mine to draw out longer than typical. By the time Will stops pumping himself below me I feel like jelly. He stills beneath me. My hands are bracing against his knees and it's all I can do not to fall off the bed. Will must sense this, or maybe my muscles are shaking, because he moves and pulls me off his body and cradles me to his side on the bed lying next to him.

We lie together, regaining our composure when a knock sounds at the door. "Housekeeping!" A voice behind the door calls out.

"What?" I whisper shout at Will.

"Just a moment," he calls to the doorway while he bolts up and strides to his suitcase. He quickly pulls on a pair of sweats as I crawl under the sheets that we'd tossed aside a few minutes ago.

I hear the door creak open and the room is flooded with light from the hallway. Will's quiet and steady tamber resonates through the room but I can't discern what he's saying to the person in the hallway.

The door clicks shut and he reenters the bed area of the room. "Well I have good news and I have bad news."

I sit up clutching the sheets to my chest and say, "Like a bandaid."

He pulls a shirt out of his suitcase as he tells me. "Good news is they'll come back in half an hour. Bad news is we overslept and at this rate, we definitely won't be making it to Aunt Julie's by eleven. We also might miss our flight entirely. It's currently ten a.m."

I jump out of bed in shock and fly into action. We both zoom around the room in a tornado of grabbing items and shoving them into either suitcase. We can sort out what belongs to whom when we get back to California.

I dress quickly while telling Will, "I can do my hair and makeup while you drive."

"Works for me. Guess we're skipping breakfast." He concludes.

"Who knows when we'll have time to eat today," I reply as I grab my discarded clothes from earlier.

Will gives the bathroom a final check and we dash out the door. We're on the road by ten-twenty and I use Will's phone to text his aunt that we're running a bit late.

After that there's no sense in stressing, Will is driving as fast as legally allowed and either we'll make it at this point, or we won't. Only time will tell.

# Six

# Hotel Hot Tubs

## Spring Term

A FEW WEEKS LATER I sit on Stefan's couch looking at our friend group. The rest of them are in the kitchen, standing around the island as dinner wraps up. I've already cleared my plate. I watch as Stefan laughs at something Will says. Ryan has integrated into their friendship as best as a gun-loving jock can intermingle with two video game nerds. Tipp has taken up a routine of hovering near Ryan when we're hanging out. I think she does it as a buffer for him in case the conversation gets awkward.

The space is dimly lit, only the kitchen light and the glow of the T.V. The couch beneath me has a few stains from various food related incidents, Stefan has shared with us over the summer. It's then that I realize Chuck and Brittney have either had sex on this couch or on the floor where my bare feet are currently resting. *Gross*. I really hope none of these stains are from them.

I shudder at that and change my train of thought to reflect on our friendships. The final two terms in California feel like they've been put on fast forward. The last few months have flown by at record speed.

Winter term finals came and went and we all settled into the new routine of Spring term.

Stefan and Mia have maintained their long distance relationship for almost two years now.

Tipp and Ryan have chosen to move to Texas in July when his service in the military wraps up. Tipp has figured out a university in Dallas that will accept a transfer nursing student so she won't have to repeat any credits in her degree.

Will and I are getting ready to move vertically across the country in June. That's only two months away. Everything feels so right with the five of us right now it makes me sad to think of how much things will be different this time next year.

Stefan breaks away from the others and comes to join me on the couch. "How's it going?"

I plaster on a fake smile for his sake. "Just thinking about how much things will be changing in the next year," I tell him as I tuck my legs into a crisscross applesauce position.

He picks up the remote and clicks the T.V. off leaving us mostly in the dark. The kitchen lighting can't permeate this far into the living space. "Well, we've got some fun to have before you all leave. Come hear what Ryan suggests we do." He stands and offers me a hand.

I take it and use his strength to pull myself from the comfy couch. We pad over to the rest of our friends and they fill us in on the plan.

"You have your suit right?" Tipp asks me first.

"Of course, we're at Stefan's. You never know when a suit will be needed."

Will looks my way with excitement in his eyes. "Just wait until you hear what Ryan says we should do tonight."

My gaze flicks to Tipp's boyfriend. "Yes?"

He sets a beer down on the counter. "So, back in Texas when we wanted to go swimming but couldn't because none of us had pools we would go to fancy hotels and use their facilities."

"But we can go swimming," I start and motion with my thumb to the house's back door and the pool that lies beyond it.

"Well yeah," Ryan agrees. "But trust me, it's more fun at a hotel."

I look at Will who still seems on board with this ludicrous idea. My brain won't wrap around any of it. "So one of you plans on spending a couple hundred dollars on a hotel room so that we can swim in their pool tonight? Whoever has that kind of money in this group should take us all to Disneyland, it would be more fun."

Stefan snickers from the sink where he's currently washing our dishes.

"Tell her," Tipp says to Ryan with a smirk.

He gives me a mischievous grin while wrapping his arm around Tipp's shoulders. "No one is paying for a room at the hotel Nikki."

"Then we can't go swimming at it." I counter.

Will wraps his arm around my waist and drags me toward him until our bodies are flush. "Babe," he leans into my space conspiratorially and clarifies, "We'd be sneaking onto the property."

My jaw drops.

It takes me a full minute to process Ryan's plan that Stefan, Tipp, and Will want to go along with.

"Okay, so you want to go swimming at a fancy hotel. We're not vandalizing anything. How much trouble can we actually get into?"

Ryan shrugs, his neck momentarily reminding me of a retreating turtle's head. "I mean, we got caught once. The hotel just kicked us out and told us not to do it again. So we went across the street to the next hotel. The trick is to not go to the same chain, they're not going to help out the competition so it was like we had a clean slate."

I nod, seems reasonable.

Twenty minutes later I've changed into my suit and covered up again with my shorts and graphic t-shirt. This one is another of my favorites. It has vampire teeth outlined by burgundy lips and there's a little blood dripping down the side of the mouth. In between the teeth, the phrase Bite Me is written in cursive. I love how the harshness of a bite from an apex predator is contrasted so eloquently with a dainty brush stroke of cursive commentary. I'm in the middle of Stefan's back seat, sandwiched between Tipp and Will with Ryan riding shotgun. He may be shorter than the other guys, but he definitely has a wider frame than either of them.

We arrive at Mission Beach soon and Stefan steers the car toward the third nicest hotel in the area.

"No resorts," Ryan tells us. "People at resorts are usually there for multiple days and the employees vaguely recognize them. The nicest hotel in the area will have a little more security than the rest. We need a place that has a detached pool with a gated entrance from the parking lot."

"I think I know just the one," Stefan says, taking the freeway exit.

In a few minutes, we're at a large brand hotel.

"Good, there's a lot of cars in the parking lot. That means the employees will be busy taking care of guests and less likely to notice our intrusion." Ryan says as Stefan picks a spot to park the car.

I peer through the back seat and take a look at the building. It's at least ten stories tall and drips with expensive taste. To the right of the skyscraper of a building is a sprawling fenced-in pool and hot tub area. The fences are well over eight feet tall, probably to prevent others from doing what we're about to try. I can't see if anyone is in the space due to vines and shrubbery that are attempting to camouflage the black wrought iron fencing.

Stefan aligns the car in the spot, kills the engine, and looks to Ryan for further instructions.

He quietly tells us, "So we need to leave our clothes in the car. No guest at a hotel is going to walk around fully clothed on their way to the pool. Obviously, we can wear our shoes."

It takes some organization but soon, Tipp and I have managed to get our shorts off. The guys have a much easier time disrobing because they only need to remove their shirts. Once we're all adequately undressed we climb out of the car.

In the still of the evening air, I hear the distant noise of the Mission Beach Boardwalk. It has to be less than a mile away from here.

I tuck my hair behind my ears and nervously look up to Will. "Are we really going to do this?" I ask with trepidation.

His arms wrap around my shoulders and he pulls me to his chest. "We can go walk the boardwalk instead if you're not comfortable." Will offers while holding me tight.

I mull over my options and bring voice to my deepest concern. "If I get arrested for trespassing I don't know if I can still be a teacher. We're not going to be arrested are we?"

He leans back and looks me in the eyes. "I don't think so. If we get caught we politely apologize and run like hell. I don't think you get arrested your first time messing up."

It's dark in the parking lot so I can't see many details of his face but I think there's a twinkle in his eyes. "You're excited to break the rules right now aren't you?" I ask him.

His lips form a sheepish grin. "You know us, we never break the rules. This is probably a once-in-a-lifetime experience."

I pinch one of his nipples and shake my head at him. "You naughty, naughty boy."

He laughs as we disentangle our arms and meet everyone else at the back of the car.

"Towels?" Tipp asks reaching to open the trunk.

"Can't." Ryan's voice stops her movement. Quietly he explains, "Hotel guests don't bring their own towels, and I'm guessing you didn't bring five plain white towels did you?"

"Actually," Stefan disagrees. He clicks the button on the keys that opens the trunk and it rises slowly and illuminates a perfect pile of five white towels.

"How?" I ask confused.

Stefan's hip rests against the car as he tells us, "My mother is a neat freak and loves her perfectly white linens, yes even with having three sons. If a towel gets a blemish, she retires it to the cupboard and buys a new one." He reaches into the trunk and distributes a towel to each of us. "These may have a small stain somewhere, but they're definitely cleaner than the couch you all choose to sit on whenever you're at my house."

"Gross dude." Will replies.

My nose crinkles at Stefan validating my earlier fears.

We all grab our towels and follow Ryan, Will and I making up the back of our group. This was Ryan's idea, so he can be the one to figure out how to execute it.

He walks up to the pool gate with the confidence of a man who has done this many times before.

"Perfect, there's someone in there swimming. Watch and learn ladies and gents." He whispers for only our ears. Then he jiggles the handle noisily before loudly proclaiming, "Crap, it's locked. Did you bring the key babe?"

Tipp chimes in without missing a beat. "No, I left it up in our room. Shoot baby, I'm so sorry!"

This has grabbed the attention of whoever is splashing around in the pool that's currently just out of our reach.

"You all wait here," Stefan calls over his shoulder as he walks away from us.

"Where are you going?" I call out of confusion and concern that he's about to abandon us without a way home.

He's halfway to the hotel entrance now. "I'm gonna go ask the front desk for a spare key!" he calls. I can tell it's a touch louder than necessary for the benefit of the swimmers watching in on our conundrum.

I see Stefan's silhouette go behind the wall of the hotel but then he stops walking. We all know he won't go to the front desk and ask for a key, but hopefully, the other guests will overhear and take pity on us.

"You guys need a hand?" A lady a few years older than us asks our group.

Ryan cues an extra thick southern drawl to drive home that he's not from around here, "Yes ma'am." He dips his chin in greeting and touches the imaginary brim of the cowboy hat he's not wearing. "We left our key in our room. Is there any chance you could please let us in?"

She smiles at his innocent country boy demeanor and comes closer to the gate. "Of course, sweetheart." With that, she opens the gate from the interior and we're in.

I hear Stefan's flip-flops hitting the pavement as he runs back to us. He's holding his hand in the air with a card in it, shouting, "I just got the— oh! You got in, nice." Then he pockets the card he was holding into his shorts.

I narrow my eyes at him knowing full well that wasn't a hotel key card. I can't question him here but I will get answers. Later.

We pile all our towels and shoes at a table and make straight for the pool. It's massive and has plenty of space for games. The entire area is secluded behind thick twining vines that cover every fence in sight.

After a little while of chatting with the "other" tourists, we suggest a game of Marco Polo. It's a blast watching the guys prank these strangers, so different from how they typically work the system when it's just Tipp and me. When I'm it, Will takes pity on my soul after a few fruitless minutes and lets me tag him to put me out of my misery. It's a genuinely wonderful time.

The boys conclude our Marco Polo session by putting on a show for the hotel guests.

There's no diving board but that doesn't stop them from performing some of their favorite dives and jumps into the pool. The finale of the show is Stefan's signature couch-laying position. He gives a wink to one of the moms supervising the chaos as he descends into the pool. I swear I can hear her swoon from across the natatorium.

We wrap up the fun evening by cooling down in the hot tub. It's secluded from the excitement of the pool by lush vegetation. Multiple vines twine around an arch that covers the hot tub and it's surrounded on all sides by walls of shrubbery. The only exception is a walkway just wide enough to walk through single-file.

"It's like they want us to fuck in here," Ryan whispers a little too loudly to Tipp.

She pushes his shoulder gently and changes the subject. "So Nikki, you told me there was drama related to getting back from Portland but we still haven't had time for the whole story."

"Oh story time! Let's hear it!" Stefan chimes in.

I feel a blush rise to my cheeks remembering the details that led up to our departing flight from Portland. I glance at Will, silently wondering if he'll take over for me. Instead, he puts his arm behind my shoulders, resting on the concrete decking of the jacuzzi, and says, "I support however many details you choose to disclose."

*What is he a fucking lawyer now?* I arch an eyebrow at his choice of words. His knowing smirk seals his fate. All the details it is. I quietly, and exaggeratedly regale our friends with the tale of Will's morning wood. I probably go into more detail than he'd prefer, but he also doesn't jump in to assist or suppress.

When I wrap up the saga of my first experience with sixty-nine Tipp's jaw is on the floor. I also notice Ryan adjust himself a bit under the bubbles of the warm water.

"You didn't!" Tipp yells too loudly for our presence to remain unnoticed.

I bite my lip, remembering how wonderful that morning with Will was. "Yeah, you should try it sometime," I recommend, trying to ease the sexual tension I've accidentally created within our group.

"Okay, so how did that result in almost missing your flight?" Stefan interjects.

"Oh!" I forgot to mention those details. "Well apparently neither of us had set our alarms. Right after the fireworks settled between us there was a knock on the door."

"Too loud for one of the neighbors?" Ryan suggests.

I wave off his comment, "Nah, it was just housekeeping letting us know we were there past check out. No big deal." I finish sarcastically.

Then Will chooses to participate in the story. "So we ran around the room and threw any item we found into either of our suitcases. We got to my Aunt's house about half an hour late."

Tipp's on the edge of her seat with our tale. "Did you miss your return flight?"

Will's hand moves from the concrete decking and he rests it on my shoulders. "This one," he says jostling me gently. "Is always early. So with the half hour sex delay, we ended up with only an hour to kill at the airport before boarding began."

I click my tongue at his jab and give him what I hope is a menacing side eye. "You tease, but if it wasn't for my planning we would have missed our flight. I don't think that's something you ever want to have to deal with."

Will kisses my temple but says nothing.

"Do you know where you're going to try to live?" Stefan asks us.

"I've been looking a little online, but you don't really know if a place has the right vibe until you see it, right?" I suggest.

Will clarifies, "We're flying back over Spring Break to see if we can find some good options."

"You have to open up a credit card before that trip!" I remind him.

He grins knowingly and nods his head at me, "Absolutely, don't want to go through that ordeal with Aunt Julie again. Anyway," he looks back to Stefan. "We figure it's about sixty days before we want to move, so hopefully people have given some notices and we'll be able to sneak in with perfect timing.

"Or we'll be living out of a hotel for a while." I shrug while mentioning our expensive backup plan.

"I don't think Will would mind that very much," Tipp mumbles to Ryan.

"Oh my Gods, Tipp!" I shout as I send a double-handed tidal wave splash her way without warning. She turns her head in my direction at the perfect moment to get bitch slapped by the water. With Ryan only being an inch or two away from Tipp my aim is perfect for drenching the two of them. I watch as a rivulet of water ricochets off her shoulder and goes straight up his nose.

My face breaks into a huge toothy grin and Stefan reaches over Will to give me a high five. "Nice aim, Nikki!" He compliments as our hands collide with a satisfactory clap.

I watch my friend regain her composure across from us; when she stops sputtering water she flips me off.

I roll my eyes and suggest to Will, "It's getting kinda toasty in here. Want to grab our clothes from the car and walk around the Boardwalk? Who knows when we'll be back here next."

His face turns bittersweet as he nods his head. "Can I grab your keys man?" Will asks Stefan.

"I think I'll go with you two," Stefan's voice comes out with a raspy worry to his tone.

I tear my eyes off Will's beautiful face and look at Stefan. His lip has retreated over his top row of teeth and his grimace is worthy of the GIF Hall of Fame. I follow where his horrified expression is originating from and see them. Tipp is all but in Ryan's lap and they're making out, well, like sloppy animals. Hands are pulling hair and tongues are everywhere except in one another's mouths. After a few seconds of frozen terror at the sight unfolding before my eyes, my face morphs into a twin of Stefan's.

Will clears his throat.

They don't notice.

I stand to retreat from the hot tub. "At least let us run away before you start fucking," I shoot at Tipp.

They keep pawing at one another without any recognition we've spoken.

When we flee the secluded jacuzzi area we notice that the pool portion has completely emptied in the late evening hours. The boys are quick behind me and we grab our shoes and towels from the table we left them piled on earlier. I pat down my skin and then bend at the waist and twist my hair up like I do after a shower. I whip the end of the towel back as I stand and put my hands on my hips waiting for the boys.

They both sling their towels over their shoulders and in the dark pool lighting, they do look like brothers.

"Nice hair," Stefan mocks.

I place my hand under my chin and pose. "I know right? It's the newest fashion."

He jingles the keys in his hand, "Shall we?"

I'm about to reply when we hear the unmistakable sound of water sloshing in rhythm and low moans coming from behind the hedges.

"No!" I whisper shout as I cover my shocked face with a hand.

Will grabs my other hand and hauls me toward the gate. "We better run before our ears are scarred with any other sounds!"

Stefan follows behind urgently. As we flee to his car we break into hysterics.

"Apparently one couple's story time is another couple's foreplay," I joke as we get dressed and head over to the Mission Beach Boardwalk.

## Seven

# Maple Drive Apartments

### Spring Break

For Spring Break we make our second trip to Eugene as planned, this time with fewer hiccups. Our rental car clunks over the rails of the train tracks that cut through the street beneath us. We exited the freeway a couple blocks back and have been blindly following the GPS directions since. We're heading to the first apartment that looked acceptable to my delicate middle-class mindset coupled with our broke-college-kid wallets.

Will turns left and drives parallel to the tracks for a couple hundred feet before the street comes to a dead end at a gravel parking lot. There are cars parked less than ten feet from the tracks. There's not even a fence for separation. About ten spots ahead of us there's a building labeled 'Manger.' Will pulls through the lot and parks in a spot reserved for potential residents.

"Ready?" Will asks as he puts the rental car in park.

I purse my lips with honesty. "It looked nicer online," I admit to him.

Will reaches across the center console and puts his hand on my thigh. He squeezes gently and reassures me, "We're only here for a tour. Maybe it will be perfect. We won't know until we get out and take a look."

I lace my fingers with his and use his warm calloused hand to center my racing thoughts.

A few moments pass quietly between us.

Then, I reluctantly let go, open the door, and step out of the car. I shut it gently behind me and hear Will's door snap shut as well. We meet at the trunk and I take his hand in mine again as we head to the manager's building.

The muddy gravel squelches beneath our feet. When we pass through the parking lot there is a paved walking path the last few steps. It's cracked and covered in patches of moss.

Will reaches out and twists the rusty doorknob and we enter.

Inside the office is pleasant enough. An average looking woman is sitting behind an outdated brown desk. Her fingers tap across a keyboard as she works and there is Country music playing softly through a speaker I can't visually locate. The space is slightly cramped with two chairs against the wall, a water cooler, and a large table in the center of the area with four chairs surrounding it. The furniture is modest and practical which matches the plain, beige painted walls.

"You must be Nikki and Will!" The lady behind the desks greets us with a cheerful smile. She stands and circles around to us extending her hand, "I'm Jenny."

I shake it automatically and let Will take charge of this interaction.

He matches her jovial attitude and replies, "Yes we are. Hoping to get a tour today."

"Right, but you're not ready to move until June is that correct?"

He nods his head. "Yes again."

She turns and bends to fiddle through some papers on her desk. When she stands she has a set of keys in her hands. "Okay, we're going to look at a unit on the first floor today. It's the same floor plan as the unit that should be available when you're hoping to move in. Of course, we can't know exactly because if the current tenant chooses to stay we can't kick them out for you, but I'm fairly certain they'll be moving out."

Will engages with her, "Sounds great. We'd love to see the similar unit."

He seems so at ease with this entire interaction, like he's been looking at apartments as a side job for weeks. Not like this is his first time.

Jenny leads us through the complex. It's located just behind the manager's office. "The laundry machines are in there," she points to a small external building. I notice there are no covered walkways leading to it. *Everything would be exposed to the Oregon rain if we do our laundry there.*

"There are two entrances to the building, if you choose to rent here you'll get a key that opens all external places residents are permitted to use."

"Why is the front entrance taped off?" Will asks.

I stop fixating on wet laundry and look for what he's mentioned. Then I see that there is caution tape exactly where he said. It's not only at the laundry room door, it's also roped around a massive tree in the middle of what I think is supposed to be a grassy courtyard. Currently, it looks more fitting to be called a duck pond.

Jenny grins at us over her shoulder. "With all the rain we get here the courtyard floods annually. No worries though. You can still access the laundry from the back door. The lock's a little sticky so just be sure to give it a jiggle when you're entering." She continues walking through the complex like these are regular problems to have. *Is annual flooding to the point of roping off an area due to safety a normal thing in Oregon?*

The apartment manager keeps walking past the buildings. It looks like they used to be a soft shade of brown, but in the years since that paint job, the colors have definitely faded. The apartment complex is made up of 6 two-story buildings. They surround the courtyard, 3 on either side. The second story is fenced in by rusted wrought iron. Residents' personalities shine through onto their patio spaces and the walkway that runs in front of their doors. Some people decorate with potted plants, others have kid's toys strewn about, and some choose only a doormat. No matter how they choose to display their personalities it feels like there's a layer of grime hovering over the entire complex.

Jenny takes us to the second-to-last building across from the tracks. She pauses in a doorway and points to the building behind us. "See that one? The unit that should be available in June is on the corner, first floor."

I follow where she's pointing with my gaze and see the unit. It's on the very edge of the property, furthest from the parking lot. That side of the complex is butted up against the train tracks, there is still no fence separating the two areas. Currently strewn in front of the door are two folding lawn chairs that are knocked over onto their sides with discarded beer bottles mixed around the chair legs.

"Ah, thanks for pointing it out," Will says neutrally. I can't tell if he's picking up on the details that I am, or if he's just really good at masking his true impressions.

"But we'll be looking at this unit today. The same floor plan, just a different spot." Jenny puts a key in the door and pushes it open.

I can hear the bottom seal of the door dragging on the carpet beneath it as the door opens with a loud squeak. Jenny pushes the door wide, flicks on a light switch to the right, and motions to the grand reveal.

I haven't let go of Will's hand since we got out of the car, except for quickly shaking Jenny's hand, and that's not about to change. He squeezes mine and leads the way across the threshold.

The first thing I notice is the odor. It accosts my nostrils and forces me to practice my poker face. The air is heavy with moisture in here. It smells of a combination of wet pet and mold. I'm about to give up and bolt when I hear Spencer Reid in the back of my mind. His voice explains that if we open our mouth and breathe through it for a few minutes then the sense of smell dissipates and we'll naturally acclimate to the new surroundings, no matter how unpleasant. So I do just that and listen to the boy genius.

I slightly open my mouth and take a tentative inhale. The odor does dampen and this allows my brain to take stock of the rest of the apartment. I look at the walls, painted a light beige. Parts of the paint are flaking off in patches and other areas are stained. *I do not want to know what created those stains.*

"Every unit is repainted before new inhabitants move in." Jenny offers after noticing where my eyes have been drawn to.

*A new paint job won't fix the things these walls have seen.*

I look down at the carpet. It's brown, black, and dark grey. The kind of carpet people get when they're trying to hide all the stains that they know will inevitably come with age, wear, and tear. Under my shoes, it doesn't have much give which means either the carpet pad is minimal or completely nonexistent.

I take a step forward and Will lets me carve our path through the one bedroom unit.

Inside the room, my logical mind takes over. I need to make a pros and cons list of this space to determine if I can live here. With this shift of thinking, I roll back my shoulders and put on my adult persona. I disentangle my fingers from Will's grasp. Then I start my assessment of the first potential apartment where my new life will blossom.

I walk across the carpeted living space in front of a large front window. In the corner of the room, there is a door. When I open it, I learn that there's a small coat closet inside. This would be where we store our jackets, on the top shelf we would place our board games.

Next.

I trail the back wall of the living space and come across an opening. I'm sure someone somewhere called this a hallway. It's an area where doors meet. To my right there's a door. In front of me, there's a door. To my left, there's also a door. My analytical brain chooses the door to the right first.

It opens to what I assume is the master bedroom. It's medium in size. I think the room would fit Will's double bed and my massive dresser no problem. If we can save and get a queen bed, that might be harder to fit in here. The wall shared with the living room has a double bifold door closet. There's no window in this bedroom.

It's then I realize that the far wall of our bedroom would be adjacent to the living room of the next apartment over. *So either quiet sex or everyone will know exactly what you're doing. Great.*

This floor is covered in the same dull brown carpet as the living room and smells heavily of the wet pet odor I first noticed when we walked in. I guess Dr. Reid left out the detail that if the scent grows stronger you're not completely desensitized to it.

It's workable. If we must.

Next.

I leave the bedroom and the door that was directly ahead before is now on my right. I choose this one and try the door but it won't push open. I have to pause, take a step back into the living quarters, and then try the door again. Instead of opening inwards like this four foot wide "hallway" needs, the door opens outward. It reveals a second coat closet. There is a single bar for hanging items and a solo shelf above it. If this door is open then anyone in the last room will be stuck inside until this door closes. That will cause a lot of unnecessary hallway traffic jams, even with only two people.

"Some people choose to use that closet as their pantry," Jenny comments from her observation spot in the living room.

"Thanks!" I call over my shoulder.

Next.

That only leaves the door on my left. This one opens into the room the way I am expecting. I take a step inside and see a bathroom. There's a small linen closet and a tub shower on the far wall. In the corner furthest from the door there's a toilet, a sink and medium sized vanity between them and the door. This room smells the dampest and I swear I see mold in the corners. It makes sense that this room would be damp, but if it hasn't been lived in long enough for all the furniture to be removed I doubt anyone has showered in here recently. That means the suffocating dampness in this air will only get worse when Will and I need to shower in here.

I pivot out of the room and turn to appraise the only space remaining.

The kitchen.

Before I'm able to take in the kitchen's pros and cons my ears are assaulted by an incredibly high pitched screeching of metal on metal. Then a deep horn blares. The sounds get louder and louder and I'm frozen in fear.

My body starts to feel a soft shaking in the apartment. My rational brain thinks this must be an earthquake, but we're not in California anymore so that can't be it.

I give Jenny a worried glance.

She stands there as if nothing is happening.

Will dashes out of the bathroom and stops in front of me in the kitchen.

Then I notice through the doorway that's still open behind Jenny there's a train on the tracks. Its presence is overwhelming to my senses. We all stand there for the duration of its passing. The apartment shakes, the screeching continues, Jenny looks unfazed.

After what feels like twenty minutes, probably closer to four or five, the screeching has dampened to a rhythmic clunking on the tracks. The apartment is still jostling beneath my feet, but not as violently as before. Will is blocking my view of Jenny with his body and his hands are resting on my hips.

"You good?" He asks quietly enough that I don't think Jenny can hear.

I stare up at him hoping that the pure terror that has settled in my gut about living here is being adequately communicated nonverbally. My fists are clenching his forearms. My eyes are bulging. My lips are worried into a thin line between my teeth. *There is no way I can live in this place.* I quickly shake my head no, hoping Jenny can't see.

Will slides his arm around my waist and pulls me close. He calls over the fading din of the passing train, "I think we're good here. Thank you very much for the tour, Jenny. We'll be in touch." He extends his hand to her in farewell and leads us to the doorway.

I'm surprised when Will doesn't slow his pace when we're outside. He's walking with purpose and only my months of learning his stride are allowing me to keep up with him.

Jenny scurries out behind us and quickens her pace to catch up before we hit the parking lot. I hear her voice call out behind us, "I know the train can seem like a lot, but they only come through a few times a day!"

Will stops on the paved walkway and turns to Jenny. "Oh no." He placates her, "Sorry for our abrupt exit, we just have another appointment to keep across town." He offers her his hand one more time.

They shake as he reinforces our exit, "We appreciate your time Jenny. Thank you for the tour."

I give a half grin and a small wave goodbye.

Jenny is still trying to pitch the complex to us as we make our exit. "Let me know if you need any help with the application!" She calls as we reach the rental car, "You'd be wonderful tenants to have here. Really bring the place up a bit!"

He opens the door for me. I slide into the clean car and breathe a sigh of relief when he closes the door behind me.

Will gets into the driver's seat and efficiently buckles up and turns it on.

"I just—"

"Not yet." He interrupts me.

My head twists at breakneck speed and I glare at him. I cross my arms haughty and try again. "I think—"

"Babe." Will cuts me off again. Then he puts his hand on my thigh in that way that always clams me. "Jenny is mere feet away from your window, still watching us. Let me pull out of the parking lot before you begin. Please." He squeezes my leg and takes his hand back to get the car moving.

I glance over my shoulder and sure enough, Jenny is still standing on the walkway in front of the manager's office.

When we clear the parking lot and cross the tracks, Will casually starts the conversation. "So, what did you think?"

I gape like a fish out of water. When I find words they come out shrill and panicked. "What did I think? What did I think?" My hands frantically wave, helping to dispel the bottled up tension created by that tour. "Will, there was mold in the bathroom. It smelled like a puppy mill. The train tracks? If we were to move into the apartment available in June that train will be rolling by less than fifty feet away from where our heads hit the pillow. What did I think? I don't know! That if we end up working different shifts I'll be murdered in my sleep at that complex!" I'm near hysterics by the end of my tirade.

My heart is beating too fast.

I feel trapped inside this moving vehicle.

My body feels like it's growing exponentially bigger and the car is shrinking at the same pace.

My hands are clammy.

I can't do this.

That apartment is not the beginning of our happily ever after.

My life would end like a scene from *Dexter* if we move there.

"Nikki," Will reaches out and takes my hands in his. "I don't think it was a good fit either." He stares into my eyes but it feels more like he's reading my soul.

His calloused palms start to center my racing mind. I close my eyes and inhale deeply. He didn't think it was a good fit either. *He didn't think it was a good fit either*. I tell him what I was trying not to think about that entire tour. "That apartment complex felt like somewhere you'll be imprisoned— not somewhere you want to build a life with someone."

He strokes the back of my hands with his calloused thumbs but doesn't reply.

"Will?" I begin once I'm centered. "How the Hell are you not crashing the car holding my hands and looking at me? Where—" I look away from him and take in my surroundings. He's parked the car in some random lot. I have no idea how we got here. "When— What?"

His face breaks into a huge grin. " I love when you get like this."

"Like what?"

"Flustered." He says. He leans across the console and gives me a quick kiss. "Your eyebrows meet in the middle, your nose scrunches up adorably, and you can't form a complete sentence. When you're flustered it's one of the rare times I remember you're human."

"What would I be if I wasn't human?" I ask confused.

He takes his hands from mine and holds my face gently. "Absolutely fucking perfect Nikki." He pulls me toward him and angles my face perfectly to meet his in a passionate kiss.

His tongue strokes my lips asking for more and I greedily open for him. One of Will's hands moves to the back of my neck and snakes its way into my hair, holding me perfectly in place for him.

I melt across the center console, longing for our bodies to be molded together.

I let him devour me with abandon. I match his strokes and nips with my own until we're both a mess of uneven breathing and heavy petting.

As I pull back from him I hear a mournful sigh escape his lips.

I lick my lips savoring the taste of him on my skin. As I look up it's pure reflex to bite my lip at the sight of the man before me.

His eyes are hooded with lust. Desire and intent etched on every line of his face. "Come back here," he growls at me.

He tries to capture me again but I lean back completely against my door. If he wants me he'll have to climb over that console to get me.

"Nikki," he growls, "Where do you think you're going?"

I smile mischievously at him. "I think *we're* going to that second complex now."

Will's face falls as if I've doused him in a bucket of cold water. He leans back into his seat and runs his hands down his face. With another deep exhale he agrees, "Yeah, cause there's no way we're moving into that first one."

I cross the space of the front seat of the car and kiss his cheek gently. "I couldn't tell if you liked that first apartment or not," I admit. "You looked so at ease with everything I thought you liked it."

He adjusts his pants with a grimace before he replies. "I could have lived there. I think Stefan would have too, but you're more accustomed to the finer things in life." He plugs our next destination into my phone's navigation system before continuing. "I'm guessing you didn't like that the parking lot wasn't paved?"

"How did you know that?" I demand as he pulls onto the street again and follows the directions toward the second complex we liked when searching online.

"Your nose was crinkled before we got to the walkway."

I look away from the road into my hands. *Am I that readable?* I think back to how I felt stepping onto that parking lot's gravel and he's right. I did immediately dislike it.

His voice jolts me from my thoughts. "I'd bet that one of the reasons you didn't like the gravel lot is because it would be hard to walk on in heels?"

I give him an exasperated exhale and roll my eyes. I suck my teeth and look away from his beautiful face. Reluctantly I utter, "Maybe," refusing to let him know how accurate he is.

I hear him lightly chuckle as he keeps driving without further comment.

The streets start to clear of the dirt and grime that was layering that part of Eugene. There are sidewalks lining each side of the road. Businesses are open and thriving with customers filtering through their doors and waiting in their drive-throughs. Trees are everywhere I can see. It's early spring so their buds are just forming, beginning the annual cycle of life and regrowth. The clouds have parted and the sun is shining down upon us as Will drives down the street. To our right is a sprawling outdoor shopping mall. To our left the street splinters off from this main drive and is lined with houses and apartment complexes alike.

Will gets to a T in the road and turns left into a driveway. I see a sign that says Maple Drive Apartments at the entrance. It's bright, clean, and welcoming.

Will turns into the lot when the road is clear and parks in a paved parking spot.

We meet at the trunk of the car like we did at the complex earlier in the day.

This time, however, there is pavement below my feet. The buildings are spread out spaciously across the property. There are grassy corridors outlined by cement walkways. The complex's paint job is fresh and crisp. It's beige like the first complex, but with dark brown accents, and nothing is flaking off or fading away.

Will's hand finds the small of my back and I look up at him with an optimistic smile.

As we head to the manager's office I can't help thinking that this is how I'd envisioned the beginning of our forever looking.

# Eight

## *Graduation*

### End of Spring Term

"It's absolutely perfect!" I excitedly shout down the line at Tipp.

"I know. You keep saying that." She replies flatly.

Our relationship has been like this in the weeks since Will and I got back from Oregon. I'm excited. I feel like our plan is working out and everything is happening as it was meant to, with the exception of one thing.

Tipp.

"Can we have an honest best friend moment?" I ask her. Enough is enough.

Her voice comes tersely down the line, "I guess?"

"What the fuck is going on with you?" I start. "Last year you were the most supportive best bitch a girl could ask for. This year I don't feel the same level from you. I love you so dearly, you are my best bitch, Tipp. But, you cancel half the time. I don't know the last time we hung out without Ryan present, and I don't feel supported like you've been in the past."

I hear her exhale but she doesn't answer my question.

I give her time to process and settle a little deeper into my cozy reading chair at Nana's house. Otis is in his favorite spot, purring in my lap. My room is littered with boxes, packing tape, and excitement for Will and my future. It would be that much better if my best friend could find it in her heart to be happy for me too.

I scratch Otis behind his ears. If Tipp doesn't say something soon this pause will become awkward.

I barely hear her whisper, "You're right."

I need more than that so I choose to wait her out. *Sometimes extending the silence is a good way to get others to fill it right?*

A cupboard slams on Tipp's end of the line. "I just—" She begins but cuts herself off just as quickly. When she continues her voice is strained, "I just can't seem to fit it all in. If I hang out with you too much, Ryan gets upset and says he misses me. If I study enough to keep up my grades, then I can't hang with you or Ryan. If I settle for passing grades, I can fit working out into my schedule. But if I try to hang out with Ryan, keep up with you, work out, and get solid grades, I feel like I'm going crazy trying to balance all the commitments." She sniffles at the end.

Tipp's explanation makes sense, and the turmoil I heard in her voice tells me this wasn't easy for her to admit. "Why didn't you tell me you were struggling? You know I would have helped you figure something out."

Focused on what Tipp was finally voicing I'd stopped petting Otis. He mewls at me, letting me know this lapse in love is unacceptable. I scratch under his chin to help him remember why he likes me as I wait for Tipp. This conversation feels like pulling teeth but it needs to happen, our friendship depends on it.

"Telling you would have meant admitting I had a problem. You know I don't like dealing with that shit."

"So you decided to shove it down until the problem exploded in your face?" My face breaks into a grin. It's true, she does not deal well.

"Maybe?" She answers coyly.

I roll my eyes at my ridiculous best friend. "Well, it's too late to do anything about it now. You'll at least be at my graduation right?"

"Yes!" she yells too loudly. My ears shudder at the assault. My heart calms when Tipp returns to her obnoxious, in your face, self. "I got the day off, four p.m. right?"

I nod my head as I respond, "Yes. You can even bring Ryan this time if you want."

Tipp's voice drips with sarcasm, "Thank you so much for the permission, Mom!"

"Bye bitch," I chuckle out.

"Bye." She sing songs before cutting off the call.

I look down and notice that Otis vacated my lap somewhere during the end of that conversation. *Guess I wasn't petting him correctly. Or enough. Whatever.* I look over what remains of my room. I spent three years living here with Nana and that chapter of my life will be coming to a close in less than a month. While I'm excited for this new journey in our life, I'll also miss dinners and late night conversations with Nana.

I stand from my favorite reading chair and placate the depression threatening to fill the bedroom when I think about my impending departure. "I can't leave yet, graduation isn't until tomorrow." Then I head to my dresser and pick up where I left off packing up my room.

♥ • ♥ • ♥ • ♥ • ♥

I hand my name card to the assistant professor collecting them and wait for two graduates to be called before it's my turn. We attended the same college, but I've never seen the students ahead of me before.

"Laura Wong." Is announced by a jovial professor and a few people in the crowd let out a cheer.

I take a step forward and Will hands his card over behind me. Stefan is on deck behind him. One thing I appreciate about this informal graduation is that we are allowed to line up with our friends. That makes waiting more enjoyable. I don't hear a word of what I'm sure dignitaries are speaking poetically about, too busy worrying about not tripping over my own feet.

I'm so far down that rabbit hole I don't recognize when our cue to move and start filing up the stage. Will interrupts my thoughts and tells me we need to follow the leader.

I'm doing it again I realize, stressing on what-ifs instead of enjoying the current moment.

"Raquel Lopez." Is next to be announced, followed by applause from her petite cheering section.

Then it's my turn.

I take a nervous step forward and shake the hand of the presenter. He smiles at me and says, "Congratulations." Then he pivots to the microphone and declares. "Veronica Welch."

Cheers from three different areas of the crowd fill my ears. I scan the audience to identify who is celebrating me. I know one section is my own family; I spotted them earlier. I assume correctly that the second group is Will's family; I see his mom and big sister standing from their seats. I don't recognize the third group as quickly. Then it hits me, it's Stefan's family. I can see Brittney's permanently pouty face staring at the stage. His mom is clapping for me along with some other people I don't recognize as easily.

"William Zoo-" The announcer starts into the mic. Then he covers the mouthpiece and I hear him ask Will how to say his name. With a quick conference, he tries again a second time. "William

Zoo-kausk-ass." The man put a little too much emphasis on the last syllable and it came out sounding like 'ass.'

Cheers louder than I received echo through the audience.

I snicker as I make my way through the line of professors waiting to shake our hands. I've never seen most of them in the years I've been at this community college. I would much rather have had the opportunity to shake Mr. Fitzgibbon's hand than any of these strangers.

I reach the end of the assembly line of handshakes and fake smiles and wait for Will at the bottom of the stairs that descend from the stage.

He's quick behind me and we walk to the complimentary photographer together.

"I'll take the lady first." The woman behind the camera suggests.

I smile up at Will and then shake my head at her. "We'll take some together please," I suggest.

She objects, "We don't really do that."

Will's quick to support me as always. "Then I guess we won't be getting any pictures taken, thanks anyway." He shrugs and puts his hand on the small of my back and starts to guide us away from her.

"No wait!"

We pause and look at her.

"I have to get a picture of all the graduates, just hurry up so no one has enough time to notice okay?" She mumbles begrudgingly.

Will and I stand to either side of the yellow X that's been taped to the ground. From this vantage point, the building that houses the Griffin Center will be in the backdrop of the picture. I smile knowing that someday this will be a wonderful keepsake from the beginning of our relationship.

Will puts one arm around my shoulders and we both hold up our empty diploma cases with cheesy smiles as the photographer starts her routine.

I had us coordinate our outfits today because I knew there would be a lot of family members wanting to get pictures with both of us. Will is wearing an olive green button up shirt with a striped green and grey tie. I'm wearing one of my favorites, an above-the-knee length pine green dress with a brown belt and cork wedges. This color choice works great with our black robes and caps.

I look up at Will as the photographer snaps a picture and love how I know we're complimenting each other. He has a bright yellow sash that says Student Athlete from when he did Dive with Stefan before I knew him. I have yellow honor cords because of my stellar G.P.A. In this moment, we are the couple that I spent my time being envious of before I knew Will.

"Wait for me!" I hear Stefan yell, as I turn to see him landing a jump from the five steps that you're supposed to use to walk off the stage.

I shake my head and laugh at his ever-present antics.

Stefan comes up on my other side and sandwiches me between the two of them. "These two are ridiculous, they forgot to wait for the best member of our throuple!" He tells the photographer.

Her eyes flash wide for a split second before she submits to his charisma and takes another photo without argument.

We stand there grinning from ear to ear as this part of our lives comes to an end.

"Okay, I think I've gotten plenty." The photographer says, dismissing our rule-breaking selves.

We turn and head back to our seats.

Shortly after we settle onto the blisteringly hot metal folding chairs the ceremony ends. "Congratulations to all of our graduates!" The announcer happily proclaims to the gathered audience.

We cheer gleefully and the boys throw their caps into the air. I would, but when they handed us the cap and gown they said if they came back damaged we'd be fined. I'm too much of a Hermione to risk that happening.

Will and Stefan find their caps, or someone else's, and we head toward the sea of loved ones looking for their graduates.

"There they are!" Stefan proclaims when he spots his people. "Coming in tall for the win!" He cockily declares. Then he high fives Will and starts wandering to his family. "See you tonight!" he shouts before he's too far away to hear.

Will's hands wrap around my waist and pull me closer now that it's just the two of us. He rests his forehead against my bangs and quietly reassures me, "We can do this."

I exhale, trying to calm my nerves. "If they helped make us this wonderful, surely they'll be able to get along right?" I ask as I grab his hand from my side and lace my fingers with his.

"One would hope." He replies. His tone doesn't offer much optimism to our impending complicating circumstances. Our families have never met before and I'm regretting choosing today for it to happen.

I try one last tactic to get out of tonight's dinner. "You sure you can't have a two hour long stomach bug? You know where you're bedridden for exactly the duration of dinner but we can still make it to bowling later?"

He pulls back to his full height and grins down at me. "They're going to have to meet each other at some point. Let's just rip off the bandaid." He kisses me on the nose and pulls me into a loving embrace.

His height allows him to spot our families and he leads me out of the sea of people surrounding us. Before we break free I tell him, "That's a horrible phrase: bandaids hurt like a bitch when you're ripping them off. No matter how fast you go."

· ♥ · ♥ · ♥ · ♥ · ♥ ·

"How was it!" Stefan calls across the parking lot of the bowling alley.

Will squeezes my hand. I feel him mulling over his words finding the fine line between truth and lies.

I decide to spare him having to talk around my family and their behaviors. I shrug, "Let's just say that Will learned why I talk to Nana and Jamie the most out of my family."

"That bad huh?" Stefan pushes as we meet up between the cars and head to the entrance.

Will steps up. "Nothing bad happened. They were very civil and polite. I guess, it is just easier to find common interests with Nana and Jamie."

"It's whatever." I try to disinterest Stefan from prodding further. "My family is an acquired taste. I'm just lucky that I turned out as normal as I did."

Right on cue Stefan jibes, "Yeah, so normal there, Nik."

He opens the door to the bowling alley for us and I slap his shoulder as we walk in.

Tonight is Retro Night and we are all decked out for it. Will is wearing his standard jeans, but cuffed at the ankle. Beneath shines a pair of bright white long socks. He asked his parents for help with an outfit and they gave him his Dad's old windbreaker. It's a dark purple and striped with pink, teal, and a lighter purple. His hair is the most ridiculous part of the ensemble. His beautiful surfer waves are greased back except for one section he forced into a curl in the middle of his forehead.

As I walk into the alley I notice Stefan's outfit is even more fitting for tonight's theme. He has on purple bell bottoms paired with orange boots. His top is a button-up white shirt that's unbuttoned low enough to reveal too much of his tan and toned surfer chest. He has an orange belt that matches his shoes and a mustard jacket finishes his outfit.

"Did you gel your chest hair?" I ask him as we walk up to the front desk.

He gives me a cocky grin. "Didn't have to Nik. They're that curly naturally."

I puff out my cheeks and cover my mouth with my hand, feigning holding back vomit. I try to start a retort but a gag passes my lips instead.

"I think what Nikki is trying to say, oh-so-delicately man, is it's Retro Night, not show us your navel night." Will mocks his best friend.

"Yes, that," I say pointing my finger at Will in agreement. "You should probably fasten another shirt button or two."

"You jus' be jelly," He sasses while flipping his nonexistent long hair over his shoulder. Then he confirms, "Ryan and Tipp are meeting up with us tonight right?"

"I think so," I reply, thinking nothing of it.

We're next in line to order our lanes and shoes. Stefan's fingers are doing a quiet count of everyone we expect to make an appearance tonight.

When it's our turn, Will and I step off to the side and let Stefan do all the talking. He has our shoe sizes memorized and generally loves being the center of attention, so it's not hard to relinquish control to him.

Will pulls me close to his side and whispers into my hair, "You look fabulous tonight."

I wiggle closer to him and a smile breaks my lips. He's right, I do look pretty spectacular. I took the time to straighten my hair and tease it to twice its normal volume. I put a chunky dark blue headband in to make it even more dramatic. I grabbed one of my favorite light blue button-ups and folded the sleeves to the elbows. I still don't like showing off my waist so I have a beige tank top on where one would expect to see midriff beneath my tied-up shirt. I found a pair of massive bell bottoms at the costume shop a few weeks ago when we decided to make tonight an official celebration. Lastly, I chose a pair of low-rise Chucks. I know they're not technically retro, but the rest of my outfit is good enough to make up for that decade slip-up.

"Lanes eleven and twelve," Stefan states as he turns from the cashier and startles me from my quiet appreciation of my outfit.

Will lightly squeezes me with his arm and turns to lead the way to our lanes for the evening.

We're in the very back of one side of the alley. Our two lanes share one operation point and the monitors are adjacent. It would be a perfect setup if we cared about who was going to win tonight. As it stands, I know Will and I are here for a final hurrah with our friends. We leave for Oregon in about a week and this is our last chance to have everyone together.

Will, Stefan, and I choose our balls and order snacks and booze from the grill located inside the alley. We all agreed to be the early group to arrive and save the space for everyone else. They're due here in about half an hour now, so we settle in and people watch while waiting.

When our food shows up I choose a seat that has my back to the wall of the alley. It gives me the perfect vantage of everything going on around us. There are some groups dressed up, others look like they had no idea it was a theme night. We are definitely the best dressed out of everyone here. I enjoy my cider and our shared nachos as the boys talk.

I'm too busy watching the dynamics of others to pay attention to their conversation. To my right are the twelve lanes of this half of the alley. We're seated a few steps up from the lanes at the tables where food is allowed. Drinks can enter the bowling space, but not food. Interspersed between the food tables are modified bookshelves holding bowling balls. The ball racks are only three shelves tall and you can see over them easily. Between the bowling lanes is a center socializing area. The very back of the space has the grill, so it's closest to us. Between that and the front desk are a couple of pool tables and a few air hockey tables. Beyond the front desk to one side is an arcade. Across from that is the pro center with lockers and some sort of repair shop.

The alley is slowly filling with people as we approach the midnight hour. Luckily, there aren't many children present. I feel bad for the poor things being kept up past their bedtime. Randomly I see a flash of neon coloring pop through the throng of people searching for balls or in line for food. A group of men is playing billiards and two teenagers are having a showdown at the air hockey table.

"Hey, man!" Will calls out, bringing me back to the present. I follow his line of sight and see Tyler and Mark walking our way. Tyler put more effort into his appearance than Mark did. He's wearing skinny jeans with suspenders and a short-sleeve white button-up. He has a red bow tie on and an eight-piece hat. It reminds me of a less sophisticated Tommy Shebly. I smile to myself and sip my cider. I'm enjoying my observations as the boys greet each other.

I remain seated during their hello hugs and shift my eyes to Mark's outfit. He's in standard jeans, which I notice is effort from him because he's usually sporting shorts to some degree. He has a turtle neck shirt on and a pair of suspenders. Maximum effort? No. However, that's more work for an outfit than he usually puts in, and I appreciate that.

When the boys finish greeting each other, I give Tyler and Mark a friendly wave hello.

"Alright man, let's put on our shoes and find our balls." Tyler narrates as he does just that. Mark follows suit and I'm left with Stefan and Will again.

We devour the nachos quickly and my drink disappears at the same pace.

"Do you want another?" Will asks from beside me at the table.

I bite my lip in contemplation. "You're D.D. right?"

He nods at me silently and kisses me gently. "Enjoy yourself tonight babe," he says as he gets up to order me another cider.

Will's space is immediately filled by the arrival of Brittney and Chuck. I know they're Stefan's family, but I can't wait for her to make some excuse to leave early. I don't know what Brittney was thinking with her outfit. She looks adorable, but there's no way she'll be able to bowl. She's wearing a lime green skin-tight dress that reaches from her collarbones to below her knees. Her heels are four-inch stilettos in a bright emerald green and her hair is in a high pony. The outfit paired together gives her short frame an additional six inches. Chuck looks like he's trying too hard. He has opted for a traditional greaser look. His hair has too much gel. He's in black pants and a black shirt. He has a black leather jacket and sunglasses on. Inside. At night. He's wearing sunglasses.

Internally I roll my eyes and groan, but externally I greet them with a fake smile. Luckily, my mother taught me how to smile on cue for her camera years ago so applying that tactic to Brittney and Chuck's presence comes as second nature. Brittney sits across the table from me as Chuck goes down to our lanes and greets Tyler and Mark.

"Hey Brittney," Stefan begins, "How do you plan on bowling in that dress?"

She pulls out her phone and unlocks the screen as she replies, "I don't. I'm only here because Chuck wanted to make an appearance." She looks up from her screen and meets my eyes, "We plan on leaving after one game." After that failed insult she looks down to her phone again.

"I'm counting the minutes," I accidentally say aloud.

Brittney's eyes flash up to mine. Her lips purse in anger and I see her grip tighten on her device. I didn't mean to say that outside of my mind, but making her look like an upset cranberry wearing a wig and dress is quickly becoming my favorite part of the evening.

Then my eyes land on the very best part of the evening: Will. He's sauntering back my way, puffy windbreaker and all, carrying my cider and a root beer for him. He gives me a lopsided grin as he approaches. *I adore this Golden Retriever gamer-boy boyfriend of mine.* I think and smile at him.

"Hey, Britt." He greets her with the nickname he knows she hates as he hands me a cider. "Come on babe, we've got some asses to kick at bowling." With that, he takes my free hand and pulls me from my chair. We descend the half flight of stairs to the lane and settle in with everyone else.

Tyler has already entered our names on the monitors when we arrive.

"Where's Sean?" I ask with my brows puzzled at seeing his name on the monitor.

"About five minutes out," Mark tells me blandly. I've known him for months now but he is still the most standoffish of the group.

The bowling alley's lights flicker off and are replaced by black lights. Cheers echo up and down the alleyway from groups excited for the bowling to begin. When they've died down, the background music is turned up until I can feel it reverberating through my bones.

I search the group and find Will. He's up to bowl and looking confident as ever. The only part of his outfit glowing are his socks and the t-shirt poking out below the slightly unzipped neck of his jacket. He grins at me, seeming to know my attention is solely on him. He turns to bowl and starts the evening strong with a strike.

He prowls straight to me once he sees his pins being swept away in defeat and pulls me close. One of his hands lands on my lower back and pulls my body flush against his while the other tangles into the hair at the nape of my neck and guides me into a passionate kiss. My hands find their way to his jacket and grip him like he'll wander off if they let go. I get lost in his claiming presence and am disappointed when he doesn't deepen the kiss. He grips my hair a little tighter and stands to his full height. It's impossible to close the distance between our lips again when he's holding my head captive with one hand.

"You're up." He seductively directs.

I sigh and bite my lip for the second time this evening. "That's sabotage." I accuse, still gripping his ridiculous windbreaker in tight fists.

He leans down and nips my bottom lip. His lips travel, leaving light kisses in their wake before finding the shell of my ear and whispering, "Nah, I call it foreplay."

Then he steps to the side and leaves me to figure out how to bowl while being so turned on by my beautiful fucking man!

I sigh, roll back my shoulders, and do my best. By the end of my frame, eight of my pins are down, That's is as good as a spare to me after how Will left me wet and wanting in the middle of a fucking bowling alley.

Tyler offers me a high five as I walk past him and I return it gleefully. My eyes narrow as I locate my boyfriend, and revenge is taking the form of Veronica Welch tonight. He doesn't get to turn me on when we have hours before any chance of sating it without being tortured a little bit himself.

Will's seated at the monitor station. One leg is bent and resting on the knee of his other leg. His arm is spread across the back of the chair to his side and his lips are caressing the opening of the bottle he's drinking from.

Seeing him look so delicious shortcircuits my brain as I try to come up with a revenge plan. When I'm less than five steps away from him he finishes his drink and he licks his lips at me knowingly.

Suddenly there's a large arm around my shoulders pulling me in a different direction.

I trip over the traction-less bowling shoes I've changed into and a hand grabs my forearm, preventing my face from finding the floor. I glance up to the face that arm belongs to and see Stefan is responsible for derailing my plan.

My eyes narrow suspiciously as I pull from his grasp. "What are you doing?"

"Preventing you from giving my best friend a hard-on in the middle of a bowling alley." He deadpans.

"I—" I start to object, but Stefan levels me with a single look and I sheepishly admit, "I may have been headed to do exactly that," I admit to him.

He takes my hands in his, it feels quite unnatural, Stefan and I have never been this kind of close. My trepidation must be written on my face because he laughs, "Relax Nik, let's put that energy to use and dance!" He quickly drops one of my hands and spins me. Then he starts doing a ridiculous sprinkler completely off-beat to the music that's playing.

I object, "You can't dance like that to songs like *Emperor's New Clothes,* it doesn't work!"

"Just dance Nik, no one cares what moves you're doing!" He calls over the music.

I shrug because he's right. I brush my hair over my shoulders and sway my hips to the music. In no time I'm letting the songs sing to my soul and guide my movements.

A hand finds my waist and pulls me back closer to the body it belongs to. I keep dancing, not caring who it is. If Will doesn't want me dancing with someone else he can come join me.

The hand splays across my stomach as a deep gravelly voice says, "You're up."

I jump a little when I realize it is Will who came to join me. I hurriedly bowl my frame, ending with a spare. When I'm scuffling back to the dance floor *bad idea right?* by Olivia Rodrigo comes over the speakers. Just like the lyrics say, when I look at Will my thoughts go, "Ahhh..."

I meet Will and his hips fit perfectly against my ass. We shamelessly grind on the dance floor our small group has created. I wrap my arm behind his neck, lace my fingers through his hair, and pull him down to kiss me.

That's how our last night, midnight bowling with friends, goes. Dancing, bowling, and enjoying every moment that we're together. Brittney and Chuck slithered off into the night after the first game like she said they would. Tyler, Sean, Mark, and Stefan joined in dancing sometimes but spent most of the evening enjoying drinks and socializing. By the time the house lights turned on and we were forced to call the game, Will was the only person sober out of our entire group.

"Shit guys, I can't fit you all in my car." Will mulls over as we are changing our shoes.

"I'm not that buzzed man, I can drive the one mile it takes to get home," Sean argues.

Stefan and Will glare him down with the same menacing expression. "Like fuck you will." Will scolds and grabs the keys Sean was fiddling with.

It makes my toes tingle seeing Will get so assertive about the well being of his friend. I tuck under his arm and take my place by his side as we head to the exit.

Stefan gets out his keys next.

"Don't you even fucking think about driving!" Will chastises his best friend.

"Calm down, dude," Stefan argues and then throws his keys to Will. "We can leave all your cars here overnight, they don't tow you for getting a ride home. In the morning you can bring us back."

I giggle at their banter as Will subconsciously rubs his hand over my forearm.

He changes our direction across the lot toward Stefan's new SUV. "That's a solid thought man, you sure you're drunk?"

"Drunk? No. I'm just buzzed right now." Stefan replies giving his best friend a sleepy smile.

We all pile into the car and I end up getting shotgun at Will's command. Stefan belts himself into the third row and we ride in a content, buzzed silence for the fifteen minutes it takes to get to Stefan's house.

Will parks where Stefan usually does, saving us a trip up two treacherous flights of stairs. Stefan leads the way into the house and Will brings up the rear. He's entered an adorable overprotective mode that makes me want him so bad.

"Everyone get a glass of water right now, I'm not dealing with you all hungover come morning," Will demands with a smile as we enter Stefan's front door.

"Already on it!" Tyler calls from the kitchen.

I enter barely ahead of Will and see all four of them dutifully downing their waters before shuffling back to the living room.

Will remains in charge of the situation and pulls blankets out from Stefan's bedroom. He points to Tyler, Sean, and Mark in turn. "You three on the floor, Nikki and I get the couch."

"No fair." Sean groans out. "I want the couch."

Without missing a beat Will challenges him, "Then next time you can be the D.D. and you can be in charge of a drunk group of fools."

Mark comes to Sean's aid. "We're not that wasted man. It's just a light buzz."

Will glares him down as he throws a blanket in Mark's direction. "Too drunk to drive, means, too drunk. If you were sloshed I'd be getting trash cans, but I don't think anyone is that bad tonight."

Tyler trudges by Will and grabs his blanket without argument. He grabs a pillow off the couch and settles in on the floor. From under the blanket he mumbles to his friends, "Mark, Sean, just shut up and go to sleep."

They take the hint and lay down like this is something they've done many times before.

I'm left standing in the living room with three grown men cuddled under blankets, Stefan has gone missing, and Will's take-charge attitude has me feeling all sorts of things. I tilt my head to the side and purse my lips as I think, *the alcohol might be helping that feeling too...*

Will holds his hand out to me. When I take it he pulls me to the kitchen. "You need to hydrate too." He says as he picks me up and puts me on the counter.

"Bread?" I ask him. "Bread is the best way for me to prevent a hangover tomorrow."

He nods and leaves me sitting there as he riffles through Stefan's kitchen.

"Where is Stefan?" I ask as his name enters my mind.

Will turns to me with a slice of bread in his hand. "He's already in bed. His house so he gets his room. We just go along with it because it's better to wake up hungover here than any of our own houses." He pauses while pouring a glass of water for me and then continues. "When Chuck turned twenty-one we had a *legal* way to get booze. Stefan's parents didn't care as long as we were safe and stayed over until we sobered up. Sleeping over here just became a routine after a fun night." He shrugs at the end. I see his face go softer and his eyes travel to a distant place where I imagine stories of their past together are playing out before his eyes.

I eat my bread quietly and finish it off with a glass of water.

Light snores float toward us from the living room. I glance over my shoulder and see the three men sleeping side by side by side in the middle of a brightly lit space. I imagine by morning they'll be spooning and I hope I wake up early enough to see it for myself.

Will kneels before me, grabbing my attention back.. "What are you doing?" I ask, confused.

His hands move to my laces and he starts taking off my shoes. "Taking care of you Nikki. You don't let me do it often, so I'm going to relish this rare moment where your stubborn independence isn't in the forefront of your mind."

"I'm not—"

"You are." He cuts me off with a cheeky grin as he pulls off the first shoe.

I bite my tongue and let him continue. I could argue my point, but that could possibly, maybe, just a little bit, prove him right. By the time he unlaces my second shoe, I have numerous scenarios where this ends happily for both of us.

My face must communicate my inner thoughts because Will tucks my shoes under the island I'm seated on and he shakes his head at me.

I bite my lip at him hopefully.

He brackets my hips with his hands and leans in close. Will kisses my nose and then uses his thumb to pull my bottom lip out from beneath my teeth.

I pathetically pout at him.

His hips nestle between my spread thighs and I feel a flicker of hope ignite in my chest again. I wrap my arms around his neck and try to pull him down to kiss me.

"No." He tells me with no room to argue in his tone.

I search his eyes and they contradict what his words communicated. I can tell he wants me, so why won't he give in?

I try pulling him to my lips again but he doesn't budge.

I think to myself, *annoying large men with muscles thinking they're stronger than us women.*

Will stops my brain from figuring out which tactic to switch to by saying, "Nikki, you could strip down to your birthday suit and I still wouldn't lay a finger on you tonight. I'd throw a blanket over you so that everyone else didn't see, but I wouldn't touch you."

I object, "But I want you to touch me. In fact, you should touch me all over, in just the right ways." I try to seduce him with an eyebrow wag.

It doesn't work.

"Nikki you can't consent right now. You're drunk, buzzed, or intoxicated, however you want to call it."

I open my mouth to argue again but he stops the words on my tongue by placing his index finger against my lips.

"I love you. We can fuck tomorrow when you're sober. But right now, tonight? Not going to happen." He steps back from me and crosses his arms. He only does that when he means business.

Still seated on the counter I deflate into a slouch. I know he's not using his love for me to manipulate me, but something feels off. I push that gnawing feeling aside and sigh at him, "Fine."

"Can you walk to the couch or do you want me to carry you?"

I slide down off the counter and take a couple of staggering steps forward. "The room was spinning a lot less when I was seated." I stammer as I feel his arms wrap behind my shoulders and under my knees. The wall before me rotates in an impossible feat of engineering as Will picks me up.

I rest my head on his collarbone and let him take care of me.

He gingerly steps around his passed out friends and places me on the couch. Then he disappears again.

I take this time to lie down on my side and try not to think about all the other people who have had sex on this couch. In the morning I might be glad I'm not joining that list.

My eyes must have closed during that thought because I startle as I feel a blanket being spread across me. Next, Will's body slides beneath it and he pulls me so that I'm halfway laying on him and only partially resting on the sofa.

His hand starts rubbing my back and my consciousness fades. I feel him kiss my hair and whisper, "I love you," right before blissful nothingness takes over.

# Nine

## Final Goodbyes

My eyes blink open slowly and I have no idea where I am. There is a pile of bodies under blankets on the floor next to me and it feels like I'm on a couch. I rapidly blink a few more times and take in my surroundings.

There is a light clanking noise coming from somewhere in the bright distance.

There's a large arm wrapped around my middle and deep breathing coming from behind me. My hand finds the arm tucked against me and I recognize the feel of it as Will's.

Then things start to click.

*We went to midnight bowling.*

*I got drunk.*

*Will is sexy when he takes over and becomes an overprotective jerk face.*

*Are the guys on the floor cuddling?*

I try to lean over the edge of the couch to get a better vantage but the thick arm holds me hostage and tightens as I try to pull away. I pick up my head further from the pillow and sure enough, the men on the floor are spooning.

*If only I knew where my phone was so I could get a picture.*

"You're thinking too loudly," a gravelly voice comments into my ear.

I freeze, hoping I haven't actually woken him. Will shatters that hope by pulling me impossibly closer to his too warm ther- furnace of a body. *He's a furnace, not a thermos,* I internally chastise, remembering the grammar lesson I got a few months ago from Will.

He nuzzles my throat and squeezes me lovingly. I close my eyes savoring his nearness before our day and the beginning of the end of this chapter in our lives begins.

I hear a door open and feet shuffling slowly across carpet. When I look to see who it is, Stefan appears in the open space between the living room and the kitchen. He's looking right at me. "Good morning guys," he greets way too cheerfully for someone as drunk as I was last night.

Someone groans from beneath the blankets on the floor and I smother a laugh.

"If we don't move do you think he'll leave us alone?" Will suggests to me.

"Not a chance!" Stefan calls louder than his first greeting.

It's my turn to groan.

"Come on," Will encourages as he partially sits up behind me. "You can go back to bed at my house later if you want, but we need to get back to my car first."

We disentangle ourselves from one another and the couch and that's when I realize I slept the entire night in my bra. It is digging in uncomfortably everywhere it meets my skin. I wince as I peel its seams from my imprinted flesh.

"You okay?" Will asks noticing my grimace.

"Breakfast is ready!" Mrs. Edwards calls from the stove before I can respond.

Instead, I shrug and slowly shuffle toward the delectable smelling food.

I don't know how long Mrs. Edwards has been working in the kitchen but she's prepared a feast for us. She's made French toast, sourdough toast, and waffles. There's a pitcher of orange juice on the counter next to another pitcher filled with ice water. A steaming coffee maker gives up its irresistible aroma. There is a platter covered in scrambled eggs, sausage, and bacon as well. My mouth starts salivating when I see all our options and I immediately understand why the guys prefer sleeping over at Stefan's house, even if it's on the living room floor.

"How long have you been working on this?" I ask Mrs. Edwards as I choose a seat.

She waves my question off. "Now you guys dig in, seems like you had a fun night celebrating?"

Stefan hugs his mother before he takes a plate from her. "Yeah, it was a great night. Thanks for making this for us."

"Thank you, Mrs. Edwards," Will and I chime in unison.

"Okay, now you kids eat off those hangovers, and let me know if you need anything else." She kisses Stefan on the cheek and goes up the stairs leading to the part of the house only family is allowed to enter. The door closes with a soft click as the pile of blankets on the living room floor starts to transition into humans. Will, Stefan, and I dig shamelessly into the platters of food as the others come to join us. We all eat in silence as we adjust to consciousness and the alcohol that's wreaked havoc on our systems.

"You all look like crap," Will announces when he finishes his breakfast.

I glare at him. That attitude will not be getting him anywhere near my beltline later today.

His eyebrows shoot up as he notices the stink eye I'm giving him. "Not you babe, you look adorable and tired."

"Liar!" Stefan shouts. "You said I'd always be the prettiest girl in the room to you!" His indignant voice fills the kitchen as he grabs his plate and walks it to the sink with his head bowed and his shoulders hunched.

Will rolls his eyes at his best friend's back. "You're impossible."

After breakfast, we all pile into Stefan's S.U.V. and head back to the bowling alley to retrieve our vehicles. I know this is the last time he'll see some of the guys before we leave for Oregon so I take Will's keys. After a quick hug goodbye to all of them, I duck into Will's car and give him some privacy to say goodbye to Sean, Tyler, and Mark. We'll be seeing Stefan a little later, he has the only car that can transport Will's bed across the Greater San Diego area.

I mindlessly scroll through my socials in Will's passenger seat. The car is a pleasant temperature, and the chill of the night has thawed in the early morning rays. It smells of Will too. It's not as enjoyable as his bedroom because the car has a mixture of his after-work and freshly clean smells, but it feels like I'm being wrapped in a delectable hug by my favorite person while I wait for him.

A few more minutes pass and I hear a car down the lot start, then two staccato beeps as it fades into silence. I glance over my shoulder and see Will still chatting with Stefan. It's undeniable that out of the entire friend group, the two of them are the closest. I see them shake hands and then give each other a quick hug.

Will gets into the driver's seat of the car quietly. He stares forward at the parking lot beyond the dash for a few moments, then I hear him sniffle.

I get as close to him as I can with the center console separating us. I put a tentative hand on his thigh and wait patiently for him to choose to share. His large calloused hand immediately grasps mine.

We sit there, hand in hand and I give him the time he needs.

His voice comes out in a croak, "We're really leaving?"

I nod my head but I don't know if he sees it.

A silent tear drops from his cheek as he continues. "I know we're leaving. We picked out an apartment. We hired movers to take our stuff up there. But I just said goodbye to friends I've had for years." Then he looks at me and I see the waterfall preparing to cascade down his face.

I take my hand from his and cup his cheeks with a physical representation of my affection for him. I stare into his water clogged eyes searching for a way to comfort him.

I can't.

We're both leaving everything we've ever known and it's the most terrifying thing we've ever chosen to do.

I think Will sees the terror on my face as clearly as he's feeling it because his tears recede and his half grin makes a shy appearance.

I lean further in and kiss him gently before folding into him. We wrap in an embrace and I'm not sure if I'm providing comfort or taking it from him, but it feels right.

Time passes as we cling to the reassuring presence of one another, but inevitably, it has to end.

"Stefan wants to help move my bed before three today. Will that work for you?" Will asks once I drag myself back to the passenger seat.

I mull over today's timeline. It's eleven now so I can squeeze in a nap after a shower, without a bra on, in a bed bathed in Will's bergamot and citrus scent. "Yeah, that should work. I think Tipp..."

My mind races. How did I not notice it before? Tipp never found me at graduation yesterday. If she'd been there she would have been in the front row cheering so loud that people around her would have lost hearing. She never made it to midnight bowling yesterday. I unlock my phone and check for messages. She never even sent me a text saying congrats or canceling. She just ghosted me.

"What about Tipp?" Will asks as he buckles up and pulls the car from its parking spot.

"That bitch!" My voice comes out pitchy and indignant. "She never showed up. She never even texted me!" I hold up my text thread with her proving my point. She hasn't messaged me since the day we snuck into the hot tub at the downtown hotel.

"That bitch." I repeat a little calmer. "Is she fucking ghosting me?"

Will's eyes are focused on the road, which I have to appreciate because I don't plan on dying this early in life. His hand finds my leg. "I don't know babe. What do you want to do?"

I heave out an exaggerated sigh and stretch my neck from side to side before replying. "She gets one more chance. We've had dinner with Nana planned for weeks. If she shows up I'll give her a chance to explain herself, but if she doesn't? That's it. I'm done."

His short term memory is working on merging onto the freeway safely so I wait to hear his opinion on the matter. Once we're seamlessly integrated into the sea of drivers on the road, he comments. "If that's what you think is best to do."

"Do you have any other ideas?" I demand.

He squeezes my leg gently. "Babe, your friendship with her has always been different. I support you in whatever decision you choose to make." He finds my hand and laces it with his fingers. Then he pulls it across the car and plants a kiss on the back of my hand before returning it to my lap.

I take my phone and type out a message to Tipp.

> Why didn't you make it to graduation yesterday?

I send that first so she knows that I noticed she wasn't there to support me. Then I type out her last chance at a friendship with me.

> Do you still plan on attending our goodbye dinner with Nana tonight? It's at 4.

I stare at my phone, hoping she replies. Maybe Ryan got in an accident. Maybe her parents had an emergency. Maybe something happened that can excuse her actions of late.

I'm still clutching my phone, internally begging my best friend to acknowledge my existence when Will pulls up to his sister's condo. He parks on the street and walks around to my door.

Once open he kindly says, "Come on Nikki, let's get inside and rest up for a bit. Stefan will be here before we know it to help move the bed and I know you want to shower yesterday off your skin."

"Can you take this?" I ask, handing out my phone to him before unbuckling my seatbelt.

He does as I bid without hesitation. Will holds his hand out to help me from his car and I take it. He wraps me in a tight embrace until I don't feel so alone.

When I withdraw from his hold he closes the car door and we head up to his sister's condo. I've never seen this place as Will's. The walls are decorated to his sister's taste, the only space where his personality shines through is his bedroom. When we're in our own apartment I'll be sure to decorate it with a combination of our personalities.

When we enter it appears Meghan and Thomas are both out so we take over the bathroom. I'm showered and cuddled into one of his shirts within minutes. A few more and I'm out cold under his sheets surrounded by his bergamot and citrus scent.

All too soon a hand is lightly brushing my hair away from my face. I try to swat at it but my arm is trapped under the blankets and can't get free.

I groan into the still room and try to find the strength to roll away from the intrusion.

"Nikki," he whispers. "You need to get up."

"No," I mumble into his sheets.

His shadow darkens the light shining behind my eyelids and I feel him kiss my forehead. "Babe, if you don't get out of bed, Stefan will strap you down and move it with you attached."

That has my eyes flying wide. "Is he here!"

"Shhh." Will's hands land on my shoulders. "You have about half an hour before he gets here but I thought you might want to be wearing more than my t-shirt when he arrives."

"Ohhh," I yawn in understanding as I stretch my arms out. "Okay, twenty more minutes. It doesn't take me that long to get ready." I flop back down onto the bed and start to burrow beneath the covers.

Will pulls the covers up off my feet and exposes every inch of my skin to the freezing air of his bedroom.

I hiss like a cat at his vile attack.

He lays on top of me and pins my claws against my chest so I can't retaliate to his cruelty. Taking all the warmth from a bed is just malicious! His face is inches from mine and the contact of his torso against mine returns some of the comfort I had from being enveloped in his sheets.

"Come on babe. We need the bed to be stripped before he gets here too." He tries coaxing me out of the bed.

A coy smile meets my lips. I'll try anything to not have to get out of this perfect bed. "How about we strip something else for fifteen minutes?" I ask in my best seductive tone.

Will's eyes flash with desire for only a second before reverting to their usual calm ocean water blue. "You may be sober, but we don't have time. If you want my dick that badly then come back over after dinner with Nana tonight."

That statement feels like a cold shower to my lusty thoughts. My grin falls from my face and is replaced with a somber downturn of my lips. "Has she messaged?" I ask him sadly.

He leans back and guides my body to a seated position. Will's hands clasp mine and he softly informs me, "Yeah, but you're not going to like what she said."

"What?" Maybe if he tells me it will be easier than reading it from her message thread.

He swallows and takes one of my cheeks in his hand. I close my eyes and focus on the feel of his pinkie below my chin and his thumb resting just below my eye. From how delicately he's treating me I can tell I've lost my best friend.

His thumb strokes my face tenderly as he tells me, "All she said was 'can't.' Not even an apology or word of explanation. I'm so sorry babe."

I bite back the tears that are trying to reveal how devastated I am by this news.

I clear my throat and open my eyes.

Will is studying every line of my face, searching for something.

I place my hand on his forearm and lower his hand from my face. "I guess it's good we're moving then. Plenty of new and better friends to make." I hop off the sheetless bed and go to the drawer he gave me to store some of my clothes in for unexpected overnight stays. Will finishes stripping the bed of its fitted layers as I change into an acceptable outfit to see Stefan in and to have dinner with Nana. I choose a black spaghetti strap tank top that has small sunflowers speckled across it in an aesthetically pleasing pattern. I'm buttoning up my ripped jeans as we hear a knock from the front door.

"You good?" He asks as he makes his way to the bedroom door.

I bend into a toe touch quickly that has my hair flying across the airspace and dangling toward the floor before replying. Through a mouth clenching bobby pins, my response is a barely discernible, "Yeah, just gotta throw my hair into a messy bun."

I hear Will chuckle as he leaves the room. He probably thinks I'm adorable right now. I tilt my head to the side so I can see what I look like in the closet mirror. He's right, at this angle, I'm a bit ridiculous which probably translates to cute for him.

I mess around with the grip on my hair a few times, making sure there aren't large lumps in the back before I'm satisfied. I whip my head back and stand as Will and Stefan enter the room.

"Well, that's a greeting!" Stefan laughs out with eyes that are a tad larger than normal, the only clue to being startled by my hair antics.

I tilt my chin at him in greeting and turn toward the mirror to finish my updo.

The boys don't even discuss their plan of attack for breaking down the bed and moving it. They pick it up and work completely in sync. I watch in awe at their reflections as I pin strands of my red hair back from my face. The one time Will helped me move a dresser in my room, it took a well-thought-out plan of attack where we predetermined who would move which way. We had no natural skill in moving furniture together. These two could be professionals.

I don't know if it's because I'm too stunned watching their telepathic communication or if they're that fast, but the entire mattress and box spring are out of the room and in the living room before I'm done with my hair. Stefan has grabbed a screwdriver and is breaking down the wooden frame as Will gets out the air mattress that will be our bed for tonight.

I switch to applying light makeup as the guys finish getting the bed frame taken apart and move everything downstairs to Stefan's family van.

Once I'm put together again, I head downstairs to help them finish moving the bed.

*Not that I've been any help this far, but maybe they'll actually need me now.*

When I round the condo that sprawls out one level below Thomas and Meghan's, I see Will resting a hand against the mattress and box spring leaning against the side of the van while Stefan is bent over rummaging around the back of the van for something. At some point, they'd slipped on the plastic protector bags we got so at least our bed isn't resting directly on the pavement.

I approach without interrupting, figuring I'll be able to piece the problem together soon enough.

"Hey," Will greets as I stand next to him. His free arm wraps around my waist and hugs me tight. "You look beautiful," he compliments me with a smile that reaches from his eyes to the fingers that are holding me close.

"Thanks." I return with a small grin. I'm still feeling tired from last night.

*Coffee might be a wise choice before I head to Nana's.*

Without missing a beat Stefan snaps his fingers triumphantly in the air. "Found them!" He announces as he steps back from the vehicle holding some tie-downs in one hand.

I want to help but it's quickly apparent that if I try to physically assist I'll end up in the way. So I supervise and provide emotional support instead. I discover that the van isn't wide enough to fit the bed frame, box spring, and mattress. They shove the frame and box spring in the back and move the mattress to the roof. Two tie-downs later and we're ready to drive the bed to Nana's.

Will hops into the passenger seat of his best friend's ride and I follow behind in my Beetle. Watching that mattress flap in the breeze on a Southern California freeway has me wondering if death by flying mattress exists in *1,000 Ways to Die*. Luckily, we make it to Nana's before anyone perishes from an untimely bed-related incident.

I pull into the top porte-cochere as Stefan guides his van in front of the downstairs triple garage doors. Nana's Spanish Colonial Home is massive and I adore it. The windows have an old school security system on them: wrought iron bars. The roof is made of red terracotta clay tiles. The walls are textured with stucco. In the last three years, its architectural beauty has made this my favorite home. It has an acre lot in the back where my mother and uncle raised sheep, chickens, and horses growing up. It's over three thousand square feet and after tonight, all that space is solely Nana's again.

Nana is greeting Stefan and Will as I walk down her driveway to the lower parking area. Stefan and Will are undoing the tie-downs and Nana is dragging a few boxes out of the way in the middle garage. I know I'm useless to the guys so I go to help Nana. We clear space to store the bed until the movers arrive.

The guys unpack the bed with the same preternatural ease with which they transported it here. Stefan is shutting the van doors when Nana offers, "Well, I have plenty of salad if you'd like to hang out for an early dinner."

"Ah thanks, Nana," Will responds, "But I'm hanging out with Stefan's family tonight as a final goodbye."

Stefan walks to the front of the van and claps his hand on Will's shoulder. "Speaking of which we better head out if we don't want to be late. You know how Mom is about punctuality."

Will walks over to me and holds my elbows as I rest my arms on his. "Stefan will drop me off at nine tomorrow, that okay?" Will asks.

I nod in agreement. "The movers will be here between nine and noon so that should be good."

I want to kiss him, but Nana is standing only a few feet away and I don't want to kiss him that badly.

Will is attuned to my hesitation and draws me closer in a warm embrace. "I'll see you tomorrow, have a fun night with Nana." He finishes his farewell with a kiss on my forehead and heads over to the van.

"Later Nik! Good to see you, Nana." Stefan calls through the open window of the driver's seat.

We watch them pull onto the street before closing the garage door and heading upstairs to the dinner Nana has already prepared.

"Will Tipp be joining us later?" Nana asks when we reach the main floor of her house.

We round the formal dining room and enter the kitchen before I respond. Nana's pulling the salad from the fridge as I choose my words. I put my hands on my hips and lean backward slightly with a grimace on my face. I scratch below my nose nervously before coming clean. "We're kind of not friends anymore."

Nana looks up from the bowl in her hands with a furrowed brow. "When did this happen?"

"Yesterday," I say as I clench my hands nervously and shuffle around the kitchen awkwardly. I pull glasses from the cabinet and pour Nana her traditional half can of Squirt. My drink choices vary more and tonight I opt for my favorite, ice water.

"Does she know about this development in your friendship?" Nana presses as she scoops our salad into individual sized bowls.

That judgment-free question has my tongue unraveling. I turn from the counter and look at Nana earnestly. "I mean, it has been building to this for a while honestly. Like before she had a friend with benefits she had time to be my friend, but then she started dating Ryan and my friendship was no longer convenient for her."

"So the relationship felt uneven for you?"

"Yeah. It stopped being reciprocal." I take our drinks from the counter and place them in the pass-through window that opens to the patio. Nana does the same with our dinners. I grab the wicker basket of napkins and we walk around the kitchen to the patio.

"I'm sensing there is more to this story." Nana gently encourages me while taking our meal to the table.

I assist and when we're seated I continue. "I called her when we were driving over here. She actually picked up and sounded happy to hear from me so that just tells how unaware she was." I take a bite of my chicken, spinach, feta, and dried cranberry salad before continuing.

Nana doesn't interrupt me as I gather my thoughts. She gives me the space I don't even know I need while also being there for me.

"I treated it like a breakup, honestly. I told her it wasn't working out for me. I used I statements so she couldn't argue with me. But the worst part of it? She didn't even try. She didn't even ask for a second chance, or admit that things had changed between us." I put my fork down a little too forcefully and tilt my head up to the shaded patio roofing while I blink away the tears trying to form. *I won't cry over a friendship that she didn't even try to fight for. My presence in her life just wasn't that important to her.*

I clear my throat before I find my voice again. "I told her it felt like she was treating me like a convenience now that she has Ryan. I said that it really hurt my feelings when she didn't make it to graduation, but it wounded me deeper that she didn't even text me an apology or let me know that she wouldn't be able to make it to what was essentially our goodbye party last night."

Nana has paused her own eating and is giving me her full attention. She approaches her question like I'm a cornered animal in need of a gentle helping hand, "What did she have to say about all these concerns you brought up?"

"She didn't even deign to give me an excuse. She said there wasn't anything she could say to change my mind, like it was a closed deal." My eyes lock with Nana's as I admit, "Then she just hung up on me."

"Oh Nikki," Nana's voice is saturated with compassion. "I'm so sorry that happened." Her gaze moves beyond my face and takes in the sprawling yard beyond the patio.

I take her shift in focus to compose myself. I didn't know I was so upset by Tipp's utter dismissal of our relationship. Years wasted on someone I thought would be my Maid of Honor. I swallow back the lingering moisture in my eyes and bite the inside of my cheek to help my brain fixate on the physical sting instead of the emotional hell I'm in.

I push a slow and deliberate breath from my lungs and stretch my neck to reset myself. "Enough about her. I won't let her poor life choices ruin any more of our evening. What are you going to do when you have this massive house all to yourself again?" I ask before digging into the delectable salad she made for us.

"I think I'm going to turn the house into a swingers club," Nana says with a straight face and proceeds to take a bite of salad like that wasn't the most absurd thing I've ever heard her say.

I choke so violently on my dinner that I swear a piece of feta tries shooting out of one of my nostrils. I clutch at my chest, take a ragged inhale, and wash down the panic that statement caused with a large gulp of water. When my eyes have stopped watering and I'm breathing normally again I look at Nana.

She's sitting in her chair looking completely innocent. Then I notice the slight smirk she's hiding behind her glass of Squirt.

"Nana!" I mockingly scold her.

She takes a small drink. "It could be fun, you never know. Besides, I always thought pineapples were cute decorations."

My jaw drops. My voice lowers to a scandalous whisper, "Nana?"

She keeps me guessing for a few heartbeats before she lets out her soft giggle. "You should see your face, Nikki! No, I think it might be time to downsize. I don't need all this space for just me, and it's too expensive to keep up until your brother is ready for college."

It takes a little while for my brain to catch up. "You want to move? Where?" My pulse jumps with excitement for her.

"I haven't decided yet. I have a lot of activities that I do around here, but I also hear that Oregon is a pretty cool place too." She replies calmly as if she has given this a lot of forethought.

I grin around my bite at the potential. "It would be wonderful if you moved somewhere near us, but I don't want you to give up all your friends down here."

She pats my arm. "That's why I need to think a little longer on it darling. However, I think there are a few more furniture items that you'll need the movers to take tomorrow."

Instead of talking with my mouth full, I tilt my head to the side like a dog trying to understand a new command. My eyes narrow and my brow arches silently begging her to expand upon that line of thinking.

Nana smiles at me, "I'm going to send you with a little more furniture than you were anticipating. Finish up your meal and we can walk around and figure out what you'll be taking to Oregon with you."

Ten

# We're Off!

"You told our intake team that it was two bedrooms worth of furniture!" The lead mover, Dennis, argues with me the next morning. The movers are forty-five minutes early, and not pleased that the intake team didn't think to ask about the square footage of said bedrooms.

I fold my arms, this full grown male won't intimidate me at my own home. "Sir," I begin respectfully. "It is two rooms worth of furniture. One bed. One couch. One desk. Two dressers. Two bookshelves. One green thing I don't know the technical name of, but it's a half bookshelf with doors. One desk chair. One cozy reading chair. Two nightstands. The contents that are typically stored within those furniture items. Two bedrooms could sleep up to three people, there are only two being moved here. I told the lady on the phone we were moving into a seven hundred and sixty square foot apartment and she assured me you'd have enough room on the truck. What do we need to do to make this situation work?"

He huffs at me and rolls his eyes.

*No tip for you then.*

Before he has time to retort, Stefan's van pulls in the drive. Will hops out before it's put into park and Stefan is right on his heels. It looks like Chuck is driving.

Dennis straightens uncomfortably as he sees two large men walking toward us with purpose. In the foggy June morning, they look like villains turned surfer dudes storming the castle to save the female main character. I may not be a woman who needs someone to come to her rescue, but watching Will approach with determination in his gaze has me feeling excited to be alone with him later.

Will approaches the moving man and reaches out his hand. They shake as Will greets, "I'd say sorry we're late, but it's you that's early."

Before Dennis gets the wrong impression that Will is the one in charge of this interaction I interject. "No worries babe. I was just informing Dennis here that we were truthful with the amount of furniture we would be moving." I hold up the paperwork I've been clutching in my hand to show him. "This is from your office." I turn my attention back to Dennis, "It only says two rooms, not that they have to be bedroom specific. So that couch," I point to the living room 1 story above us, "Counts as contents from one room. How can we work together to get our furniture onto your truck and up to Oregon?"

He looks at Will and Stefan standing still as statues flanking either side of me. "Let me see what we can move around inside the truck to make room for all your stuff." He mumbles as he turns and walks to his coworkers.

Stefan, Will, and I step into the open garage area and have a hushed conversation.

"Okay, so what is going on?" Will asks me once we're out of earshot.

I glance over my shoulder to make sure none of the movers are nearby. I word vomit the details quickly, "Nana gifted us some additional furniture last night. It will all fit in the apartment, but the movers seem to think that we lied about how much we needed to transport. I'm glad I had a copy of the original agreement because they said they'd have to get a second truck since there wasn't enough room on this one. I guess there are three different consignments' stuff inside the truck, and since we're last, we get the least amount of space. But that stipulation isn't in the fine print, and we're only moving two rooms of furniture. It just so happens to be a master bedroom and a living room, but they didn't specify the difference between specific room types, so that's on them." My shoulders lift quickly to my ears and I move my hands, palms up, toward the guys.

Their faces split into identical grins.

"Way to read between the lines Nik." Stefan compliments my analytical thinking.

Will gives me a side shoulder hug and the three of us wait to see what magic the movers can create within their semi-truck.

Two hours later, our lives are loaded into a truck being driven by strangers. It's scheduled to arrive at our new apartment in Oregon in seven days.

· ♥ · ♥ · ♥ · ♥ · ♥ ·

The final day with our family and friends goes by too quickly. Yesterday morning was spent watching the movers load up our lives. Nana made Will, Stefan, and me a quick lunch before we crammed into my Beetle and went to finish packing up Will's room. His parents took us to dinner later, and we ended the evening packing up my car with what we'll need before the movers get everything else up to Oregon. Now we're on the road.

We passed through the Grapevine an hour or two ago. Now that we're out of true Southern California, we're surrounded by farmland. No mountains, little scenery, and judging by the state of the brown landscaping: no rain either. I drove from Will's sister's condo to North of the Grapevine and now it's his turn. He's currently driving the heavily loaded Beetle up the desolate two-lane highway toward Oregon and our new life.

"How much longer until the hotel?" Will asks, drawing me from my thoughts.

I pull up the GPS and give it a second to load. When the directions say go straight on the road you're currently on forever, there's no need to drain the battery by leaving the directions on. "It says we have about two and a half hours left today, but the directions don't change for another hundred and fifty miles," I click off the phone.

Will's silent for a beat. "So we should be good on gas til we make it back to some sort of civilization. We'll probably get to the hotel by eight tonight."

I nod my head, "Sounds about right. Tomorrow we have to leave earlier. I talked to Trevor yesterday, he said that we need to be there by five p.m. or we won't be able to get keys until Monday."

"Trevor's the apartment manager?" Will clarifies.

"Yeah. If we backwards plan, let's estimate arriving at four p.m. so there's wiggle room. Seven hours of driving would mean leaving at nine a.m."

"You know we're going to need to stop for gas and food though." Will reminds me.

I purse my lips as I further my calculations. "One hour would probably be enough for two fill-ups and going to a drive-thru?"

"Yeah, probably."

"Okay, so we need to leave by eight in the morning. I'll get up at seven and you need to be up half an hour after that?"

He moves his hand from the steering wheel to rest on my leg. "Sounds good, babe."

The rest of our day of driving passes uneventfully. No semis abusing their size. No crazy commuters when we get closer to the city. We get to the hotel a little after eight and settle in for an early evening.

As we carry our suitcases to our room I comment to Will, "I didn't know sitting down and driving all day could be so exhausting."

He puts his free arm around me as I let out a huge yawn. "Good thing we can shower and be in bed in no time."

The elevator dings as it opens up to our floor. We exit the elevator and follow the signs to our room. The hallway is lit by traditional hotel sconces and the carpet is another pattern designed to hide all of the stains and scuffs it has accumulated over the years. We find our room easily and Will uses his key to unlock the door. The electronic entry flashes green and we push inside.

We have one king sized bed and that's what matters. I fling my suitcase down on top of the dresser forcefully enough to worry it may have scratched the surface, but Tomorrow-Nikki can care about that. Tonight-Nikki needs the bathroom, a shower, and sleep. Stat.

Will's at a counter space between the bathroom and bedroom area situating his luggage. "Can I use the bathroom before you shower?"

He's so courteous. "Of course, just let me pee?"

He nods and I take care of business.

When I exit, he passes quickly by me, not even sparing a second for a kiss. *Guess he really needs to go.* I head to the chair across the room and pull out my phone as I wait to shower. I sit with one leg bent beneath me and the other folded up in my coziest reading position. I pause at that and realize this is a great substitute for my chair.

I scroll through socials for a few minutes and see an image of Tipp and Ryan on my feed. They're smiling and looking so happy together. Ryan is kissing her cheek and her grin takes up the rest of the frame. Her caption reads: *Spend time on those who matter in your life.* Now

I feel like an idiot. Like one of those people who saw someone else's status and immediately think it's about them when in reality it could be about a million other things.

My fingers click and tap across the touchscreen of their own volition. My eyes are following their moves, but my brain is not making these decisions. They finally freeze and my mind catches up when the block button is one click away. If I press my thumb down, it's over. If I press my thumb down, I don't have to see shit like this anymore. I look up from my phone and stare at the ceiling, longing to find the answers I need written across it.

"You okay, babe?" Will's voice asks as he walks toward me from the bathroom.

I push a breath through my lips and admit, "I don't know if I should block Tipp on socials or not."

"Ah." He confirms he heard me while scratching his neck looking uncomfortable with this subject.

My gaze tracks over his taut frame. "What's up? There's no way my friend drama has you feeling this uncomfortable."

He refuses to meet my eyes and sidesteps nervously.

"Will, what's going on?"

His voice is barely audible, "Do you think if we call the front desk they'll bring up a plunger?"

I try to hide my immediate smirk, but my lips wobble every time I try to cinch it down. They let out a smacking noise and I surrender to how adorable he looks feeling like this. "Forgot to double flush?" I gently tease him.

"Yeah."

I get up from the chair and walk to him. "Do you need me to make the call down?"

He finally looks at my face and his eyes are struck with humiliation. "Could you please?"

I wrap him in a hug that he doesn't return. I take a step back and rest my hands on his shoulders. "Babe, we all shit. It just so happens that you're large, so I'm guessing your poops are too." My hand moves to his cheek as I ask, "Next time can you double flush please?"

He sighs. It seems as if my enjoyment in his apparent despair is grating on him. "Nikki, just make the call. Please." Then he turns on his heel and slinks back to the bathroom.

*I don't know why he wants to hide in the room that smells like feces right now, but that's his choice.*

I pick up the room phone and dial the front desk. "Hi, could someone please bring a plunger to room one seventeen?"

"Sure." The lady's voice hints to no surprise at this request. "Do you need someone to plunge the toilet too?"

I internally cackle with laughter. "I think my boyfriend would die of embarrassment if you did. Just the plunger will do please."

"Someone will be up soon."

"Wait!" I call so she doesn't hang up. "How often does this happen?"

She pauses. "At least three times a week. Mostly it depends on how booked the hotel is."

"Okay, thanks," I reply and set down the receiver.

I cautiously walk to the bathroom door and knock tentatively. "Babe?" I call out.

He cracks the door enough for me to see his face. "Yeah?" His expression is so somber it hurts to see.

"Come here." I hold out my hand and beckon him to leave the bathroom.

Will reluctantly follows my request and sits with me on the edge of the bed. His head is bowed and he looks completely defeated.

"Why are you so upset by this?"

I rub my hand up and down his arm as I wait patiently for an explanation.

"Poop is gross." He quietly admits to me.

He may be the cutest thing I've ever seen right now. My head tilts to the side in confusion. "And?"

Will lifts his head and looks at me with furrowed brows. "You're not repulsed?"

"Why would I be?" I lightly laugh as I shake my head. "We all do it, I'm just glad I was able to go pee before this happened."

Will's face relaxes before my eyes. His brow softens and his eyes get their normal spark back. He's sporting a half grin and sheepishly says, "Thanks for being chill about this."

There is a knock at the door, and his calmness fades with each knuckled thump.

"I got it." I pat his leg as I stand.

Once the door has closed behind me Will emerges from his hiding spot. I hold the plunger out to him, "Well, go fix this mess."

Will makes a show of it and rolls back his shoulders. He takes his battle weapon from me and enters the stinky beyond. When the door clicks behind him I roll my eyes, find my phone, and decide to scroll in the comfy chair until he's done.

Sitting there I begin to feel like it's been an unusually long time since Will went off to do battle with the toilet. I don't remember the last time I plunged a toilet, but it's supposed to be two or three precisely placed punches of the plunger and that's it. Not ten minutes worth of distraction and noise.

I set my phone down and go check on my boyfriend.

My knuckles rap on the door twice. "Babe?"

"It won't work!"

I push an exacerbated breath through my lips. *Enough is enough.* "Time to let me in then," I tell Will through the closed door.

"Not happening," comes Will's mortified reply.

"Fine." I cross my arms and lean on the wall adjacent to the bathroom door. "Then you can be the one to tell the receptionist why our room smells like shit in the morning."

A groan emanates from behind the door.

There is a click, and the handle pushes down slowly.

An inch of light shines through the crack created by the open door.

I take a deep breath of fresh air and enter the poopy room of doom.

"I tried like fifteen times but I can't get it to unclog." Will points to the toilet where the plunger still sits submerged in a dark plume.

"Were you getting it to suction right?" I ask as I try to ignore the foul odor giving my nostrils a suffocating hug.

"I— What?" he stammers.

"The plunger isn't to liquefy your shit, if you get it to suction correctly to the exit of the toilet you can push your shit through the piping with one or two perfectly placed thrusts." Without comforting him any further I take the plunger and find the right position. My arms tense with the effort needed. My feet are hip wide in the fighting stance so commonly mentioned in my favorite books.

I push.

Once.

Twice.

Then a slurping sound bellows from the toilet and its entire contents are sucked away.

I flush the toilet a second time for good measure and let the clean water give the plunger a rinse before removing it and placing it to rest on a towel in a corner of the bathroom we can avoid for the next twelve hours.

We take turns washing our hands and head back to the room that smells decent. Will's gone back to looking dejected, and I'm kind of over it. I sit in the chair and pretend to be on my phone until he breaches the uncomfortable silence that's settled between us.

"Are you sure you still want to do this?" His voice is so uncertain it takes me a moment to comprehend what he said.

"We're already halfway there, it's a bit late to turn back now." My voice comes out harsh, but serious. Is he having cold feet right now? I take a deep breath and convince myself to hear him out before I let him know how I feel about him backtracking. There are plenty of airports I can drop him off at on the way if that's what he wants.

"Nikki, you just had to plunge my shit for me!" He's distraught. His brows have crinkled together again and his lips are turned down in the corners. His shoulders are hunched over. This is not a version of Will I'm used to.

I stand from the chair and meet him in the center of our room. I cross my arms in challenge and look up at him. "And?"

He runs his hands through his hair before replying. "That doesn't have you disgusted with me?"

I put my hands on my hips and let him have it. "The only thing about this entire situation that is disgusting me, is that you think my opinion of you would change over something so trivial. You took a shit. Congratulations. It was too big and we dealt with it." My hands have started supporting my argument and I know my eyebrows have receded above my bangs. He needs to know the truth. "Newsflash, I picked you, out of every other person I've met, to move to Oregon with me. I know you. As long as you don't cheat on me we're good. Cheat on me and I'll chop your balls off." My face splits into a savage grin. "Oh, and I'll make sure it's with a rusty knife and jagged slices so there's no option of reattachment. You're mine, massive shits and all. Savvy?"

"I'm yours, huh?" Will repeats as he prowls forward. He pivots our bodies and pushes me down onto the bed beneath him.

I brace his chest with my hands, preventing him from claiming a kiss. "Out of everything I just said that's what you're fixating on?"

He cracks his neck while staring down at me. "Cheating means I lose my balls, blah, blah. That doesn't matter. You said I'm yours."

I lick my teeth in arousal and disbelief. My leg has snaked beneath him in preparation for my next move. "You are, but I also just saw firsthand what comes out of that ass. So we're both showering before you pursue this line of thinking any further." I tuck my foot under his sternum and push him off of me. I roll off the bed while he's still frozen in shock and saunter around him to grab my toiletries. I click the bathroom door shut and lock it behind me just before hearing Will try the handle. I look at myself in the mirror and my cheeks split into a shit-eating grin. *He's mine, and I'm his. The beginning of our forever is starting very entertaining, shitcident and all.*

# Eleven

# Our. Own. Apartment!

My Beetle is in our assigned parking spot fifty feet away. Will is steady behind me with a hand on the small of my back. I'm staring down the door to our very own apartment. Our first apartment. Ours.

With trembling fingers, I unlock the deadbolt and doorknob. I look over my shoulder to Will. He's practically vibrating with excitement. My favorite of his grins is plastered across his face. It radiates pure unhindered joy for life.

"Ready?" I ask him.

"Ready." He confirms.

I place my hand on the doorknob and twist it open.

I look into our first home together and feel like it was meant to be. The carpet is freshly cleaned. The windows are slightly open, allowing an early evening breeze to filter through. Will follows me across the threshold and we explore our new home.

The front door enters into the living space. To the left is space for a dining room table and in the corner a small coat closet. To the right of the front door is the living room. It's about twice the size of the dining area. A glass door leads to our private patio big enough for a couple of chairs and a table. The wall of the living room is lined with four large windows that overlook a grassy, tree filled community area. I go over to the windows and realize this apartment's location will allow us to see sunsets shining through the trees daily.

Will is ahead of me, in the kitchen area. There's a cut-out in the wall so the space is physically separated but you can see through from the living room to the kitchen. I go through the hallway entrance and meet Will. It's a small square room. The wall shared with the patio and living area has a pantry. To the left of that is a sink and dishwasher with a window above them that looks over our patio. A ninety-degree turn of empty counter space takes you to a combination stove and range. On either side, there are narrow cupboards that will fit the baking sheets we will someday buy. Another quarter turn and you're facing the standard white, fridge on the bottom, freezer on the top, appliance. There's a small counter section to the left of that perfect for a microwave. The floors are covered in pretty grey linoleum and the lighting is one long fluorescent strip. The cupboards lining the walls are painted white and the countertops are grey laminate that match the floor.

I leave Will to his daydreaming about the kitchen and walk down the hallway. The first door on my right opens into a spacious bathroom. There are twin sinks below a mirror that covers the rest of the wall. The cupboards below the laminate counter match the styling of the kitchen as well as the flooring in this room. A toilet is placed in the corner. On the opposing wall, across from the toilet, is a stackable washer and dryer unit. To the right of that is a standard white tub and shower.

Back in the hallway, I go to the next door on the left: the master bedroom. In the far corner, there are twin windows overlooking the parking lot. There's one closet that Will and I will have to figure out how to share. While that may be an issue, the ample floor space for all of our furniture will not be. The window sills are about six inches wide and I can already visualize a cat sunbathing in them. One of the windows in here is also cracked open and I realize this is how there's a cross wind gently blowing through *our* apartment.

I enter the hallway and see that Will is still hanging out in his kitchen. I veer to the left and enter the last room of the apartment. It's another bedroom, a little smaller than the master but has a closet, enough space for a bed, and anything else we might need it for. There's a solitary window in here also looking over the parking lot.

This is our home. This is all ours. "Babe!" I call to Will.

He finds me still standing in the second bedroom. He asks, "What's up?"

I draw him close and wrap my arms around his neck. "We're home."

"Yeah." He leans down and kisses me in that soul consuming way he's so good at. We stand there leaning into one another, cherishing the safety provided by the other's comfort. When Will draws back to catch his breath, I'm equally winded and still reeling with excitement.

"Let's go unpack your car." He suggests. My body has other ideas for breaking in our place, but I guess unloading everything we managed to stuff in the Beetle is a slightly more responsible first move.

One of the first things we locate is the air mattress and our bedding. "How about I get this set up while you get the rest upstairs?" I suggest as we pass by one another on the pathway that leads to the car.

"Sounds good." He agrees and kisses me on the cheek.

There are only a few more loads that need to be carried up; it's not like my Beetle could fit much of our stuff, so setting up the bed sounds like the next logical decision. I lug the box upstairs and plug the mattress into the wall as I disentangle the bedding from its haphazard ball. "Will must have been the one to pack this up," I joke to myself as I find the fitted bottom sheet.

"You know it!" He calls jovially from somewhere else in the apartment.

I roll my eyes and keep working until our bed is inflated to my liking. There's no point in shoving it against a wall since it's the only furniture in the room besides our suitcases. I think once everything arrives, my dresser will end up furthest from the doorway and the bed will be on the wall that's shared with the other bedroom. We won't have anyone sleeping here with us, so it doesn't matter if we're noisy or not. I shove the suitcases that Will brought up over to where my dresser will be and open them. We don't have any hangers yet so our closet can't be used correctly. Already this space is becoming our own with these small adjustments.

I head to the bathroom next and find a box on the counter. It has some toilet paper, soap, and other miscellaneous items needed in a new living space. Our brand new light purple and burgundy towels are hanging on the rack along the empty wall bringing character to this room. I set up our full sized toiletries in the medicine cabinet, store the spare toilet paper within reaching distance if you're seated on the toilet and realize you've run out, and put my makeup and hot tools in their drawers. I reserve the top drawer for Will's items, he'll only have a fraction of the number of products I do, so at a minimum I can give him the top pull out drawer.

I hear the front door close and go find him.

"Hey!" I greet cheerfully.

"Hello there," he purrs as he stalks forward.

My eyes bug out when I hear the intent in his voice and I turn and run. Not that there's anywhere I can escape to. I head to the spare bedroom and slide into the closet, waiting for him to discover me. I hear his feet pad softly across the carpet when he enters the room. He turns the light off and the room goes dark. I wait in anticipation of what comes next.

"We know you're here poppet. Poppet." Will's sultry voice quotes one of our favorite movies.

I bite my lip in anticipation of the fun he's instigating.

"Come out... and we promise we won't hurt you." He sings out as he gets closer to the sliding closet door.

My breath quickens from just his words, his hands haven't even touched me yet. His eyes haven't seen me yet. Gods, this is a wonderful new kind of foreplay for us.

The door creaks in the still air and Will's fingers curl around it. He slides it fully open and gives me a Cheshire grin. "Ello, Poppet."

I take a step back and run into the closet wall behind me. "Parlay!" I shout to him, wondering where the hell he'll take this next.

Will steps into the closet and grabs my waist in his strong hands. He hauls me out of the closet, twists us, and pins me against one of the barren walls of the room. "Sorry lass, there's no parlay here." He purrs at the base of my throat before nipping and biting his way to my mouth.

Will devours any protest I pretend to have with a kiss. He starts tender and slow but that's not what I'm wanting with our pirate scenario. I encourage him to deepen his kiss instantaneously and he greets my tongue with reverent strokes of his own.

I make quick work of his belt and reach inside his pants to find his thickening member, already damp at the tip, waiting for me. I begin stroking him roughly but am hindered by his jeans.

Will yanks my hand free and I whine in protest. He pulls my shirt over my head in one effortless motion and throws it to the floor.

As he grabs his own to do the same, I kneel before him and slide his pants down to his ankles. I see his cock tenting his boxers and coax it out eagerly.

I start off teasing him and lick down his shaft. His hips buck forward involuntarily as my tongue flicks over the tip of his head.

Will leans his forearms against the wall he just had me braced upon and sucks in a pained breath. "Nikki," he groans as I continue to play with him with light licks and gentle strokes of my hand.

I grin up at him through lowered lashes, "Nikki's not here right now, my name is Poppet."

Will opens his mouth to respond but before he can I close my lips around his cock and begin sucking him off properly.

As my hands, mouth, and tongue work in unison to bring him closer to the edge, I feel Will start to lose his restraint. His hips are quickening, thrusting deeper down my throat and I take everything he has to give.

I ease off his tip just enough to lick down the full length of him again and that's when his control vanishes.

Will puts his hand around my throat and uses a soft but firm pressure to bring me back to standing before him. He pushes me against the wall again and pins his cock against my stomach.

"You want to tease me?" He taunts haughtily, "Two can play at that game, lass."

He in turn kneels before me and hikes one of my legs over his bare shoulder. Then he starts to truly worship me.

He starts off lazily, tasting me and greeting my clit like an old friend he needs to reacquaint himself with. His hands grip my ass and hold me in place as he slowly and methodically explores the center of my body.

One of his hands roams up to my breasts and he pinches and rolls one nipple until it's a sharp peak.

Then he flattens his hand across my stomach and changes his focus back to my clit. His tongue stops its lazy exploration and hones in on exactly what I need. It licks at my core and sucks at all the right frequencies to have me in a mewling puddle, barely able to stand above him.

Only when I'm quivering on the only leg that's holding me up does he insert two fingers to help me teeter on the precipice of release. Right as I'm about to come he withdraws all contact and slides my body down on top of his as my legs collapse.

He perches me on his thighs, inches away from his glistening dick, and leans my back against the wall. "Not so fun when you're on the receiving end is it love?" He demands as he licks his lips.

I don't have enough moisture in my throat for my vocal cords to work so I settle for a defeated nod of my head.

"How about we both get off now?" He asks as he lifts me a few inches and lines up his head with my entrance.

I brace my hands on his shoulders and use my legs to take control of some of my own weight. I let out a low moan as he guides me down onto his shaft and rest there as I stretch to fit all of him.

At this angle, he's as deep as he can possibly get and I savor how full it makes me feel.

His calloused hands slide up and down against my sides as he waits for my cue to continue.

I roll my head back against the wall and start grinding down on him.

Will meets my grinding by thrusting up into me and we find a rhythm together.

The empty bedroom is filled with our moans and the slapping of our skin against one another as we build closer and closer to our own releases.

"Nikki," he warns me as he gets close.

I take a bracing hand from his shoulders and use it to rub my clit with the perfect amount of pressure to help myself get closer to the edge we're both chasing.

"Yes," I groan as Will takes control of all thrusting.

His rhythm becomes sporadic. He pumps into me at a punishing pace and it's all I do to hold on.

My own ministrations break rhythm and I feel it. The beginning of my release. "I'm," is the only warning I'm able to give him as I see stars and fall headfirst off the cliff into oblivion.

Will thrusts into me two more times before he comes with a shout of my name on his lips.

We stay there, panting and connected, as we come down from our high and find our breaths.

I find my strength and gingerly ease off of him and sit down on the carpet at his side. "That was—"

"Exhilarating." Will finishes for me.

I swat at his bicep as I laugh at him. "I was going to say fun, not having to be quiet for once."

"Oh yeah, that too," Will replies as if he's still off in a faraway place.

I lay down next to him giving my limbs a chance to stretch out as I think aloud, "What possessed you to do that role-playing all of a sudden?"

He copies my sprawled position on the floor before replying. "I didn't think it through," he admits with a half grin. "I saw you run, *Pirates* popped into my head and I just went with it I guess."

I prop my head up with one hand and trail my fingers down his chest and through the light dusting of hair there with the other. "Mhmm."

"You seemed to enjoy it enough." He says, sounding smug with himself.

"The thought of you dressed as a pirate, ab-so-fucking-lutely. The thought of Pintel," I shake my head for dramatic emphasis. "He's not my type. Not enough hygiene going on there."

Will gasps and puts a hand on his chest. "Are you discriminating against pirates of the eighteenth century? That's very unkind Nikki, they did the best they could. Even with limited hygiene resources." He ends his joking at a higher pitch, sounding like he's about to cry on the pirates' behalf.

I roll on top of him and sit on his stomach so his cock doesn't get too many ideas about a round two. "Come on," I brace on his shoulders and stand above him. "Let's go get cleaned off."

"Nah," Will says as he swiftly sits up and gives my core another lick.

My jaw pops open, "Will!" I shout as I step over him and get out of reach.

"Nikki?" He drawls, still sitting there looking smug.

"We need to get dinner." I remind him. "So I'm taking a shower."

"Sounds like—"

"Alone."

He lays back down and chuckles. "Fine, let me know when you're done. I'll just wait here."

I sashay my hips, knowing Will's eyes are glued to them as I walk down our hallway to the bathroom. I turn left and enter it, temporarily blinded by the bright fluorescent lighting I flip on. I use the toilet quickly to prevent any U.T.I.s from occurring and wash my hands. I pivot and turn to the shower. It's a simple faucet. I twist it up, surpassing the cold settings on the right of the circle, and settle in the medium heat range. I figure that's the best bet until we figure out the right angle to get a perfect shower temperature. My muscle memory had my left hand pulling for a shower curtain but it finds air instead. I stick out my arm, further, thinking it's just out of reach but my fingers still don't gain purchase. Then I look to figure out what the heck is wrong with the shower curtain.

Turns out there is nothing wrong with it.

It's not there. Neither is a bar to hang it from. "Will!" my voice echoes off the barren bathroom walls.

The door bursts open as he enters in a rush. "Nikki! What's wrong?"

He's still naked and I'm swept up in his glorious form before I remember. I clear my throat and suck in my upper lip. I gesture to the shower behind me, "Well, we don't have a shower curtain."

His eyes look behind me as he takes in my words. His head nods once and he bites his inner cheek. "That... appears to be an accurate statement." He agrees and claps his hands together.

I shrug, "So what do we do?"

"Bath?"

I shake my head, "No plug."

He walks across the room and grabs a towel. He opens it up and spreads his arms wide. "Okay, hop in, angle the head as far to the wall as you can. I'll hold this up and try to keep the spray from getting everywhere. You can do the same for me. We can dry off the floor with this when we're done too."

"So we'll be drying off using the same towel?" I confirm with him.

"Yup. I think after dinner we need to go to Target for some essentials we forgot about."

I agree and get in the shower. I make it a quick one that skips any type of hair care. As I'm taking one of the fastest showers of my life I keep thinking, *at least we're in our own apartment, and we're figuring out how to make it work.*

Will is equally efficient as he showers. We use both towels to mop up the shower splatter from the floor once we're dressed and throw them in the washer.

"We need laundry soap." I declare as I realize we have no way of washing them so that they'll be clean before we shower tomorrow evening.

Will pulls out his phone and a moment later I hear my text chime go off in the other room. "Added to the list. Shall we?" he asks and puts out an arm for me to grab hold of.

We exit our apartment and Will locks it up tight behind us. Keeping all five of our current possessions safe. We walk across the private landing that ends at our door and head down the wood railed concrete stairs. They're exposed to the outdoor air but the entire space between the buildings is covered so we're protected from the elements. When we get to the ground floor, an elderly gentleman is leaving the apartment that's located directly beneath ours.

He looks up from his walker and grins at us as we descend the last step. "Well hello there!" He greets us a little too loudly. "Thought I heard someone new rummaging around up there."

I swallow back my horror that this old man heard us going at it merely half an hour ago.

Will doesn't miss a beat. He has a genuine smile on his face and sticks out his hand to our neighbor. "Good evening Sir. My name is Will, this is my girlfriend Nikki. We just moved in upstairs about two hours ago."

"Pleasure to meet you, Will and Nikki." The elderly gentleman shakes Will's hand. "I'm Walter, but you can call me Walt. Practically deaf though so you might have to tap me on the shoulder to get my attention."

I shake his hand next, "Hi Walt, nice to meet you." Internally I sag with relief that there's no way he overheard our pirate themed scene a little bit ago. Not the first thing I want a new neighbor to know about us.

"Well, aren't you two a striking couple? Where ya from?"

I grin at Will and let him explain our past and our goals for moving to Oregon. It's a quick conversation and Walt is dismissing us soon. "Well you kids go get some grub, there's plenty of spots at Corridor Mall across the street. Hurry on ahead of me, I'm out for my daily walk to get the mail, but you don't want to be stuck behind this walker of mine."

His self-deprecating humor has me smiling light heartedly with him.

Will says goodbye to Walt and we hasten to the car. Standing there talking with him reminded my stomach of exactly how hungry it is right now.

I let Will drive my car over to the area Walt called Corridor Mall and we choose the sub shop located in the heart of it. Not quite fast food, which we've been living off of for two days now, but also not as expensive as a sit down restaurant. After eating the subs and wrapping up our leftovers for lunch tomorrow, we hop back in the car and drive a little closer to Target located at the far end of the strip mall.

As we enter the bright store with its red accents everywhere I can't help but feel nostalgic. This is the first shopping trip that we're taking together, to get supplies for our own place. It doesn't feel real yet. Like if someone pinches me I'd startle awake from this dream.

We do a lap around the perimeter of the store and realize it's the same layout as the one we used to frequent back home.

"That will make this easier." Will comments as we search for today's necessities. They're gathered quickly along with a few generic grocery items and we head back to our place.

As Will enters the Maple Drive Apartments road and drives down the section that leads to our building I'm caught up looking at our new home. Trevor told us there are about two hundred and fifty units total. The complex spans an entire city block. There is a road that cuts directly through to the two main streets but it's fenced off close to the manager's building. We were told that people who didn't live here would use it to cut through the stoplights on the main road so they created the barricade to make it safer for residents and their children. Each building only has four apartments, two upstairs and two downstairs, so we only share one wall with a neighbor. Lucky for us, that wall is in the second bedroom, which may also be the room we recently had loud christening sex in. Hopefully, our wall neighbors weren't home yet.

Will drives slowly through the covered parking spaces and pulls into the one reserved for our apartment. The sidewalk immediately meets the parking lot but there is a small area of grass and shrubs before the walls of the apartments. Trees are planted everywhere at the complex and I already adore looking at them as we walk up the sidewalk that leads to our building. Our building is second to last on the very edge of the property. Trevor said it's a nice location because we won't be bothered by many neighbors, if any. He also said being on the outskirts of the complex can feel like your secluded slice of paradise. At the time, I thought it was a sales pitch, but based on how few people are around us right now I think he may have been right.

That's not the best part of our new home though. What I love the most is that the beige walls serve to compliment the larger color scheme, instead of being the only color. There is green grass. The buildings are painted beige with dark brown trim. The trees are all living and covered in brilliant leaves. The shrubs are a deeper emerald in the shade of the setting sun. Everything is alive and full of color and that vibrancy is translating directly to my soul.

Will and I pack up our groceries into our arms and trudge up the stairs in one trip. It's not much, but our bathroom is now showerable without a disaster happening. We can do laundry, wash dishes when they show up in a few days, and have a couple of options for breakfast in the fridge now.

"My parents will probably take us shopping when they get here. You know how my mom loves to help out where she can." Will reminds me as I stand in our empty living room.

We close the blinds in here and check that the front door is locked before heading to the bedroom. "When will they be getting here?"

"They wanted to give us a few days to settle in, but also to be here to help when the furniture shows up. I think my dad said that five days from now would be best."

Will closes the blinds in our room before I nod my head at his comment and proceed to change into my pajama tank top.

The second my bra is unlatched Will is on me again. He walks me backward until I'm against yet another wall in this apartment and I can't even be mad about it.

We have six more rooms to break in, after all.

# Twelve
# Missing Furniture

"No. You said that our furniture would be here by June eighteenth!" I argue on the phone with a representative of the moving company. Will and his parents are all seated at our temporary dining room setup: patio furniture they bought for us after the first delay notification we'd received about our belongings. We'd been sitting on the floor and using a cardboard box as a table for the first few days, but his parents wanted at least a chair to sit in while they were here. I couldn't blame them. So after a trip to Fred Meyers, which we quickly learned is affectionately called "Freddy's," we have four patio chairs and a small table. It looks ridiculous in our living room but someday, maybe, we'll be able to move it outside to the deck and eat at a real table.

The employee restates the same line we've been hearing for over a week now. "Ma'am, there are a lot of people moving during this Fourth of July, and unfortunately your furniture is being delayed. I'm sorry but there's nothing we can do about it. Your belongings will be delivered by July tenth."

I wipe my brow with the back of my hand in frustration. "I can't cook. You have my pots. I can't go job hunting. You have my interview clothes. I can't do *anything* until our stuff gets here." I try to say it calmly, but this company is ruining our grand plan of having jobs within a month of moving.

Their nasal voice chirps in a rehearsed line, "If you have any expenses directly related to the delay in your shipment you can look online for a reimbursement form. Attach your receipts, fax it in, and the company will refund any justifiable expenditures on your part."

"And in the meantime, I get to keep sleeping on an air mattress and eating off paper plates," I murmur to Will and his family with my hand over the speaker. "Okay," I sigh. "Thanks, I guess."

"It's been a pleasure doing business with you."

I end the phone call before I tell the employee what I really think about who they work for. I know it's not their fault that someone over-scheduled clients, or they're understaffed, or whatever the excuse for not getting our stuff to us is. I just want my shit. Please.

"Well, it's out of your hands now. Let's go get you both some interview clothes since your belongings will be here so much later than you anticipated." Will's mom suggests from her lawn chair.

They've already been overwhelmingly generous that it feels wrong to take more.

"Nikki, wipe that look off your face," his dad directs me. "We're happy to help you both out. You're our family now too, and family helps their own when they can."

I give them a grimace of a grin and try to object. "It's just—"

"What family does." Will's mom interrupts me. "You're basically a Zukauskas now. If Will deems you worthy of moving across the country for I get the feeling that you'll be my daughter-in-law soon enough. Let us support you in this move." Will's mom says before taking a sip of her coffee.

They've bought us so much already, but I'm also not one to kick a gift horse. We are just starting out. We won't even have a table when our furniture does arrive. "Okay," I sigh in defeat at their generosity.

Will's dad claps his hands together, much like his son does when he's got an idea. "Ladies, you stay here and bond for a bit, Will and I need to run an errand before we all go clothes shopping."

I look at Will with raised brows but his face is just as confused. He grabs his wallet and heads out the door after his father.

"Well dear, it's just the two of us now. I don't plan on staying put like my husband suggested though. Let's go have some fun." She puts her cup down on the rickety table and picks up her purse. "You don't mind driving do you?"

Two hours later, I can't manage to carry half the bags up the stairs of our building in one trip. Will's mother went on a shopping spree. We started at a cute store I've never been to before and she bought me over five hundred dollars worth of clothes! The woman asked me my sizes and just started throwing items into a dressing room for me. If it fit, and looked cute she bought it without looking at the price tag. We put those bags in the car and she took us next door to a large chain for men's and women's clothing. She had me try on some business casual items there and bought me four different interviewing outfits. Then we headed to the men's department and worked together to pick out colors that would complement Will's blue eyes and natural blond highlights. I was terrified at first when he left me alone with her, but in the last two overwhelming hours I had gotten to know Marie, as she asked me to call her, better now.

I see Will's car parked in the spots for guests. His parents drove it up for us, packed with a few more things they thought we'd need. Little did we know what that actually meant. When they got here a few days ago it was filled to the brim with a microwave, brand new pots and pans, a toolbox for Will, a few pairs of adorable shoes for me, the list of gifts goes on and on. Then they took us on a pantry filling spree. Will and his dad spent at least thirty minutes discussing all the seasonings we needed in our basic kitchen. That trip had taken the four of us three trips to empty the car and a half hour to unload and put everything away in the fridge or pantry.

*I'm drowning in generosity and if this keeps up I will be overwhelmed,* I think.

"Hey!" Will's voice rings out from above where we're unloading my car. "Hold up, we'll come down and help you."

I'm finding the handles to all the reusable shopping bags that are much more popular here in Oregon than they are back home as Will and his dad, Paul, get to the car. Will puts his arms out and has me load him up just like before. Paul takes most of the remaining bags after his son departs. That leaves Marie and I to grab the few stragglers and follow behind them.

When we reach the apartment, Will and his dad put all the bags against the pony wall that separates the living room from the kitchen. Paul is standing next to him and they're wearing duplicate mischievous grins. In this setting, Will does look just like his father, only a few years younger.

Paul claps his son on the shoulder and instructs, "Show her, Will." He takes the remaining bag from his wife's hand and kisses her hello.

Will grabs the bag from my hand and puts it with the others. He doesn't seem at all shocked by the sheer amount of things that his parents have bought for us. He takes my hand in his and leads me down our hallway.

I look at him, confused to find our bedroom door closed.

"You have to close your eyes." He instructs as he stands as a barrier to me opening the door.

Instead, I roll them at him, cross my arms, and pop my hip in defiance. Then I close my eyes, with a jut of the chin for a touch of attitude.

He kisses my nose before I hear the doorknob turn. My face is lit up by the light coming from the bedroom and it takes effort for me not to open my eyes instinctively.

Will pulls my hands free of their crossed position and guides me a few steps into our bedroom. His presence moves from in front of me to behind me. He places his hands on my hips and instructs, "Open."

I do just that and am shocked at what I see.

There's a bed!

A queen-sized bed, on a bedframe, covered in a brand new comforter. All of it is immaculately made.

No words enter my mind.

I'm shocked. Utterly and completely speechless.

"Did we guess the right comforter set?" Will asks. He's moved beside me and is staring intently at my impersonation of a gaping fish.

I look at him and gesture to the bed, still unable to form words.

"Well, what does she think?" Paul's voice comes from the doorway.

I spin on my heel and see him and Marie standing there grinning at us.

I blink rapidly trying to form any coherent thought, but it's a blank space in my brain.

"I think she's a bit surprised." Will offers his parents.

His hand rests on my back and he rubs soothing circles, giving me the time I need to process. I close my eyes, take a deep inhale through my nose, and expel it through slightly parted lips. "I just—" I start but end up having to try again. "You're just so generous. Thank you, thank you for everything. But, please tell me there aren't any more surprises. I don't think I can take any more."

Marie laughs lightly. With a jovial grin she replies, "Only one more, get changed into one of your new outfits, we all need to head out to dinner before Paul and I fly out tomorrow morning."

I wrap my arms around Will. "Wait til you see what your mom and I picked out for you."

He grins down at me and then looks at his mother. "You're going to make me do a fashion show aren't you?"

"How else would we know if your new clothes fit?" She asks, feigning innocence. Before her back is completely turned I see the blatant smile written across her face. Paul follows her out of the doorway and we follow them to the living room.

Will and I take the bags of new clothes and put them on our new bed. I rummage around the purchases until I find a pair of black slacks and a nice black tank top. I pair them with a dark green blazer that hangs down to mid-thigh. *Something I could wear to a job interview or working in a classroom*, I think as I look at myself in the full-length mirror, an addition to our home that has magically appeared since Will's parents' arrival. I finish off my ensemble with a pair of ballerina flats. It's a bit warm for the summer evening, but it looks so good I'm unwilling to change into something more fitting for the weather. The sun will be set soon enough.

By the time I'm finished piecing together my outfit, Will is in his first ensemble. He's wearing a standard pair of jeans with a black button-up shirt. "Come on." He urges and sticks his arm out for me.

We walk into the living room side by side to see Marie and Paul lined up three chairs for us to watch Will's fashion show. Marie is beaming seeing us in the clothes she purchased. "Lovely dear," she comments on Will's outfit. "Now Nikki come here and watch the show." She pats the open chair next to her and shoos Will away to try on his next set of clothing.

The three of us sit there and chat about Will and my upcoming plans for the next month or so as he sporadically comes out in different looks. He struts in front of us and puts on a good show for his parents with each new outfit. His current look is my favorite so far, dark black jeans with a purple long sleeve dress shirt. However, the button-up isn't solid purple, it's checked with black underneath. Somehow the pattern brings out his eyes better than blues typically do.

"Show us your Blue Steele," Paul pretends to cheer as his son complies pursing his lips and jutting his chin out for added runway style.

When Will makes his exit with a kiss over his shoulder and a smack of his own ass Marie and I pick up where our conversation had paused earlier. "I have an interview set up in two days with the same chain I worked for in El Cajon, so hopefully my previous experience will make me an obvious contender."

"Oh, I have no doubt sweetheart. They'd be fools not to hire you." She compliments me and pats my knee.

Paul leans forward in his lawn chair to be able to make eye contact with me. "I chatted with Will and it sounds like he's found some leads with a temp agency. I think he mentioned something about working campus security until another opportunity arises."

I nod my head. We'd talked about that possibility before his parents showed up. Since their arrival, we've both kind of paused our job hunting efforts. Starting tomorrow that will have to become a top priority.

My face must have turned serious without my noticing because Marie waves her hands in the air. "Enough serious talk from you two. Let's enjoy our last evening here. I think Will is down to his last outfit if my memory is correct. Nikki, do you want to head in there and make sure all your clothes are hanging up on those new hangers so they don't get wrinkled?"

It's clearly a dismissal so she can discuss something with Paul. I smile at her dutifully and take my leave. "Sounds like a great idea." I walk down our hallway and knock on our door. I'm still getting used to that line of thinking, *ours*. Will opens up and I relay his mother's instructions about our clothing.

We open the closet and work together to hang everything up. Will's side is the left third, he graciously gave me the right two-thirds knowing that when the movers get our belongings here I'll be pressed to fit all of my stuff into the closet. Once our clothes are all put away we head out to the living room.

Paul and Marie are standing at the windows that overlook the grassy area behind our building, linked arm in arm. Marie looks away from our view first and asks, "Ready?" with a forlorn smile on her face.

"Ready," Will's voice comes out a little tightly.

Then I realize this is Marie and Paul's way of wishing their son good luck. He's a thousand miles away from home now. Tonight is their last dinner with their baby boy for the foreseeable future.

## Thirteen

# *Actually Adulting*

OUR FURNITURE SHOWS UP on exactly July tenth and I'm still annoyed that we went three weeks longer than predicted without it. The queen bed is in the master. Its bigger size makes me miss Will at night even more than ever. It's like part of me is missing every time I lay down to go to sleep. I'm alone in that brand new bed right now, debating whether I can hit snooze on my alarm again and still make it to work on time. My boss hired me as the opening shift manager. She decided since I'm from out of town to put me on a thirty-day trial period before paying me a managerial wage. I sigh as I remember this responsibility and decide that I need to get up and put some effort into my appearance as the opening shift manager. I flick on the light and immediately regret it. Four in the morning seems so much harsher in Oregon than three a.m. did in California.

I let out a groan as I roll out of bed and start getting ready for the day. Will isn't due home from his night shift for another hour. I'll end up leaving fifteen minutes before he walks through the doors. The last time I saw him, he told me that our paths had crossed so recently that by the time he'd showered and collapsed into bed, my side was still warm. I miss my boyfriend, but we're just starting. Someday our schedules will align better.

I pad down the hallway to the bathroom and catch a glimpse of the spare bedroom. We now call it the guest room because of the double sized bed we put in there. Coupled with Will's desk and chair, it's basically at max capacity for furniture. I flip on the fluorescent light of the bathroom and regret that action even more than I did the lamp on my nightstand. I squint in the bright lights and take care of business. This room has more character now too with a fun, French inspired shower curtain. It's designed like newsprint and has images of cafés drawn alongside popular French tourist traps. Nana picked it out for me before we moved, one of many items I've enjoyed quietly unboxing in the afternoons when I get home and Will is still sleeping.

I tie my hair back into a low pony and put my sandwich mogul baseball cap on. My standard burgundy shirt with a green collar is tucked into black pants and my bulky non-slip tennies are laced on nice and tight. It's a horrible uniform, but it's what I have to do to pay the bills. I turn off all the lights in the house except for the living room corner lamp and our bedroom lamp. I like leaving some light on for Will to see when he gets home. I head downstairs quietly so I don't disturb any of our neighbors who work regular hours and hop in my car.

The sandwich shop is a few miles from our apartment, but this early in the morning there is very little traffic on the road. I park in my designated spot in the back and let myself into the shop. The smell of the bread in here hits me like a tidal wave every time I enter. How can something that tastes so good smell so horrendous? My body reacts from habit after the week I've been here as I disarm the chirping alarm and turn on all the lights. Time to get the shop set up for the morning and lunch rushes.

I go to the walk-in fridge and pull out the meats and cheeses that belong in the sandwich making station for customers to see. The setup at this store is different than the location I worked at in Southern California. There, I did all the prep in the morning before my coworkers showed up. Here, I'm supposed to work on things like the weekly schedule, planning advertising campaigns and deals, and payroll before other employees show up. Alice, the owner of this shop, told me that I shouldn't be prepping any of the food. The only problem with that is I don't need all the morning time for the duties that she leaves me. I got the schedule done in two hours last week and when she reviewed it before posting she said it looked better than most schedules she'd ever made. I also met her quota for hours for each of the employees. Payroll was also checked in a single morning once I learned how to do it. I don't want to tell her these things though, because I'm not getting paid for my managerial duties yet, and I'm not going to take on more work for free.

My makeup bag is in my purse and I spend thirty minutes every morning applying my face. The manager's office doesn't have any cameras, which is weird because that's where the safe is, but I use it to my advantage. Once the shop is set up for customers, I take thirty minutes, on the clock, and do my makeup.

Fifteen minutes after I finish, my first and favorite coworker shows up. The first time we met he was polite enough, and Alice was teaching me all the interworkings of the store. I'd be fake polite in front of my boss too. The second time we interacted I was flying solo, and James dropped all pretenses of niceties. So naturally, I met his sour attitude with my perky morning personality.

"Good morning!" I sing-songed to him as he walked in for his shift. Instead of a greeting, he had grunted in my general direction. It was only the second day, and it was five in the morning so I gave him one more chance to treat me like a human.

On our third interaction, he was still a jerk, so I fought fire with caramel laced kindness dripping in sarcasm. "What's the matter?" I'd asked him in a motherly tone.

That had gotten James's attention. His gaze flicked to me as he pieced together what I was getting at.

So I got even more annoying, "Rough morning?"

"Not a morning person, unlike you apparently," he'd grumbled at me.

"Aww, cheer up buttercup. You get to work with me today!" I said perkily as I spread my arms out giving a visual aid to how fabulous I am.

"Don't call me Buttercup, Princess." He replied to me flatly.

That morning I must have had some extra sass added to my coffee because I did not back down. "If I'm a princess, then you're officially Princess Buttercup."

"No."

"Whatever you say, Princess Buttercup," I replied and went back to my work.

The next day his attitude had changed. "Morning Princess Sunshine," he greeted me almost nicely on the fourth shift we worked together.

Now, over a week since our first honest interaction I'm Princess Sunshine and he's Princess Buttercup. We have a strange rapport with each other and it feels like we've known one another for years. Early morning conversations with James are the highlight of my work shift.

Since payroll is done, the schedule is written, and I have an advertising pitch for Alice whenever she deigns to show up and check in on us, I join James in prepping the backstock for today.

I grab the bell pepper slicer and get to work as James regales me with the antics of his life. "Did you know I've had a vasectomy?"

"Of course I know that. It's a standard question on all employee applications." I deadpan without looking away from the bell peppers.

"Yeah. Bad intro, that." He says slamming down a large box of tomatoes on his prep station.

As much as I hate it, my curiosity is piqued. I take his bait reluctantly, "Why the fuck are you telling me you got a vasectomy?"

He chuckles softly behind me. I hear the tomatoes squelching through his slicer before he responds. "So that chicks can't baby trap me."

"Has that happened?" I ask, honestly worried about his answer. My bell pepper cutting pauses as I wait for his answer.

"Once," his voice turns dark. "She almost succeeded too, but I had her get a paternity test once the kid was born. Longest four days of my life, wondering if I'd have to raise a kid with her."

"Not a match made in Heaven?" I ask him jokingly, hoping to lighten the mood.

James glances over his shoulder and gives me a half grin. "Nah Nikki, we can't all be as in love as you and Will. But I can hook up with whoever I want and not have to worry about it anymore." He turns before finishing, "My ex taught me that I'll never be able to trust anyone other than myself."

I don't know if it's because I don't have a bestie right now or because he sounds so dejected but I put down the pepper I was planning on slicing next and clear the distance between the two of us. I put my hand on his shoulder and he pauses his work too. We stand there looking at each other for a moment before I clear my throat and tell him my thoughts. "I know we just met like a week ago, but I promise you can trust me. Alice may have hired me as *a manager* or whatever, but I value this friendship more than the distance that she wants me to keep from all of you."

"Management is a lonely position." He mimics her signature saying to me.

I cross my arms and lilt my voice to Alice's cadence, "I am a wonderful boss."

We break into twin grins and get back to our stations. James is an interesting character to get to work with. I never know what's going to come out of his mouth, that's for sure.

The rest of the shift passes quickly with more of our coworkers showing up for their shifts and the breakfast and early lunch rushes. I clock out at one thirty and head home to Will's unconscious body starfishing across our queen bed.

I sneak into our room as noiselessly as I can and hug him. I wince as I accidentally stir him from his slumber. He rolls onto his side and pulls me down into a full embrace. I lean there half on the bed yet still supported by my feet planted on the ground. He nuzzles my hair and groans. "You smell like sandwiches, did you bring me any to eat?"

I die on the inside at that comment. Dead. Done. Keeled over. I hate smelling like sandwiches! "Shhh," I cajole him. "Go back to sleep, I'll see you when you wake up." I withdraw from his embrace and kiss him on the cheek before grabbing my lounging clothes and immediately jump into the shower. I lecture the bathroom about my woes as I rinse off the grime my skin has acquired from work. "If I have to smell like a sandwich, Alice better be offering me a good pay raise when this thirty-day trial period is up. I could make the same wage brewing coffee or cashiering at Freddy's and smell a whole hell of a lot better."

"Is that so?"

I shriek at the sound of Will's voice coming from the other side of the shower curtain. I rinse the shampoo from my hair and pull it back a few inches to glare at him. "You could have knocked to let me know you were up." I grind my teeth in annoyance with him for scaring me.

He's leaning against the sink wearing only his boxers. He looks way too good for someone who just rolled out of bed. A knowing snicker forms at the corner of his lips. I swallow and resume my hair care routine. He has no business making my mouth go dry like that.

I finish washing and turn the water off. When I pull back the curtain to exit the shower, Will is standing there holding out my towel. I take it and notice the tent pitched in his boxers. I pat dry my skin and lean over to twist my hair up to keep it out of the way until I'm ready to deal with it.

Only when I'm standing naked and exposed to Will does he find something to say. His voice comes out huskily as he suggests, "You know, we haven't broken in this room yet."

I fold my arms in defiance, doing little to hide any of his favorite parts of my body. "And we're not going to be breaking in this room." I point to the shower I just exited, "That's too small, and there's no way you're getting me to go at it on this floor."

"That leaves the counter then." He closes the distance between us and crushes me with a fierce kiss. His hands claim my body, snaking their way around my waist and grabbing my bare ass. I wrap my arms around his neck and bring our naked torsos together. The damp friction created by my nipples brushing against his abdomin elicits a low moan deep in my throat.

That sound is all the encouragement Will needs. His hands squeeze my hips, turn me around, and prop me onto the bathroom counter. Somehow in the same fluid motion, his boxers are abandoned because when I open my thighs to wrap around his waist there is no fabric between his cock and my center.

He brushes it against me tauntingly and I whimper from wanting more, needing more.

My hand reaches down and strokes him roughly. He sucks in through his teeth in response to my touch. "Feeling greedy today?" He asks before nipping at that perfect spot right behind my ear.

"Always," I breathily encourage him.

"I want to experiment though. Take it nice and slow with you." He plants kisses down my neck and across my collarbones as he informs lazily of his plans for our afternoon.

I pinch his chin forcing him to pause and look at me. "You can play after you get me off."

His eyes darken with my command. He kneels before me without another word and perches my ass on the edge of the counter. With agonizingly slow precision he drags his index finger down my folds without parting them.

My hips grind dangerously close to falling off the counter in their yearning for more.

Will chuckles devilishly at my body's involuntary reaction to his teasing touch.

"Fucking finish me," I growl growing angry at his enjoyment of my torture. It's been over a week since our schedules have let him fuck me properly. This won't be finished until I've cum so hard and so many times that I need another shower.

He teases me again and only lets one finger slide into my sopping core.

*That's fucking it.*

I grab his wrist and shove his hand knuckle deep into me and hold it there. Will looks up at me with wide eyes, clearly shocked at what I just did.

I growl at him, "Either get me off right, or I'll get Belladix and do it myself. With the first option, you get to participate. The second?" I pause for emphasis. "I'll lock you out of our bedroom and force you to listen."

"You wouldn't," he argues with me as I keep his wrist firmly gripped in place.

I thrust his hand into me again forcefully as I argue, "Just try me."

He growls in response and then gives me what I've been needing so desperately. A second finger joins the first and Will thrusts into me mercilessly. I moan at the fullness the sensation provides. His mouth devours my clit in time with his finger thrusts and I writhe under his ministrations. I tilt my head back and rest it against the bathroom mirror as he brings me closer to the edge. With a few perfectly placed licks of his tongue, I cry out and fall into oblivion with his name on my lips.

"Better?" He questions while licking his lips and grinning up at me.

I can't form coherent words yet so instead I nod my head in agreement.

"Good, because now I get to play." He opens the bathroom drawer we haven't designated for anything in particular yet and pulls out two familiar items. "I found these when I was unpacking a box labeled 'bedroom' the other day. Thought I'd hold onto them until a good time." I see my gorgeous black, grey, and white marbled dildo, Belladix emerge first followed by my bullet vibrator. Will has a gleam to his eyes, hinting at the mischievous ideas I know are lurking just below the surface.

I bite my lip as I sit there in the afterglow of my first orgasm. The look on his face all but guarantees there will be more to follow.

He dips the bullet gently into my juices and it comes up glistening. He licks it clean before telling me any of his scheming thoughts.

"Do you think you could take Belladix and me at the same time?" He asks.

"Probably not," I answer him honestly.

He tsks softly. "That's a shame because this bullet doesn't have a flared base, so we can't use it anally."

I lick my lips at that idea. We haven't tried anal yet, but the idea has potential. "I guess we need to go shopping for more toys then."

"Well, we don't have any of those toys here yet, so I think it's time we put that mirror to use Nikki." Then with all command in his tone, he directs, "Get on your knees and turn around."

I eagerly follow his demand to see what he has planned for us. The counter is narrow so I have to spread my legs apart in order to be on my knees. It feels like I'm resting more on my shins by the time I get into the position Will has asked for.

He slides a hand up my stomach, reaches between my breasts, and grips my neck gently. His hand slides a little higher and forces me to look at myself in the mirror.

At this angle, I'm completely on display. My tits are practically rubbing against their own reflections and my clit is on view for both of us to see.

"I want you to see yourself when you come apart for me again." Will commands while slowly exhaling onto the shell of my ear.

It causes my back to arch and my body is put even more on display for the two of us.

Will's free hand slowly traces the curves of my body. It slows as he reaches my center and slowly plunges one, then two fingers into me again. I draw out a pleased moan as I let him explore at his leisure this time.

He gives delicate attention to my clit with his thumb and works me into a small frenzy again. When I'm about to combust for a second time he withdraws his hand, reaches behind me, and starts rubbing his head in the juices dripping from my entrance.

"I need you to lean forward just a bit babe." He guides me while gently pushing me to brace against the mirror.

Our eyes lock in the reflection and I see the pure desire written across his face. He was wrong, seeing myself come undone in this mirror isn't what I needed. Seeing him close up is what will be my undoing this time.

Will lines his cock with my entrance and pushes in slowly, one inch at a time. When he's fully sheathed, he pulls out and repeats the process a few more lazy strokes. When there's no resistance to our bodies meeting he starts to really pump into me.

He drags my back to rest against his chest and kneads my breasts greedily as I grip onto his hair.

"Nikki, use the bullet on yourself." He directs me.

He slows his thrusts as I bend sideways and pick up the bullet from its resting place. I click it on as Will pounds into me more forcefully than before. He grips my chin in his hand again and forces me to look at our reflections in the mirror.

I want to temporarily turn invisible so I can see his abs contracting with each thrust but those powers evade me. Instead, I'm greeted with the view of watching him slide in and out of me repeatedly while his jagged breathing comes hoarsely from behind me.

I take the bullet and drag it across one of my nipples, then the other before sliding down to my clit. When the silicone vibrating device makes contact I let out a mewl that would be embarrassing in front of anyone else.

"Yes baby, just like that." Will encourages me as my inner walls tighten around him.

When his brow starts to furrow and his thrusts become erratic I pull it away to draw out his torment like he did earlier to me.

He hisses behind me and I meet his irritated scowl in the mirror.

"Not so fun when it happens to you is it?" I taunt him while I bite my lip.

"Nikki—" he starts right as I drag the bullet across his balls.

"Fuck," he groans, "Do that again."

I bite back a laugh and do as he begs. Then I drag it up to my clit again and search for my release.

Will pounds into me with abandon. Our moans echo throughout the bathroom. I watch my tits bounce in the mirror. My gaze travels from my own body to meet Will's heated gaze. He nods at me in warning. I grin back at him in encouragement. I click the speed on the vibrator and it increases in frequency. I roll my head back to his shoulder and let him take control of my entire body. I flick my clit with the perfect pressure from the bullet and cum so hard I see stars on the edge of my vision. Will grabs onto my body and holds me tight around my center as he continues to pound into me from behind. Three more thrusts and a flick of the bullet have him coming with a roar that is only dulled by his biting of my neck.

He thrusts gently into me as he comes down from his orgasm. When he's sated, his knees begin to wobble and I pull off of him, resting against the mirror. "I think we both need a shower now," I inform him with a drugged smile.

"Not yet," he replies with that same devilish grin. "I'm just getting started."

## Fourteen

# A Cure for Loneliness

I sit 'crisscross applesauce' in my favorite reading chair in the living room as I process the last few weeks of our lives. The sun is shining through the window, warming my skin. A cup of iced coffee sits on an end table we got for cheap at the grocery store. We're doing it. We're here in Oregon, holding down jobs, paying rent, and sort of succeeding at being adults. I would think we were actually succeeding if either of us somewhat liked our jobs.

Princess Buttercup is literally the only thing I enjoy about the sandwich shop. When I spoke to Alice on the phone, I asked when we would meet to discuss my pay raise since I've been manager for a month now. She was vague and noncommittal. I ran into her in person shortly after and she told me that she was going to stretch out my trial period to sixty days. When I asked if there was a problem with my performance or if there was something she thought I needed to improve upon she had no critiques to offer.

My finger snags on the lip of my chair at that thought. I start tapping the armrest irritably, remembering Alice's next words, "I need more time to make up my mind about you and our working relationship."

In the moment, I'd managed to remain non-fussed. However, once I got home, Will heard every opinion I had, completely unfiltered.

I'd started looking for new jobs that night.

I pick up my iced coffee and take a smug sip, knowing that my revenge on Alice will happen sooner than later. I've heard from a grocery store in town where the employees always seem happy. Most importantly, the store doesn't have that nasty signature scent.

Through some self reflection and journaling, I've discovered a few more issues that are eating away at me. I wrote out my list of biggest complaints last night and decided on my days off this weekend I was going to work on them. I pick up the paper and reflect on the words listed.

1. *New Job*

2. *Loneliness*

3. *Lack of friends*

"Well, job applications have been sent into the ether," I inform the empty living room. Talking to myself has become an unfortunate norm with Will usually sleeping when I'm home. We only have about three hours of consciousness together on days that we work which brings me to issue number 2: *Loneliness*. The sparkling sunshine and birds chirping through the open windows listen to my thoughts this time. "With Tipp's friendship ending, and the fact that she hasn't reached out with an apology or desire to fix things between us even once, I have no friends other than Will and James. But James and I really aren't friends beyond work. He's like my work husband," I explain my friendship to the chattering birds. "So what can I do in the meantime? I know I'll stand a better chance of making friends with a new job, and also once classes start at U of O." I sigh with frustration, "What about until then?"

"Talking to the trees again?" Will's sleepy voice asks from the hallway, startling me from what I thought was a private conversation.

I grin up at my fresh out of bed, shirtless, boyfriend. *He's all mine.* "They were giving me advice on how to solve some of my current problems."

He strolls across the room and kneels before me. "And what would those problems be, babe?"

I offer him some of my iced coffee to help clear the sleep that still lingers near his sea-blue eyes. I mull over my options of how to phrase this before deciding brutal honesty is the best policy. "I'm lonely."

His eyes jump from the coffee he's consuming to mine. He doesn't speak but asks me to continue with the gentle placement of a hand on my outer thigh.

"We're both working, we're both making it work. But at night when you leave for your shift and I'm in bed. That's it. It's just me and whichever character is written into the books I'm reading."

Will's hand starts massaging my leg lovingly as he asks, "So you want someone to warm the bed when I'm gone?" His half-smirk belies the innocent tone he uses.

I swat his bicep. "No! I just, ugh!" I inhale deeply trying to figure out exactly what I mean.

"Want someone to talk to so you feel a little less alone?" He offers.

I nod my head, feeling pathetic. "Like not a roommate or anything like that. But I know if Tipp and I were still friends we'd be talking. I never know when Nana is available so I feel guilty calling her up impulsively. I need a damn friend."

"What about James?"

"He's a friend, but he's not a call-up at night when you're lonely, friend." I pause and wrinkle my nose. "Am I looking for a platonic booty call?"

Will lets out a full belly laugh. His awkward laugh of our first date has been long abandoned and hearing his joy now brings a smile to my face.

"Let's put a bookmark in the platonic booty call idea." He suggests while patting my leg and standing. He holds a hand out and steadies me with it as I disentangle my legs from beneath me. When I'm standing he says, "What about a pet?"

I look up at him with hope in my eyes. My cheeks hurt with the width of my smile. My hands clap together the way the members of his family do when they're excited. "Do you mean it?"

"You know our rule: no yard, no dog. So I guess that means we can either get a ferret or a cat."

I shake my head in disbelief. "We are *not* getting a ferret!" I shout at him.

He shrugs, "It was worth a shot, it's legal here in Oregon you know."

I shoo him away. "You go get dressed. I'll make you a coffee before we head out."

"Where are we going?"

"We're getting a cat! You don't work until nine tonight right?"

He hesitates, then nods.

"Great. That gives us five hours to pick one out! I'll search for local shelters while you get ready."

Forty minutes later, Will's coffee sloshing around in a To-Go cup, we pull into the local shelter's parking lot. Blue Skies Humane Society is written in a bold script across the front doors. It's located on the edge of town and has great reviews online. Most importantly, it's a no-kill shelter.

As soon as Will puts the car in park I hop out excitedly. "I feel like a kid being taken to a candy shop without a budget," I tell him as he rounds to meet me at the trunk, moving slower than a sloth. We link hands and I pull him to the shelter doors. "No! I feel like a book lover set free in a store where her significant other is going to buy her everything she can carry." I can feel Will's eyes roll at that comment. "Nope. Still not good enough. I feel euphoric!" I open the door for us and we enter the shelter.

The employees are situated at various desks to the right. To the left is a small shop set up with a variety of pet supplies.

"How can I help you?" The young lady at the front desk asks us.

"We'd like to get a cat please!" I call out a little too excitedly.

She smiles at me kindly and gives us directions. "The Cat Room is out those doors and to the right. Just follow the signs along the path. There will be people in there to talk to you and answer any questions you have."

I practically skip through the doors and leave Will to catch up.

I'm hit with the smell first. Cats. Healthy cats, but a lot of them. Once my nose adjusts, my eyes take in the scene before us. It's a massive room filled with cat trees, cat toys, and of course cats. The edges of the Cat Room have eight private rooms total. Inside those rooms are also cats.

"Where do we even begin," I hear Will ask nervously from behind me.

"That's up to you." A perky employee offers as she appears from nowhere. She's in sweats, covered in cat hair, and rocking a sweatshirt with the shelter's logo on it. "The first thing you should probably decide on is what age of cat you'd like."

"Two kittens please." I immediately answer her.

Will's eyebrows shoot up. "Two?"

"Yeah! So that when we're both at work they have someone to play with until we get home."

"Makes sense." He replies, draping his arm over my shoulders.

"Okay, so most of our kittens are located in the glass-walled rooms on the perimeter of this room. The kittens are mostly too small to hang with the adult cats so we keep them separated for their safety." The employee explains. "Go ahead and walk around. Let me know if there are any that stand out to you." She turns on her heel and leaves us to look for our cat.

The first two rooms we walk past already have people inside playing with different litters of kittens. When Will and I approach the third room, its only occupants are of the furry variety. We wait for them to play in the far corner of the room and slip through the sliding door quietly.

"What do we do now?" Will asks once we're sealed inside.

I motion to the plastic chairs. "I guess we take a seat and get to know them," I suggest before sitting on the ground, more on level with the hoard of kittens.

"I've never had a cat before." Will confides as he takes a seat.

"I didn't know that."

He picks up a stick with a string attached. At the end is a feather. One of the kittens eyes the movement of the toy and chases it. Will deftly twists and pulls the stick, keeping the grey tabby kitten engaged. "Yeah, we had an outdoor cat once when I was younger. But it just kinda showed up one day. My parents figured it would find enough food from the vermin running around the neighborhood so they didn't get any food. It wasn't skinny or anything like that. Then one day it was just gone. We only had dogs really, and a turtle."

I nod while listening to him. Another kitten, this one completely black, has decided to brave the new strangers in their room and is beginning to climb on me. I scratch it between the ears and under its chin. Soon it has crawled into my lap, cuddled into a ball, and is now taking a nap. When the kitten settles, I answer Will's train of thought. "I grew up the opposite. I wanted a dog but my parents couldn't agree on a way to potty train it. They were both working, it was peeing on the carpet, it didn't work out. We always had cats though. My mom loves orange tabbies. We got one when I was in eighth grade and Jamie and I both asked our mom, without previously talking with each other about it, if we could name it Tigger. Everyone knows he's basically my cat, but we were worried about how well he'd get along with Otis so I left him behind when I moved out."

A second cat has joined in with Will's feather on a stick game and is competing with the grey tabby for the toy. "So how do we choose?" he asks.

I shrug and continue petting the kitten snuggled into me. "I think this one has chosen me. Maybe now we wait to see which one chooses you?"

We stay in the room and I watch Will play with the kittens. They're a variety of colors and sizes, making me wonder if they're from a few different litters. No matter the case, they all get along. Some of the kittens come and go, but the original grey tabby keeps pace with Will's playing. Its little sides are heaving in and out with exhilaration when Will puts the toy down.

"Try picking it up," I suggest.

Will's hand stretches out and strokes down the little cat's back. The tabby turns and looks up at Will with curious eyes. I wish I had my phone ready to get a picture of this moment, they're absolutely adorable. He wraps up the kitten with one hand and brings it to his chest. Immediately, it snuggles into the crook of Will's neck and closes its eyes.

"You have no idea how cute you two look right now," I tell him when they're settled. "I think we've both been chosen, want to go tell the employee?"

His lips turn down at that idea. "Do I have to put him down?"

I beam at him. "No," I pick up my kitten from her ball and hand her to Will. "You're going to take my kitten too. I'll go tell the employee. Just, don't move."

When he has both the kittens snuggling either side of his neck I give him a soft kiss and sneak out the sliding door to find the sweet lady that was helping us earlier.

I'm instructed to fill out some paperwork and provide our landlord's information. Once it's all completed they say, "Okay, go hang out with the kittens for a bit. I need to make sure everything checks out. I'll come get you when I know."

Before entering the kitten's room again, I get out my phone and prep it for taking a picture of Will snuggling the little fur balls. I slide open the door and snick it shut behind me. It's then I realize that the felines aren't the only ones in this room sleeping. A soft snore is emanating from Will. His chin is tucked into his chest and his hands are propping up the butts of either kitten. All three of them are sleeping, and it's one of the cutest things I have ever laid eyes on. I snap a pic on my phone before disturbing his cat nap.

"Hey," I whisper as I put a hand on his arm.

Will immediately jolts awake. The movement startles the kittens and suddenly 6 eyes are staring at me in confusion. I take the black kitten from him and hold her to my chest, my breasts making a soft shelf for her to rest on. I go back to my spot on the floor and lean against the wall.

"What did they say?"

"We have to wait a bit for some paperwork to process. She said she'd come get us once everything checks out."

There's a light tapping on the kitten room's sliding door and I look up to see them. I give my kitten back to Will and poke my head out. "What's up?"

They swallow, "Unfortunately, your landlord has a strict one pet per residence rule. So you can get a kitten, but only one of them."

My brows furrow, "Oh. Okay, we'll have to talk this over."

They nod and back away to give Will and me a moment. I relay the information to him and we both agree not to choose one kitten over the other. We put them both back into the corner with the rest of their siblings and sneak out, hoping that a better fitting family will adopt them together.

Once outside the room, Will takes my hand, "Let's go find a cat that works for both of us."

# Fifteen

## *Toph*

"Ow!" Will whisper shouts and tugs his hand away from a grey tabby with white patches.

"Did she draw blood?" A man wearing a t-shirt with the shelter's logo asks us.

"Nah." Will lies to him. "Just startled me is all."

The man's face looks like he doesn't believe Will so I ask him, "What happens if they do draw blood?"

Flatly he answers, "We have to quarantine them for thirty days." Then he turns and walks away like that's no big deal.

"Thirty days?" I ask Will incredulously. I reach my hand out and pet the cat that apparently just broke a very serious rule.

"Good thing it was on my hand and I could shove it in my pocket." He laughs, joining in petting her.

She nuzzles into our affections and starts purring loudly.

The first, sweet, employee still covered in cat hair comes over to us. "Ah, this one is Rebecca. She's only been here a few weeks. Came in with her litter of kittens. They've all been adopted and now she's waiting for her own forever family." She bends her head down to nuzzle the cat, who immediately paws at her dangly earrings.

I look at them while still petting Rebecca and ask, "How old is she?"

"Only two or three from what our vet can tell," she says, looking up from the tabby with white patches.

"Is she the one?" Will asks me.

"I think so."

"Great!" she exclaims happily, "I'll just take her and get her boxed up for you. You can go back to the office where you entered. When they're ready they'll call out 'Rebecca,' and you'll be able to take her home." She approaches Rebecca and picks her up with finesse. Rebecca squeals with indignation at the interruption to her pets as she's carried out of our sight.

"I guess we go wait?"

"Yeah," Will agrees, eyes still watching the door the employee took our cat through. "I should probably wash out where she scratched me though."

Twenty minutes later, yet another employee calls out, "Rebecca," signaling the end of our trip to this shelter.

We take her in a cardboard box out to the car and Will drives us back into town. "You know we have nothing for a cat right?" He asks after a few minutes.

Rebecca is situated in my lap, still contained in her box, much to her disappointment. She's been yowling since the car started moving. I've been sticking my fingers through some of the holes to try to comfort her, but at this point, she's lost all her babies, is in a terrifying car, and with two people she's known for all of five minutes. Sticking my fingers into her box isn't going to help anything. "Well, they gave us a week's worth of her food, pellets for her litter box, and a temporary litter box. We'll be able to survive one night at least. I can run to the pet store tomorrow and get other items after my shift."

"What time?"

"I'm off at one-thirty; I was thinking I'd stop by on my way home."

Rebecca's cries have quieted slightly since our conversation started.

Will merges onto the freeway before responding. "Would you be willing to wait until four or five so that I can join you?"

My arm crosses the center console and my hand rests on his leg. "Of course babe, all you had to do was ask."

We drive home in companionable silence that is frequently interrupted by Rebecca's meowed opinions.

At home, we toe off our shoes at the front door and carry the cardboard cat box into our large bathroom. Will brings in her supplies and we start setting everything up. Once Rebecca's litter box is shoved against the wall, some food and water are poured into little dishes that sit across the room, and the door is closed, locking all three of us into the room, Will opens the box. Rebecca's head pops out immediately and her little nose twitches as she sniffs her new surroundings aggressively. Her eyes are huge and her ears are shifting at every little noise that catches her notice. She stays within the safety provided by her box while she takes in her strange new home.

Will and I settle in side by side, leaning our backs against the edge of the bathtub. "What now?" He asks me.

One of my brows lifts toward my hairline. "I don't know. I only remember having one new cat. We had to lock Tigger in my room for the first thirty days we had him because he was an alley cat. He couldn't interact with our other cat until we knew he was free from street cat diseases. Rebecca doesn't have that problem."

"Maybe we start there then."

"Where?"

Will laces his fingers with mine. "We have to choose a better name for her than Rebecca."

I laugh softly, trying not to scare her. "Okay. She's tough, since she drew your blood."

"She's not afraid to tell you her opinion, all that meowing on the drive," Will adds.

Just then our cat jumps out of her box and walks over to our legs. She sniffs us in turn and then goes to explore the perimeter of the bathroom.

I continue listing her attributes. "Apparently she's curious about life, and won't be scared into submission."

"What if we were to give her an Avatar name?"

I cross my arms and rest my hand on my chin. "What, like Katara or Azula?"

He counters my idea. "No, neither of those are right. She's not nurturing enough to be Katara, and not enough of an insane power hungry bitch to be Azula."

"What about Toph?" I ask.

We watch her sniff her way around the base of the counter space that Will fucked me so well against a matter of days ago. She rounds the base of the toilet and crosses the room to our stacked washer and dryer unit. She jumps onto the closed lid of the bottom washer and then disappears behind the unit.

"Oh shit." Will breathes out.

I pat his leg, "She'll be fine. There's what, a power cord and exhaust piping back there? Give her time, she just wants somewhere to hide for a bit." I suggest and stand. We leave the room and keep the door cracked for our cat to explore the apartment when she's feeling up to it.

"I guess she is a bit like Toph." Will explains his thinking, "If she had earth bending powers she probably would have dug a hole to hide in."

I elbow him as we walk down our hallway and go to the kitchen to figure out what to eat for dinner. "You're ridiculous." I tease my favorite human and kiss him.

We heat leftovers from last night's dinner and eat them on our lawn chair dining room setup. We figured it was best to do something simple and quiet rather than scare Toph more with loud noises and appliances going off in the kitchen.

Toward the end of our meal, we hear a distant meow from the recesses of the bathroom.

"Do you think she's okay?" Will asks.

I finish my bite before replying. "Probably. Let's give her a little bit more time before we disturb her safe space."

We finish our meal and are cleaning up the kitchen when he hear Toph meow again. It's louder and more distressed this time.

Will tosses the plate he was putting into the dishwasher in my direction and practically runs into the bathroom. I barely manage to catch it and put it down safely on the counter before following his panicked path.

When I enter the bathroom I see he has already pulled the stacked unit halfway out of its alcove. Another meow comes from behind it and I realize, "She's stuck?"

He pulls on the unit again but it won't budge any further. "I think so," he grunts trying to be stronger than metal.

I hurry over and look between the unit and the wall it's sandwiched against. "Okay, you won't be able to pull it any further without disconnecting it. Hold on." I tell him and analyze the situation. "She's small, I think if you push it all the way to one side she'll be able to squeeze through the space created."

Will doesn't answer me with words. Instead, he swiftly pushes the unit to the side and waits for more directions from me.

They're not needed though. With the extra two inches provided, Toph wiggles her body out of its former jail space. She goes to the middle of the bathroom, sits down prim and proper on her haunches, and looks up at us seeming to say, "I meant to do that."

Will pushes the unit back into place and turns to look at our new cat. He asks her, "You're going to be a handful aren't you?"

She blinks up at him once, turns around, and leaves us alone in the bathroom to contemplate how our lives are about to change.

# Sixteen
## Friendships and Expectations

It feels like we've just settled into the routine of work, and caring for Toph when reality comes crashing back. School. I have to keep on track with my timeline and get my education degree, no matter how much I'd rather stay home, cuddle up with Toph, and get lost in a good book.

The bus that passes directly by the University of Oregon also goes right past our apartment. It's less than a five-minute walk from our front door to the bus stop, and today, my snoozing turned into a challenge of trying to make it in three minutes. I round the corner, wishing my backpack wasn't weighing me down as I see the green bus pull away from the stop. My steps falter and I pause on the sidewalk, watching my ride leave without me. "It's fine," I breathe into the cold morning air. "The next one will be here in thirteen minutes." I slow my pace and regain a steady breath as I use the crosswalk and approach the bust station. The weather hasn't turned yet. It may be cold, but that's only because the sun hasn't risen yet. I go to the middle seat at the bus stop and sit. My legs bounce in the cold morning air. My eyes scan my surroundings.

If Turner and Brock from my past life in California dared to treat me so poorly, and they knew me; then who knows what some random person would be willing to do to a complete stranger waiting at the bus stop before the sun rises? I don't listen to music, but I do have headphones in. I saw on social media that it's the ultimate lure to make predators think that you can't hear them. Then they're louder with their intent, and sometimes even say what they're going to do before they do it.

Before I can go too far down the dark hole of my assault history, another bus pulls up. I enter the first door and sit near the driver. My back is against a wall looking into the middle of the bus. I hate that this is how so many members of our population have to act in order to prevent an assault, but I can't afford the four hundred dollars a term the university wants for a parking permit.

The bus pulls away from the curb and I let my body sway with its movements across the road. The seats are dark blue with patterns to hide the disgusting secrets besmirching their surfaces. The floor of the bus is shades of grey that tell many of the stories they've seen. I clutch my backpack to my lap doing my best not to touch my surroundings. On days when I'm lucky, someone else hits the button for my stop as well, nullifying my need to sanitize when I step off. I sit and stare at nothing in particular in the quiet of the morning commuters and wait the forty-five-minute drive it takes to arrive at my stop on campus.

I'm still navigating the various buildings on campus. Everything seems so different now than when Will and I were here less than a year ago. During the middle of the day, thousands of students hustle between classes where the walkways were previously piled high with snow. When the sun is shining, students will call to people they know. I imagine professors standing around talking to one another. An angry protester stands in the heart of campus, telling us we're all sinners and going to Hell for it. Most of the action happens later in the day when I'm headed home. Currently, the campus is eerily quiet.

I make the trek to the far corner of campus unaccompanied. The education department is sequestered in the back. It takes me fifteen minutes to get from the bus to the building that houses most of my classes. I usually stretch that out to twenty. I feel a natural tilt of my lips into a soft smile as I choose my path for the day. I weave through the heart of campus easily and take a left toward the library building. If it were later in the day, there would be students sprawled in front on its massive lawn. They would be laid out sunbathing and reading their textbooks. Some would be sitting in the grass eating their lunches. Others would chat. More still would nap. At this early hour, I walk through the deserted campus without interruption.

I arrive at the Department of Education and take up residence in my favorite study booth. There are four options and I choose the second in from the front of the building. I deposit my backpack, go to the cafe around the corner, and order myself a coffee. I'm over an hour early for class, the curse of working openings, but it's a great time to fit in homework.

I slide across the dark green bench seat and get out my supplies for the morning. Somehow, I'm already behind on the assigned readings and it's only the second week of classes. I'd like to blame my newest monster romance with Esther and her many enticing suitors, but it's really my self-control that's the issue. I needed to know what happens next and about Amon's curved...

A tall redhead with a smattering of freckles breaks my daydream. "Hi, you're in EDST 412 right?" She asks me.

I swallow and clear my mind before replying. "Do you recognize me, or is it the book I was about to read that gave me away?" I ask her while pointing at our assigned reading sitting on the table before me.

"Both," she grins. She sticks out her slender hand, "I'm Shona."

I grin up at her and reply, "Veronica, but everyone calls me Nikki." I gesture to the open half of the booth across from me. "Want to join?"

Shona slides her bag along the bench and follows it with. "On one condition, we actually get some studying done. If you have no self control we're doomed, because I'd love to do anything other than study right now."

I like her honesty, it's a good quality in strangers who might become friends. "Done. We're not allowed to talk until fifteen minutes before class." I pick up my phone and turn on music in my earbuds for the first time today. Shona takes my cue and gets her work out.

For a woman who spoke so little of her self control, she doesn't try to interrupt my reading once during our study session. I wrap up the mandatory reading five minutes before our agreed upon chatting time so I pull out my planner and make sure all my other assignments are completed. The summer off was a nice reprieve from this level of workload. I'm already counting down the days until our month long winter break.

My new companion puts down her book as soon as our predetermined study time is over.

She leans in across the table and meets my gaze. "So, you're not fresh out of high school either are you?"

*Well, that's a conversation opener.* "Uh no. I took a year off, and also spent three getting my Associates at a community college."

"Smart." She nods her head at my answer.

"What path did you take?"

"Wasn't sure where I wanted to go exactly, so I got my Associates locally and then took some time off to figure things out. Long enough to save up for my tuition, so at least that was a bonus."

I'm honestly impressed. "Wow, that's some dedication."

Shona brushes off my comment and we start discussing where we're from and where we're hoping to go. Too soon, it's time for us to head upstairs with the other students who have started filtering in for our eight a.m. class. Shona and I sit with two other friends she's already made. For the first time since classes began, I feel like it might be possible to become friends with some of my classmates.

· ♥ · ♥ · ♥ · ♥ · ♥ ·

In the last twenty-four hours, I've made new friends at school, had a job interview, and now there's even enough time in our schedule to have dinner with my boyfriend. I'm currently seated in my cozy reading chair with my legs folded under me. Sadly, I'm not reading for fun, I'm surrounded by homework. Toph is purring across the room on the antique couch Nana gifted us. The afternoon sun is toasty, but with fall filtering through the open windows the gentle breeze is preventing me from overheating.

Will's keys clink down onto the piece of furniture we've affectionately named "The Green Thing." It's probably older than I am, which also means it was made well. Not like the plywood crap in all the stores these days. *Oh my gods, I sound like a cranky old person.*

"How did your interview go?" He asks me with a closed kiss hello.

I jump up from my reading chair and spread my arms wide. "Well enough that they called me before I'd even made it home and offered me a position!" I run toward him with a huge smile plastered across my face. He catches me easily enough and swings me around our living room in a congratulatory hug.

"That's so awesome babe! Did you tell Alice yet?"

He sets me down and I laugh conspiratorially at him. "Even better, I've figured out the best way for me to exact my revenge." I bite my lip at my own devious idea.

He kisses my forehead before walking to our room. "I'm glad that look isn't directed at anything having to do with me."

I follow him and sit down on the bed next to Toph as Will changes from his errand clothes into sweats. *If he's going to offer a free show I'll watch it shamelessly.* When Will's shirt comes off I cover Toph's eyes. "You're indecent in front of the fur baby." I tease him.

He scoffs at me. "Well then you might want to get some cat ear plugs because we were a lot more indecent last night."

I shake my head at him without reply.

"So what's your plan?" Will asks when he has a shirt on again.

I waggle my eyebrows at him. "You sure you're ready for it?"

"That's what she said."

I heave a sigh through my lips at his outdated reply. "Okay, so delivery day is Tuesday right?"

Will nods his head.

I pull my legs onto the bed, sit crisscross applesauce, and pick up Toph. I stroke her fur like an evil genius before continuing. "Well, she has me work Tuesday openings so I can put delivery away. I told James a little while back that I'm quitting as soon as I get a position. He told me he'd just follow me out the door. It just so happens that somebody, *no idea who of course*, wrote the schedule so that James is the second to come in on delivery days." I pause, waiting to see if Will catches on to my plan.

"And?"

Apparently it's not spelled out enough. "Well, we're both quitting without notice on Tuesday. Alice will have to drop everything she's doing to come over immediately to save the order."

"How will she even know if you're not there?" Will asks.

"That's the best part of it. The store won't open until our third person shows up, and they don't have a key. Alice will be so fucked."

Will scratches the back of his neck as he always does when he's uncomfortable. "Are you sure that's how you want to end things with Alice? Like I get it, she sucks. But do you know for certain you want that bridge completely burned?"

I set Toph down on the bed where I originally disturbed her. "Babe, even if things don't work out with Grocery Select, I never want to be a sandwich artist again. I'm tired of coming home smelling like a sandwich. That isn't my signature scent."

He wraps his arms around me and gives me a tight hug. "You know I'll always support your decisions." He says into my hair. He takes a step back and looks me in the eyes. Admiration laces his tone as he says, "Nikki, you're fucking savage."

I bounce on my toes because he hasn't heard the best part yet.

"Why are you still so excited?"

I rock back and forth, unable to contain my excitement. "Because! The best part is that I'm going to work closing shifts now. I won't have to wake up at four a.m. anymore. The earliest I'll have to get up is six, and that's only two days a week for my earliest class!"

"You mean I get to see my girlfriend two more hours a day?" He clarifies with a smile.

I bite my bottom lip and nod my head vigorously.

His hands grip my sides in the way I've come to love all the way down to my toes. Will lowers his lips until they're an inch away from mine. His voice comes out gravelly and his eyes have darkened a shade, "I think this calls for a celebration."

I twist back and forth expectantly in his grip. "Yeah?" comes out of my mouth, sounding more like a moan than a word.

Will stands to his full height and takes a step back. "Mac 'n cheese with garlic bread for dinner?"

My jaw drops as Will breaks all forms of contact with my taut body and leaves our bedroom.

I look to Toph, confused. "Were you reading that situation as wrong as I was?" I whisper to her.

She looks up at me and laces her responding meow with judgement.

"Harsh," I tell her as I pet her, turn the light off, and we follow Will to the kitchen.

We eat our fancy dinner on the couch and watch some reruns of The Witcher. In the middle of a lull in the episode, Will randomly says, "You know this is it for me right?"

I sit up from where I am resting my head on his lap to better look at him. "What do you mean by that?"

He pauses right before Jaskier is about to break into another song and takes my hands. "I don't need any time to think it through. I've been thinking it through since our first date when you made a logical decision and dumped me. Moving to Oregon just proved what I already knew even more. I love you. I love our life. We rent an apartment together. We've adopted a pet together. You're officially stuck with me, Veronica Welch."

That phrase, 'I love you,' brings a flash of Turner across my vision. I suppress him from my mind and focus on the gorgeous blond giant in front of me. I nervously draw a breath through open teeth. "This better not be your idea of a proposal William."

He squeezes my hands and laughs. "Nah, I don't have a ring picked out yet."

I take one of my hands and pause him. "Wait, wait... That doesn't even begin to cover my expectations."

"What else do you need?" He asks with a hint of a smirk.

I imagine a filing cabinet in his brain getting ready to catch everything I'm about to tell him. I tick off my requirements on my fingers as I list them. "My nails have to be done so they look good in pics afterward. I have to be wearing a cute outfit. No going on a hike to the top of a mountain and proposing while I'm a sweaty, heavy-breathing mess. And I want someone getting a picture of you proposing as it happens."

"That should be achievable." He replies calmly as if I didn't just provide an extensive list for my perfect proposal. "Any specifics that you want in a ring?"

I twist to stare at him with breakneck speed. "Really? You want to talk wedding rings?" My voice squeaks out an octave higher than typical.

He gives me a lop sided grin. "Yeah, I only plan on proposing once in my lifetime Nikki. I have some ideas, but if there's anything else you need or want you better fill me in on those details."

I beam up at my amazing boyfriend and pull my phone out. "You might want to get yours out, I definitely have ideas about what kind of ring I want. The actual proposal is all yours to figure out though."

Will smiles at me and comes to sit down. "Consider me a sponge. Tell me everything you've dreamed of, babe."

# Seventeen

## Lying to Yourself

As I settle into bed on Monday evening, I pull up the alarm app on my phone. I click off every single setting that would normally wake me for an opening shift. Then I turn my phone to vibrate. Last, I put it on sleep mode, ensuring that the vibrating won't be able to wake me until after seven a.m. The smirk lining my face must rival the Joker. I'm pretty sure I can feel the beginnings of two tiny devil horns sticking up from my scalp as well.

"You look smug." Will comments as I lay down next to him.

I snuggle into his body, separated only by our blankets. "Something tells me I'm going to sleep like a baby tonight."

He leans over and kisses my forehead. "Wish I didn't work tonight so I could enjoy the morning with you."

"Me too, maybe someday soon."

"Deal, get some sleep, Nikki. I'll probably be home before you wake up."

We give each other the passing kiss that we'll exchange for the rest of our lives and Will gets up from the bed to head to work. "I'll never eat a sandwich from that chain again." I declare to our bedroom before sleep pulls me into its familiar embrace of nothingness.

I feel a warmth join me in the bed that isn't usually there. Behind my eyes, I know that light is streaming through the small cracks in the blinds of our bedroom. *We really need to invest in some curtains so we can sleep in.* A strong hand snakes over my waist as a large body molds seamlessly against mine.

"Morning," Will's tired voice kisses into my neck.

I roll over so we're pressed chest to chest and kiss his sternum. "Good night."

He softly chuckles.

I slide out of our bed slowly, letting my body adjust to the crisp morning air. My feet slide across the carpet, knowing their path by heart in the near dark of our bedroom. I grab my phone and head into the bathroom. While I'm going about my typical morning routine, I glance at my phone's illuminated lock screen. It's bright with an incoming call from Alice. I stare at it blankly and let it ring through. When she's hung up I see the slew of notifications, five missed calls, and seven text messages. My fingers drum on the bathroom counter as I watch another text pop up on the screen from her. I unlock it to see what words Alice has chosen to say to me.

> Where are you?

> You didn't show up to opening. James didn't show up either. What is going on. Why did I get a call at 7 saying the store isn't open!!!!

> Veronica. Get to work. NOW!

There's a fifteen-minute pause between her text messages. I leave the bathroom and head to the kitchen to leisurely make myself a nice cup of coffee. *Nowhere to be for hours today.*

> You have 15 minutes to contact me if you still want a job.

> 10 minutes.

> 5.

> I am a wonderful boss. You were lucky to work for me.

My coffee finishes brewing and I take it to my reading chair. I have so many options for how I want to break her down just a little bit. Working for Alice for all these weeks has sucked. I fold into my chair with my phone in one hand and my coffee in the other. Toph announces her presence with a meow and climbs onto the wide arm of my chair for pets. I put my coffee down and indulge her.

"Did you know when they interviewed me at Grocery Select they asked if I'd ever had a boss I didn't like working for? They followed it up with how I dealt with those professional differences."

She purrs at my ministrations.

I take it as a sign to continue my story. "I brought up working for Alice by name. The interviewer asked the location of the shop and paused me on the spot. She said if I'd managed to work under Alice for more than two weeks without quitting I showed remarkable self control. Guess Alice is known around here for being one of the worst employers."

My fingers dip under Toph's chin and she closes her eyes in ecstasy.

"So, it's only fitting if I tell her that right?"

Toph doesn't tell me not to, so I do it.

I pull out my phone. It takes a few tries before I get the wording correct. When I'm certain it will drive my message home as clearly as possible I hit send.

> Thanks for checking that I wasn't in an accident or something before you decided I needed to be threatened with firing. Nice to see what months of hard work and perfect performance has made you think of me. It is with a smile on my face and joy in my heart that I tell you: I quit! Most importantly, if you were actually a wonderful boss you'd be hearing that from your employees, you wouldn't have to lie to yourself about it daily.

Within seconds Alice's contact is popping up on my screen with an incoming call. I send her to voicemail. Toph's soft fur brushes against my legs as she moves to my lap. We stay there for hours. My phone blissfully ignored. My cat in my lap. I crack the spine of *Crescent City* for the first time and am immediately sucked into the world of Bryce Quinlan and Danika Fendyr. The only negative about my morning? My coffee cup isn't magically refilling itself.

Reluctantly I put my book down when my alarm lets me know it's time to head off to campus for my afternoon classes. At least the University was kind enough to have our program's schedule be flexible with both morning and evening shift workers. Mondays and Wednesdays our classes are from eight a.m. to five p.m. I'm not crazy enough to work after a full day like that but I know some people are.

I head into our room and change into clothes for walking around campus. Will is still dozing in bed so I get dressed quietly by the sparse light emanating into our room from the hallway.

Toph follows me into the room and snuggles into Will. It seems that she's happy with anyone who will provide warmth. "Traitor," I whisper at her and she tucks her nose under her tail next to my boyfriend.

I go into the routine of fixing up my hair and doing some light makeup while thinking through my change in employment and how that will impact our lives. With my new job being closing shifts I told them I could work three days a week. They agreed to give me ten-hour shifts on the weekend, so in total I'll be working twenty-eight hours a week. It's definitely less than at the sandwich shop, but I think the joy I have will make up for it. Will and I chatted about the possibility of me bringing home a little less money working fewer hours and he was fine with it. After all, our rent was lower than we had anticipated and his parents had been incredibly generous in helping us furnish our apartment.

I tiptoe back into our room and kiss Will goodbye. "Love you," he mumbles in his sleep.

I freeze in the dark, being momentarily brought back to Turner's manipulations. He used those words to guilt me. He warped a kind phrase into a weapon and used it against me strategically until I'd comply. His love for me was conditional.

My head shakes back and forth vigorously, bringing me back to our bedroom. I pat Will on the shoulder and exit our apartment. I step into the stairwell in my sweats, tennies, and t-shirt to immediately find that there will not be enough layers for today. "I guess Fall is officially here," I say to myself. I duck back inside, grab a sweatshirt that's quickly becoming my favorite, and pull it over my head. "Defy the Stars" is now sprawled across my chest in a whimsical font and it brings me some inner strength purely inspired by Tory and Darcy Vega.

This time when I close our apartment door behind me I also lock it shut and head off into the world of the University of Oregon.

· ♥ · ♥ · ♥ · ♥ · ♥ ·

"Veronica!" Shona calls to me in greeting from our favorite bench seat in the education building. She's accompanied by the two friends she introduced me to last week, Kiara and Jenn.

"Hey everybody," I greet them cheerfully.

Shona scoots to the side and makes room for me on her side of the booth.

Kiara reaches across the table with a flourish. "Okay Veronica, you have to tell us about yourself, meeting you with only five minutes to introduce ourselves was literal torture last class."

I laugh at her dramatic nature but give the table a play-by-play of my relationship with Will and how we've ended up in Oregon.

"Girl," Jenn draws out in her somber tone, "I love how you told him what was up. Either join me or don't because I won't be waiting around for you."

I grin at her. She's almost what I would consider petite, but not quite. Her hair is a sleek medium brown that's been straight and down the two times I've been around her. If I'm not mistaken she's also wearing a different pair of glasses than she was last week at class.

"Enough about me," I tell the table. "What about all of you? How long have you known each other?"

"Oh can I tell this part?" Kiara asks her friends.

Shona laughs, "Sure, not that there's much to tell."

"Don't give it away!" Kiara shoots her a stink eye for letting even that small detail slip. She spreads her hands across the table and takes a deep breath. "Well, it all began about two weeks ago, on our first day of classes. We met, and now we can never be separated. Instantaneous best friendships!"

Jenn flicks her dirty blonde hair over her shoulder. "That's it, Veronica. We happened to sit at the same table together on the first day and bam! Now we're study buddies and the closest of friends. Want to join our gang?"

I gasp in mock shock. "Sounds a little dangerous."

"Oh, it is! For your wallet," Shona giggles. "We're all going out to eat next Saturday night, want to join?" She asks.

My lips turn down, "I wish I could. I work nights on the weekends."

"Then let's do lunch!" Kiara offers cheerfully.

I look at the three of them, in turn, to make sure that Kiara's idea is acceptable to their schedules. When no one speaks out against it I reply. "Sure, if we meet around eleven that would work for me."

Jenn's nails clink against her phone screen. "Done. It's in my calendar. Officially, no changing it now."

We dive into our homework once the getting-to-know-you conversation dies down. I decide to break into another reading assignment. I'm learning rather quickly that I do much better with splitting my home reading and my school reading. At school, I read for academic purposes. At home, I can escape to some far-off fantasy series. I have the feeling the two should remain apart, almost like separation of church and state.

I pull out the next chapter we've been assigned, lean back into the bench seat, and highlight any bits that may be important for papers as I go. Doing homework with these three feels right. Like the start of something that could last beyond college.

# Eighteen

# Haunting Wakefullness

I CAN FEEL HIS round face, sticky with sweat, resting against my neck. He places a kiss there, thinking it will coax me into being a more willing participant. My hands try to push him away but he grabs them with just one of his and pins them above my head.

I try to break away from his hold but he pins me in place.

I try to close my eyes and block away the feeling of his hands grazing down my body. The proof of his enjoyment at my torment pushes into my hip.

I writhe under his grip again but he takes it the wrong way. "Yeah, baby? You know you like that." His damp breath speaks against my neck.

*How can he be misreading my body language this horribly?*

Turner's hand slides under the waistband of my pants.

*Why can't he understand this isn't what I want?*

His fingers find my bare skin beneath my underwear.

*Where has my voice gone?*

"Shhh, baby. The fun is just about to start." He tries to console me before sliding his fingers past the point of no return.

"No!" I shout as I find consciousness. I sit up straight in my bed and fight to calm the instincts that the nightmare has brought forth.

My heart pounds in my chest as my eyes fight to take in my surroundings.

My eyes shoot to the familiar twinkling of light from our bedroom blinds in the early morning.

The sheets under my fingers are the same smooth constant that I crawled between last night.

It smells like the pleasant mingling of two people's scents combining into one.

I haven't been haunted by Turner since Brock. *What the hell brought that on?*

Something isn't right. As I calm my panicking mind, I notice that I am not alone in bed. "What the fuck!" I shout as I scamper off the bed and turn on the overhead light.

A massive form crawls from under the sheets.

I grab the first weapon I can find. A book. Let's hope that Danika's star sword can come off the pages. At least it's a hardback.

I hold it above my head, preparing to attack the intruder as a familiar face is revealed.

Will.

"What the fuck are you doing?" I shout at him, still holding the book prone for self defense.

He uncovers his entire body and I see that he is in our bed naked. He picks up his boxers and steps into them before replying.

"Nikki." His hands are open and visible. He approaches me slowly, the same way one would approach a wounded animal. He starts again, "Nikki. It's me, babe. What's wrong?"

"It's you," I whisper back to him. When the words register, I lower my book and drop it onto my nightstand.

With my weapon discarded, Will moves within arms reach. He reaches to hold my hips but I flinch back from him. "Nikki, what's wrong?" His voice pleads for me to open up to him.

I fold my arms around myself and shake my head. *I can't tell him. He'll never look at me the same if he learns what Turner did.* I avoid the truth and deflect, "Why were you at the foot of our bed?"

He scratches the back of his neck nervously. The familiar motion I usually find adorable helps my mind leave my nightmare.

I focus on Will.

My Will.

My.

Will.

He looks at me, eyes laced with apprehension. "You know how you woke me up from sleep that morning at the hotel months ago? When we almost missed our flight?"

I nod at him, wanting to know more, but still not trusting my own voice.

"I was hoping to return the favor. But I don't think it worked out so well." He takes a step forward and this time I let him touch me. His warm hands rest on my upper arms and slide up and down with a reassuring rhythm. He pleads with me, "Nikki, please. Tell me what happened. What did I do wrong?"

His assumption that he's the reason for my reaction guts me. I feel the tears well up. How could this man, this wonderful, thoughtful, amazing man ever think he's the cause of my nightmares?

He kisses my forehead and pulls me into the sweetest of embraces.

He holds me and runs a soothing hand down my back as my emotions flow freely.

My tears streak down my face like rain down a window pane. My sobs rack through my entire body as I fall apart in his loving embrace.

Will holds me tight and lets me feel all of it.

Only when my crying has subsided and my tears have halted do I pull away from Will. I stare at his chest and see it glisten with the evidence of my weeping. "Sorry," I say motioning to his damp torso without meeting his gaze.

His fist slides up my arm and rests below my chin. He gently grips it with his thumb and forces me to look up at him. "I don't care that your tears are on me, babe. Please don't shut me out. What happened?"

"Okay," I agree to tell him. "But first we'll need coffee and some clothes."

We both put on sweats in companionable silence. Will makes us coffee while I hide in the bathroom and prepare to tell him my darkest secret. When I'm as ready as I'll ever be I open the bathroom door and sit on our couch. I fold my legs under me and give Will my full attention.

He doesn't move a muscle as I tell him the full story of what happened with Turner. How I went to the party. How I trusted him. I fell asleep thinking I would be safe and how helpless I felt when I woke up and Turner was on top of me. Worst of all, I tell Will about how ashamed I am that I let myself get put in that situation.

Will pulls me into his arms when I'm finished and lets me cry out everything that's bubbled to the surface. He gently rocks us back and forth while kissing my hair. All I can do is clutch him as the emotions I've suppressed for years spill from my eyes. My biggest shame. My darkest secret. If Turner had loved me and done that, how can I expect any other form of love to be different? I want to love Will. If I give him that piece of me, he'd have the power to destroy me. After that nightmare of a night, I promised myself no one would ever have that kind of control over me again.

When my sobbing dissipates to a trickle of tears I sit up and look at Will. He asks, "Did you press charges?"

I shake my head. "What would have been the point? He was my boyfriend, the sex wasn't a new thing. We'd done everything before and I was willing."

"You say, 'No,' and that means no." He objects, "Doesn't matter when or why. You want something to stop and it does."

"I know, and you showed that this morning. Tipp didn't even know about this. I didn't want anyone to know. On campus, people would have heard and I would have just been another girl who changed her mind and got blamed for it. They would have asked what I was wearing. Why I was staying over at his house so late?" My foot starts tapping with my discomfort. "Honestly, I don't know that it really was assault. What I know is how I felt afterward and how I feel about it now. Can we just drop it?"

Will takes my hands in his and stares into my soul. "Of course Nikki. Let me take care of you today, okay?"

I dip my chin in agreement.

Will gets up, pushes the footrest closer so I can prop my legs up, and tucks me in with a large fuzzy blanket. "Would you prefer T.V. or phone while I cook us some breakfast?"

A small grin pulls at my cheek. "Neither, can you grab my book? I want to know if Bryce will ever go on a date with Conner. He seems so perfect for her."

"The red one you were ready to kill me with this morning?" He teases me.

"Yeah. You're probably lucky we don't have any real weapons in that room." I call after him as he disappears down the hallway to retrieve my book.

We spend the day like that. I decide a mental health day from my Thursday afternoon classes is warranted and send the group chat that Shona, Jenn, Kiara, and I created, a text asking them to let me know what I missed. Will and I hide from the world watching movies, taking reading breaks, and enjoying each other's company. I find solace in his quiet strength until he has to go to work. Then I'm on my own to keep the demons of my past at bay.

# Nineteen

# *Heavy Breathing*

LATER THAT WEEK WILL and I capitalize on an alignment in our schedules and decide to take a 'fun' hike. Well, that's how he presented it, currently, it doesn't feel too fun to me.

"How was your first weekend at the grocery store?" Will asks without any strain in his voice. I take a deep breath and try to hide how ravaged my lungs feel. "Pretty good, haven't connected with other employees the way Princess Buttercup and I hit it off, but it's only been three shifts so far."

He holds a branch back from the path and lets me pass him. "Makes sense, it's always hard to make friends when you're the new kid."

"Thanks," I say as I pass by his courteous gesture. "There's one person I think I might connect well with. She's our age, but seems a bit like a terrifying badass."

"What's wrong with that? Sounds a bit like Tipp, and you two were thick as thieves."

I hide the twinge of pain I feel at the mention of her name. That abandonment is still fresh, and I can't quite believe she threw our friendship away like that. "Yeah well, hopefully, a badass blonde makes a better friend than a badass brunette did."

"What's her name?" He asks, giving me a flirtatious smack on the ass as he passes me and takes the lead on the trail again.

I smack his butt back in retaliation. To my delight, he yips in surprise. "Something like Harvey? Harriet? Definitely not Helga. Something with an H, I'll have to pay better attention this weekend."

We continue hiking on without conversation. I listen to the rustling of the trees in the light breeze and the birds chirping in the crisp fall air. Will said this hiking path was recommended to him by a fellow security guard the other night. We made plans to try and fit in dates between our work schedules and my classes, which has resulted in this ridiculous eight a.m. hike. Will hasn't even gone to bed yet and his pace is smoking mine.

He veers off to the right of the path and follows a smaller trail that twists around some bushes and trees. When it ends, we're standing at a bench in a secluded section of the forest. I know the main path is only a matter of feet away, but the nature encapsulating everywhere my eyes wander provides the illusion of privacy.

Will sits down on the bench and looks up at me.

I close the distance between us, wrap my arms around his shoulders, and lean down for a kiss.

Will's tongue strokes in that familiar way he asks for entrance and I grant it.

Our kiss deepens.

Will grips the back of my neck and guides my head exactly how he wants me. His strong hands hold me in place. One on my cheek, one at my neck. My mind isn't there though.

My chest starts heaving and my breaths come faster.

Will mistakes this as a cue to pull me onto his lap. He grips my neck a little tighter as I spread my legs, one on either side of him, and sit on him. I must create friction for him as I lower myself because he groans into my mouth.

That snaps my ability to control the terror haunting me. I abruptly break our kiss. "Stop."

Will's hands freeze.

He lets go of me with a jolt like he's been shocked. His gaze travels from where his hand hovers inches away from my cheek and looks me in the eyes. He must understand the pits of despair that I feel because his face softens. The confusion of his knitted brow melts to understanding. His shoulders sag downward. He takes my hand in his and guides my body to sit on the bench next to him.

His voice comes out soft and concerned, "I misread that Nikki, I'm sorry."

I shake my head. "You shouldn't be apologizing. You were trying to make out with your girlfriend and here I am falling to pieces over shit that happened years ago. Why is Turner coming back to haunt me like this all a sudden?" I wipe tears aggressively from my cheeks angry that they deigned to fall in the first place.

His fingers tighten around mine before he asks. "Can I give you a hug?"

I nod, not trusting my words at the moment.

Will twists his leg over the bench so he's straddling it and pulls me to his chest. I lean into him and listen to the forest around us. His bergamot and citrus mingles well with the natural scents around us. His strength, his smell, and his presence slowly soothes my panicked mind and brings me back to reality.

*Turner is an issue of my past.*

*Will is the hero of my present.*

I repeat those two sentences until they sink in.

*Will is the hero of my present.*

When my breathing has slowed, my eyes have dried, and my mind has cleared, I sit up. I turn to face him and tuck my legs to crisscross applesauce.

Will takes my hands in his warm, calloused ones and waits for me to speak first.

I stare at our hands rather than his face, knowing that the love I see in his eyes will reduce me to a pile of tears all over again. "I'm sorry I'm broken like this," I whisper to him.

His fist and thumb work together to gently coax my shattered soul into looking at him. "Nikki, you're not broken." I can't stand the way he's looking at me right now, so full of concern. "I love you as you are. Can I ask, is there anything that I do to trigger this?"

My eyes fly wide in shock, "No, never!"

His thumb strokes along my cheek placating me. "Not like that babe. Is there any way that I touch you where your mind might associate the movement with Turner?" His eyes flash with a momentary rage at the mention of my past.

I don't like the idea of this wonderful man before me somehow triggering memories of that night, but I close my eyes and think back to what we were doing. I focus on what I was physically feeling before my mind dragged me away.

Our kiss.

His hand at my neck.

My hands resting on his shoulders.

Sitting on his lap.

Those are all things we've done in the past that were fine, and they don't scare me as I think of them now.

My eyes open and I see him staring patiently. "I can't think of anything."

"Can I try to help you, with my touch?" He offers.

"Okay?"

He clears his throat. "Alright, let's do this again. Slowly, methodically, without any sexual intent."

I stand before him and we reenact the scene.

I wrap my arms around his shoulders.

"Is this okay?" He asks and he places a hand at the back of my neck.

"Yes."

Our foreheads meet, our lips less than an inch away from kissing.

Will uses his free hand to help me straddle him.

"Is this okay?" He questions again before proceeding.

My breathing is picking up in pace, but I think it's due to his desire to help me work through this and not because of how we're touching. "I think so," I admit with a little uncertainty.

I close my eyes and feel his hand travel the curves of my body. He's done it countless times before and once again the only thing I feel is passion and desire for the man beneath me. Nothing close to the paralyzing terror that night elicits.

With one hand at the back of my neck and one hand wrapped around my cheek and jawbone Will pulls me closer to him.

The pressure on my head has me freezing up.

My body goes rigid, locked in place on top of him.

"No."

Will's hands immediately disconnect from my skin. He rests them on my thighs while I regain myself.

I count my breaths in and out until both inhale and exhale exceed a six and then I look at him.

"That was it." He confirms, his voice solemn.

My throat is dry. I swallow my nonexistent saliva and croak, "Yeah."

His hands rub my legs reassuringly. My hands lace behind his neck. Will lets me stay perched on his lap finding solace in his presence.

*He wouldn't do that to me. He's better than Turner. Will's love isn't manipulative like Turner's.*

"Seems like one hand on your head is fine, but when two get involved, your subconscious takes you back there."

I draw my lips between my teeth and dip my chin once in confirmation of his hypothesis.

"Okay. One hand above your neck only. Easy enough." He smiles tentatively at me. "Nikki, we can work through this. Now that I know one thing that triggers your memories I can prevent it from happening."

Where I'd just felt a barren desert there's now a lump. I swallow and take a shaky inhale. "Why are you so cool with all this?" I tilt my head back and look blankly into the canopy of tree cover.

One of his hands, only one, moves back to my face. He softly pulls my gaze back to his and says, "Because Nikki, I love you. I'm here for you. I'll always be here for you, no matter what."

Another tear runs down my cheek at his words. The way Turner manipulated me with those words in the past tries to seep in, but I push it aside. Will's love for me is pure.

Will means it, that promise he made to me all those months ago at Balboa Park. I can't tell him here. I can't tell him like this, after having just relived my assault, again. Instead of validating his commitment to our future I lean down and kiss him gently. He doesn't move to deepen it. He leaves me completely in control.

I sit back up, finally noticing the tingling starting in my knees. "I think we've got another problem." I laugh at the change in conversation.

"What's that?"

I move to stand up on shaking legs. My right leg remembers how to work, even though I can't feel any of its muscles engaging. When my left leg dismounts from Will, my body tries to crumble to the forest floor. He catches me, my ever present knight in a beige Camry, and helps me sit down on the bench. "Both of my legs have fallen asleep." I grit out through clenched teeth.

The tingles running up and down half of my body are next to unbearable. Yet there's nothing I can do to subdue them.

"We just need to wait it out," Will says. He looks like he's trying not to laugh at me with that stupid smirk at the corner of his lips.

"You wouldn't be so smug if you'd been the one mounting me." I bite at his undeniably entertained face.

He tilts an eyebrow and an idea flits into his mind. "I think we have two options, babe."

My legs are no longer tingling, they feel like they're being stabbed repeatedly with needles now. My teeth clench as I whine, "What would those be?"

Nonchalantly he suggests, "Either you can sit there and suffer, or we could try our hand at exhibitionism."

My jaw drops, all the way to the ground. "Will!" I shout before continuing at a quieter level, "You never know who will come around that corner."

He shrugs. "We've been back here for what, fifteen minutes now? No one's come yet. Let's give it a shot babe." He gives me a wink. "I'll even straddle you if you think we could work out the angles."

I swat his arm. "Absolutely not! I get caught doing something like that once, then I get arrested, and there goes any chance of being a teacher. If a kid came around that corner we could be charged as sexual predators. Are you insane!"

He stands up and leans over me. An inch away from my face he dips in and gives me a peck. "Nah, I didn't mean it. But it got your mind to think about something other than the pain in your legs right?"

I snap my mouth shut and purse my lips. He did distract me from the worst parts of the pain. "But, you don't want to fuck me in the woods?" I ask, somehow feeling disappointed.

Will rolls his eyes and draws back to his full height. He places a hand out to help me up and I take it. When I'm close enough he brings his lips to my ear and rumbles, "I'll fuck you anywhere, anytime Nikki. As long as the when and where don't jeopardize either of our futures."

My skin crawls with goosebumps at the promise in his voice.

He leaves me standing there processing his words as he takes off back toward the main trail. "Come on," he calls, "This hike won't be finishing itself."

Half an hour of pure vertical climbing later, I can barely catch my breath. Will is ahead of me on the trail looking like a natural mountain man, all he's missing is a plaid shirt and an axe. I stop on the side of the trail, for the millionth time and try to catch my breath. I brace my hands on my knees and focus on slowing my breaths. My elementary school P.E. teacher's voice runs through my mind, *in through the nose, out through the mouth.*

I feel Will's hand rub between my shoulder blades. "You okay babe?"

I nod my head as a pathetic wheezing sound leaves my lips.

"I mean we could head back to the car if you need, but I think I can see a break in the tree line up ahead."

I stand and put my hands on my hips. "Nope." My words come out labored. "We are finishing this hike. Even if it kills me." Then I stick a finger in his face, "However, the next time a work buddy tells you which path is harder, or longer, or more intense. We're going to do the exact opposite of that."

He bites toward my finger, missing it by less than an inch. "Deal," he agrees with a soft chuckle. "We can start up again when you're ready."

I look up at him under a sweat covered brow. He's standing there all calm, cool, and collected. It's unfair how good he looks working out. I wipe my forehead with an equally gross forearm and ask, "Can I lead so you don't leave me in your dust?"

"Sure thing babe." He leans down and presses a kiss to my sweaty temple. The gesture is equal parts adorable and disgusting when I see him pull away with lips glistening with my perspiration.

When I've regained oxygen entering my lungs at an acceptable pace we set off again. We're slower than before with me in the lead, but I also don't tire out as quickly. I shed my lightweight zip-up ages ago and retighten it around my waist as my boots crunch dried leaves that have flitted down to the path from the canopy above. If I wasn't so focused on my basic human needs such as breathing I might have better noticed the beautiful fall foliage we were immersed in.

We round another bend in the trail and I see it. Clear, open, skies just ahead of us. My throat is too dry to say anything so instead I pump my fist in victory.

Will lovingly swats my ass cheeks in encouragement as we crest the butte.

Having spent so long in the shaded forest below, I'm forced to blink at the startling brightness of actual sunlight. My vision slowly clears from the blinding light and I'm able to take in the view. The top of the butte is rather ugly. Covered with a smattering of boulders and dirt, it's not much to see.

My nose wrinkles up in disappointment. "We hiked all that way for this?" I ask Will despondently.

He doesn't answer me, instead, he takes my hand and pulls me around a pile of boulders. I stare at his shoulder, wondering what he's up to but let him have this moment. "What are you?" I ask as he fully rounds the boulders and the view is revealed.

Will pulls me in front of his body. He steps closer and brackets my feet between his. His hands caress around my stomach and pull my back flush with his torso. I lean against him and take in the sight before us.

Unlike the hikes we've been on in Southern California, this view is completely green. The city of Eugene is sprawled out below us but it's not the same as a city from back home. Here the buildings are vastly outnumbered by trees. It's not a concrete jungle like I'm used to. Beyond the city are mountains speckled with more trees. They're luscious and alive, not the dead shrubs I've grown used to seeing in San Diego.

I take in the beautiful oranges, reds, and yellows of the fall adorning the trees below us. Some of them will remain green like their names, Evergreen. The smattering of color reminds me of speckled paint on a canvas. I've heard Vermont is the best state to see fall foliage, but looking out over the Willamette Valley makes me think Oregon is a close second. In the sea of color, I see a green backdrop with a yellow "O" on it. Immediately I know it's Autzen Stadium. A smirk pulls to my face as I think about how my time at the university will lay the foundation for the rest of my life. Our lives.

My eyes scan the view while my body is wrapped up in Will's safe embrace. We stand there taking everything in for a few minutes. Our breaths even out, our bodies relax from the grueling hike to get up here, and we fit perfectly like this.

The words are on the tip of my tongue. I can feel my body committing to them, for him. "I—"

"We gotta fit hikes like this in while we can." Will's voice cuts me off.

His words bring confusion to my mind. "What?"

"Yeah, this hike and view are awesome. Gotta fit as many in as we can." He squeezes me and kisses my cheek.

I twist out from his hold to look directly at him. He maintains contact with me by shifting his hands to my sides. I rest my arms on his and grip his forearms before asking, "What do you mean while we can? We have our whole lives ahead of us."

He gives me a soft grin. "Of course, we have our whole lives for hikes together. But we only have a couple years for you to get your teaching degree and we move back home."

My brows draw together and my head slowly shakes back and forth. "No, Will. I'm never moving back to California."

His touch drops away and leaves me isolated. Suddenly the soft breeze dancing along the butte is harsh and cold. I wrap my arms around myself to try and ease the loneliness created by Will withdrawing from me.

He runs an agitated hand through his glistening golden locks. "What do you mean you're never moving back? We're only here long enough for you to get your degree."

"No. It wouldn't make sense for me to get certified in a state different than where I want to teach. I'd literally have to redo all of my licensing tests. That would be such a waste of time and money." I've thought it out plenty of times. Oregon is my home now. Up until now, I thought it was *our* home too.

Will's lips thin into a straight line.

The love I was feeling moments before crumbles to ashes and falls out of my heart. My voice comes out sounding meek, "I thought you knew that."

"I didn't agree to that, Nikki. Two years. You told me your degree would be done in two years. That's what I agreed to." He crosses his arms and paces away from me. After a few strides, he turns and comes toward me again. "I thought this was temporary." He pauses in front of me. His eyes scan my face before he takes a deep breath.

My posture has left my shoulders. I'm curled in upon myself, using my arms to provide a semblance of reassurance.

I thought he was my forever.

I thought he was my last, first kiss.

We'd discussed wedding rings.

With one damn statement that's all gone.

Will's thumb brushes away the silent tear I didn't know I'd shed. He tilts my head to meet his gaze and kisses my forehead. "I'm not saying no. I'm also not saying yes. I need some time to adjust what I thought our lives were going to look like together okay?"

I nod my head. His request is reasonable. So why does it feel like this is the beginning of our end?

# Twenty
## Strawberry Lemonade and Burgers

Life hasn't felt right since Will and I got into that fight.

My body is driving down the street headed to burgers with my friends from class. My soul, it's stuck in limbo. Will and I have only talked in passing for the last week.

"How's class?"

"Good. How's work?"

"Good."

Such a riveting conversation for two people who were discussing wedding rings a few weeks ago.

My hands turn the steering wheel of my Beetle and maneuver it into a parking spot. My brain chooses a space in the shade while my consciousness is preoccupied with feeling sorry for myself. I look down to find that my car is already in park and huff out an exhale. I tilt my head back and muster a fake happy face. These friendships are new. I can't go to the deep and heavy before we've even gotten to know each other well enough to determine similar interests.

My fingers pick at lint pilling up on the sleeves of my sweater of their own volition.

Shona noticed something was off with me during classes a few days ago, but she didn't pressure me into sharing any details. She just gave me a sympathetic grin and patted my arm, letting me know she was there if I needed it. I'm just not ready to trust them yet. Who knows, they could get a boyfriend and suddenly lose any desire to be my friend whatsoever.

I twist my neck from side to side, hoping to let out some tension. It does nothing.

I roll my shoulders back, trying again. Nothing.

"Guess this is my current state," I inform the car dejectedly.

A tap, tap, tap, comes from my back window. I look in the rearview mirror and see Shona standing there smiling.

I pull my keys from the ignition, grab my stuff, and climb out of the low sitting car.

"Hey!" she calls to me.

My purse rests heavy on my shoulder and I round the car before replying. "Hi," I say, quieter than typical.

"I'm glad I recognized your car, I wanted to check in with you before we met up with the others."

"Oh?"

She pushes a lock of bright red curls behind her ear. It does nothing to contain their volume. They pop back out almost immediately after they're free of her finger's grasp. "Yeah, you've just seemed kinda down this week. I wanted to make sure you're okay, and ask if you need anything."

My lips pull into a resigned grin. Her kindness has me wanting to share, at least a small detail. "Yeah, no. Will and I just got into a huge misunderstanding. But I don't want to overwhelm you with my drama."

She bats down my reasoning with a smile and sweet response. "No overwhelming, we're friends. Friends help one another through things, even relationship struggles."

I laugh lightly at her. I open up a bit further as I nervously adjust the strap of my purse on my shoulder. "I guess he thought we were moving back to Southern California when I finished at UO, but I never plan on moving back home. So basically he's having to decide what he wants to do with the rest of his life and if I'll even be a part of it. Nothing big." I shake my head in dismay, "Nothing important, at, all."

"Oh shit," Shona whispers in response. Then she flips on a dime with a dimpled smile stretching across her face, "Well, I did hear one wonderful piece of information in all of that!"

I roll my eyes at her. "How was any of what I just said positive?"

She turns and starts walking to the restaurant entrance before replying. "Well, if you never plan on leaving, I guess I just gained a lifelong friend." She elbows me gently, "That's pretty awesome, if you ask me."

With that kind remark, we turn and head across the parking lot to the restaurant. As we enter the heavy double glass doors of the burger joint I feel part of my soul reattaching to my body. I want it to be Will and me up here, beginning our forever. If he doesn't decide that's what he wants for his life, at least I've found some pretty awesome friends.

Shona takes point with our group and follows directly behind the hostess as I trail behind, lost in my thoughts. We go up a ramp, curve around a wall, and the space opens up into the bar area. In the center of the room Kiara and Jenn are already waiting for us.

"My friends!" Kiara calls louder than necessary. Heads in the section pivot with curiosity at her outburst as we walk over and take the two remaining seats at the counter height table.

The bar lends itself to a light hearted nature. All interior walls are adorned with art so various it can only be described as eclectic. To our side, the exterior far wall is lined with windows. Lingering fall sunshine streams through them not willing to fade away for winter storms just yet. The bartender is lively and makes a show of the drinks that he's making. Most importantly, my friends are here and we're getting to know one another beyond school. We settle in and order our meals quickly.

"Only four weeks of classes left before finals." Jenn reminds us.

"Boo," Kiara comments. "No talk about classes when we're having fun."

We laugh at her blatant dislike of shop talk.

Shona offers an adjacent conversation, "That also means only four weeks until we get to have a break for a month."

"Now that's what I'm talking about!" Kiara exclaims loudly enough for the whole restaurant to hear. I'm beginning to wonder if she's why we're in the bar area and not the restaurant. "Justin and I will be going up to Washington with the kids to see his family. It's so nice that he's been stationed on the West Coast so that we can see everyone. It's been years since we've been this close to home." She flips her hair over her shoulder and takes a sip of her strawberry lemonade.

"There's so much to unpack there I don't even know where to start." I chuckle. "How about with all of it? Husband? Kids? Family? Stationed? More details please."

Kiara too happily jumps into a summary of her life story. Her face lights up even brighter than normal when she speaks about her family. "We met in undergrad and it was insta-love. We were married within seven months, and he shipped out three weeks later. The first time he was on leave I found out I was pregnant with our oldest, Izzy. We lived with his parents in Washington for a few years so they could help me with her." She hasn't even come up for breath yet. Her eyes twinkle with every detail she reveals about their life. "Then about two years later he got stationed stateside so Iz and I moved into military housing with him. That's when little Sarah happened." She pauses her story with a wistful grin. Whether that grin is about her daughter, or the antics involved in her coming into existence is unclear. Before I can determine which, she dives back in. "For the last ten years, we've been lucky, ending up mostly on the West Coast. We're here for at least three years so we decided it's a perfect time for me to go back to school and get my teaching degree. So he goes to work, I go to school, and the girls go to school."

"What branch is your husband?" Jenn asks.

"Oh, that's the best part. What's the sexiest branch of the military?" She asks us with a hair flip over her shoulder and a leading smirk.

Shona guesses first, "Marines?"

Kiara bites her lip and nods her head. "And what's the hottest position one can have in the Marines?"

I try this time, "Uhhh, one where he wears a uniform?"

They all laugh at me but I'm not sure why it's so funny. I smile and wait for someone else to speak and draw the attention away from my accidental humor.

Kiara splays her fingers across the table and slides them forward like she's pushing a secret document toward us. "He's an M.P."

"You married a literal Marine M.P.? Like the cops of the Marines?" Jenn asks sounding a little impressed.

"That's like the badass of the badass," I comment, impressed.

"That's not all," Kiara is practically giddy with the attention from all of us. "He's an incredible lay."

We all burst into laughter at her blatant appreciation for her husband's talents.

When we've quieted down the bartender comes around his counter to our table. "Another round ladies?" He asks.

A chorus of agreement chimes from all of our lips.

"You got it, four more strawberry lemonades coming your way." He turns with a wink over his shoulder at Jenn.

"Girl, you've got an admirer," I tease her.

Her cheeks go crimson and she ducks her head in embarrassment. "Don't say that, he was just flirting with all of us. Probably wants a bigger tip," she objects.

"You are considered one of us. Go for it." Shona encourages.

Jenn shakes her head. "Things are a little rocky with Jordan right now. I'm not going to complicate that by flirting with a bartender."

"Shit my bad. Didn't realize you already had a person." I apologize to her.

"No worries, Jordan and I are, well it's complicated. Her family is really upset that she's dating a woman... Can we chat about something else?" Jenn ducks her head again and I shift in my seat uncomfortably.

I grimace at Shona and Kiara showing that I know I fucked up, but also not knowing what to say now.

Shona saves the meal with a graceful topic change, "So what does everyone have planned for our month long December break?"

Our meals arrive as we discuss our holiday plans. I dig into my grilled chicken wrap as I listen to the others. My heart is feeling lighter than it has since Will and I got in that fight. This also might be the first time I've tasted the food I'm eating since that day as well. Everything else since then has been eating out of a human's need to survive, not enjoyment of the meal.

I rip off another piece of my wrap as Jenn updates us about her plans. "I think to keep things civil between our families, and because our relationship is so new, Jordan and I will be celebrating separately this year."

"Makes sense," Kiara says with a reassuring half-smile. "For what it's worth, I hope that her family gets their heads out of their asses. Do you plan on doing anything special with just the two of you?"

This brings a glint to Jenn's eyes. "Actually, yeah." She takes a sip of her strawberry lemonade before continuing. "I was hoping to take her to Portland for a night. It's so magical if you know the right places to go. I just want us to be able to be us without the worry of running into her family in town." Jenn looks down and bites at her lip before continuing. "It's our first holiday season together. I want it to be as incredible for her as she makes me feel every second we're together."

Our whole table goes uncharacteristically quiet.

"If you tell her exactly that there's no way you won't achieve your goal," I tell Jenn.

She looks at me with gigantic hopeful eyes. "You really think so?"

"I mean I don't know Jordan, but if I heard those words from Will I'd simp real freaking hard. Like, what was that ridiculous position you were trying to convince me to try the other day because I'd be swooning hard enough to give it a go."

The whole table erupts into laughter and I see nods of agreement from Kiara and Shona.

"Well, Jenn has all these elegant plans of sweeping her lady off her feet, my holiday will be a bit more basic." Shona pivots our attention to her.

"Which would be?" Kiara asks.

I bite into some of my crunchy sweet potato fries as I listen to Shona.

"Caleb and I are kinda local. My parents are like a ten minute drive from our apartment. His parents are only a three hour drive away. So travel-wise it's not too much effort. But my family celebrates Christmas and his family celebrates Chanukah and Christmas. So really it's a whole month of celebrating multiple cultures and combining both of our seasonal traditions. It was complicated at first, but we've figured out how to make it work so that all parts of our spirituality are honored."

"That's cool," I start. "Would you ever be willing to educate us, or at least me, about that? I haven't had a friend who celebrates Chanukah before and I'd love to know more about it if you're ever willing."

Shona's face breaks into a wide grin showing off both of her dimples. "I'd love to. I'll have to have all of you over then, I feel like it's best explained with some visuals to accompany the explanation of traditions and whatnot." She pauses and takes a sip of her drink, "That would be really lovely someday."

My heart warms up a little bit more at seeing the joy my question has brought to Shona's face. With her openness, I decide to offer some of my history to the group. "I wasn't raised religious. My parents would say that we were raised with Christian values, but really that means we were taught not to be dicks to others. Admittedly, I'm incredibly ignorant about all religions. So, I'd absolutely love the chance to learn about yours."

"So the vibe that I'm getting here is that our hangouts need to transition from this restaurant to one another's houses so we can learn even more about each other?" Kiara chimes in.

"That would be fun!" Jenn agrees.

"On one condition," I object. "I get to host the first one."

Kiara narrows her eyes at me. "Only because you called dibs first Nikki. Now spill, what are your plans for break?"

I put down the sweet potato fry I was about to consume and take a deep breath. "Well, Will and I were planning on going home for a week or so. I'm not so sure that will be happening anymore." I finish quietly.

"What's up?" Jenn asks me so sweetly it has the wall that Tipp built around my heart cracking.

I want to be close to these women, I really do. The first step will be trusting them and then I'll find out if they'll betray me or not I guess. I take a sip of my lemonade before deep diving into my relationship drama. I tell them about the hike, our misunderstanding, and the space that Will is needing right now. All of it. "He's still making food for me because I can't cook. But that's it. Our conversations are stilted and formal. I know I need to give him space and let him figure it out. The waiting is slowly killing me, though. I wish I could just fast-forward to when he's made up his mind and hit play from there. So that's why I'm not really sure what our break will look like anymore. I'm not even sure if I'll have a boyfriend at the end of it." I mess with the napkin placed in my lap, uncertain if I've shared too much.

The girls sit quietly and take in everything I said. Shona puts me at ease first. "I think you're doing the right thing, Veronica. Give him the space, I'd bet with how you have talked about him in the past that he's going to choose you."

"I agree," Kiara chimes in. "You don't want to pressure him into a decision, no matter how hard it is to wait patiently. You want to know that he's choosing this life with you because he wants it, not because you coerced him into it."

Jenn puts in her two cents last. "I don't have anything as eloquent to add as these two," she jerks her thumb at the other half of our group. "I will say if you need to hang out to take your mind off of it let me know."

I wasn't expecting support from all of them, I honestly wasn't expecting it from anyone other than Shona. I sniffle back a tear before it has time to fall from my eyes and look at my new friends. "Thanks, guys, I'll let you know what he says whenever that conversation happens. How about we talk about less heavy topics now." I shift my gaze pointedly to Kiara, "We all know you've got some elaborate plan for the break. Let's hear it."

Kiara flips her hair over her shoulder, yet again. While she answers my question, I get lost in thought. She must have her stylist cut her hair perfectly for it to fall back in front of her shoulder every so often to allow her yet another flick. It seemed a little overdone at first, but now I notice, it's just part of who Kiara is.

Our meal wraps up quickly after Kiara divulges her state hopping, five different house visits in four days plan to us. Just listening to her talk about corraling the girls and her husband from family to family has me feeling exhausted. The smile that hasn't left her face the entire time she's been telling us of her plans says she feels the exact opposite. I get the feeling that she's going to be making the three years they're stationed in Eugene count.

"Okay so meet up again in January?" Shona asks once we've paid our tab and are walking back to our cars.

"Sure." I say, "How about the Sunday before classes begin again?"

"Oh yes." Kiara draws out the last syllable to make her response match her dramatic personality.

Jenn chimes in, "Works for me."

"Deal," Shona confirms.

"Alright then, I'll let you know what time closer to the day of," I say.

We wave goodbye to one another and part ways. We've all got different plans for our breaks and it will be interesting to see how theirs go, and whether I'm even in a relationship when the new year comes about. My body goes through the motions of driving home without my brain providing guidance. Halfway there, I realize I don't feel as dark and twisted as I did when I met the girls for lunch. I swear somewhere deep down there's even a small spark of hope trying to catch fire. I rock out to LoSpirit and Taylor Acorn as I remind myself Will didn't say no, he just asked for time. I can give him that, and hopefully, in return, he'll give me forever.

Twenty-One

# Selective Amnesia

A FEW DAYS LATER, when I pull into our complex after running errands I see Will's car, which isn't right. He's supposed to be working tonight. I park my car in the spot reserved for us under cover. A smile pulls at my cheek as I remember when Will offered the spot to me.

"You love wearing fancy heels and your hair is always done. You should get the covered parking spot so you don't have to rush in or out of your car." He said without me even having to bring the subject up a few weeks ago.

I steady myself for what is awaiting me upstairs. There are three logical options. One, he's packing and getting ready to move back to California as soon as he can. It's definitely the most likely of all his options. Two, he's sick and had to stay home for the night. I don't know if I've ever seen him sick before, so that's not very probable. Or three, the least likely of all, he's planning on staying in Oregon with me and wants to have a conversation about it.

I get out of the car and roll my shoulders back, preparing to be dumped. I'll have to find a roommate to afford rent and keep my same work schedule. I'll need to learn how to cook too, but it can all be done.

My feet lead me up the stairs and I pause in front of our door. Is this about to become my door, no longer ours?

I twist the key in the lock and cross the threshold nervously. I snick the door shut quietly, toe off my shoes, and put my things down next to the door. Then I turn, so slow it feels comical, and survey the apartment. There are no packing boxes or suitcases strewn about. He must be starting his departure by packing his belongings from our bedroom then.

Toph lifts her head from her paws on the cat tree near the wall of windows and greets me with a soft meow. I walk over and give her a reassuring pet. I'm not sure if the gesture is meant to soothe her or me. Too soon, I know I need to find Will and figure out what he's doing and why he's even home tonight.

I pad to the hallway and see our bedroom light on. I try to take a deep breath but it gets caught in my lungs. It feels like a car is sitting on my chest and I don't know how to get relief from the crushing worry that's beginning to overwhelm me.

The door to our bedroom is slightly ajar and I see Will packing his clothes into a suitcase.

That's it then, he's calling it quits on us.

Tears well up in my eyes and streak down my cheeks.

I stand there and watch him packing as he listens to an audiobook. He's so calm, like this change isn't breaking him at all. Will folds his shirt up neatly and lays it down next to his luggage. He must have been at this for a while because he's surrounded by neatly folded clothing.

Toph silently approaches me from the living room and announces her arrival to Will with a cheerful meow. He looks up from his packing and smiles at her. Then his face shifts when he lays eyes on me. His previously neutral face hardens with worry as he looks me over. Will rounds the foot of our bed, I guess just his bed now, and he stands directly in front of me. Will moves to take me in his arms like he's done a hundred times before, but he stops himself before he makes contact. "Nikki, what's wrong? What happened?"

I sniffle and shake my head before I can find my voice. "What do you mean what happened? You're packing." I gesture to the bed that's currently littered with his clothing. Toph has settled in and made herself a nest of his freshly folded belongings. It's like she knows she needs to make the most of his presence because it won't be here much longer. I turn and walk back to our living room with my head buried in my hands. I never should have let him in. I should have known, I'm not the kind of person that people stick around for. Especially not the kind of person a guy would move away from his family for. I slide onto my cozy reading chair and fold my knees into my chest. Hugging myself will be the only comfort I can find for a while, guess I better get used to it now.

Will follows on my heel and kneels before me. His hands still don't touch me, instead, they rest on the arms of my chair.

Gods how I wish I could feel his warmth on my skin just one last time. If I'd known that alcove in the forest would have been the last time we were close, I probably would have been an exhibitionist for him. My chest shakes as I try for another deep inhale only to be disappointed as my grief consumes me. He hasn't even said the words yet, I'm going to be cut into a million pieces when he says it aloud.

"Nikki, of course, I'm packing—"

"Really?" I shout at him, "Of course? Guess I should have known it would be so easy for you to choose to leave me. Go on then, go finish. I won't get in your way." I point for him to leave me alone but he doesn't budge.

Will sits back on his ankles and his hands fall to his knees. He closes his eyes and inhales deeply.

I watch his every movement, knowing this will be one of the last times I get to see him.

He opens his eyes and levels me with a look that reminds me of a parent scolding their child. "Veronica, will you let me get a sentence out before yelling at me again please?" His voice is even and steady, yet demands I obey his request.

I nod my head and prepare to be ripped to pieces with his next statement.

"Yes." He says one word.

I stare at him blankly, waiting to hear the rest. Yes, he's leaving me. Yes, he's packing up his belongings. Yes, I can keep the double bed so I at least have somewhere to sleep that isn't on the ground. My confusion must shine through because after a few heartbeats, he elaborates.

"Yes, I choose to move and stay, in Oregon. Yes."

I search his eyes, trying to find the trick. My knees are no longer a barrier between us as I pivot and sit crisscross apple sauce. I look away from Will and notice a string sticking out from the cuff of my socks. My hands drop to my lap and I fidget with it as my brain catches up to what he just declared. An uncertain sniffle breaks the silence between us. When I look back at my boyfriend it's through waterlogged lenses and with a huge smile spread across my lips. "You mean it? You choose me, and Oregon with me?" I hopefully ask him.

His hands touch me for the first time in days. They slide up my arms and wipe away the tears streaking down my cheeks lovingly. "Of course I choose you. I just needed time to readjust to knowing that meant I was also choosing Oregon. I have a few conditions though."

I swallow back the lump in my throat and nod for him to continue.

"First can we move to the couch babe? I haven't touched you in so long." He stands and offers me an assisting hand. Will sits down first in the middle of the couch and crosses his legs at the ankle on the footrest. "Come here." He pats the cushion next to him and I oblige. I drape my legs over his lap and we sit as connected as possible while still being able to have a conversation.

"So what are your conditions?" I encourage him to begin.

He twists his neck from side to side and I hear it pop multiple times before he starts. His eyes find mine and his face softens with love that I feel in my soul. His hands rub up and down my sweatpants as if reminding himself that I'm actually here. His voice is calm and steady, a sound that I might be lucky enough to hear for the rest of my life. "I don't like the idea of never moving back to California. So there are two big things that I'd like you to agree to before I can solidly say I'm in it one hundred percent. First, I want us to visit home at a minimum of once every two years, assuming we can afford it."

My eyebrows draw together in confusion. "I assumed we'd be going home closer to every year since both of our families are down there. Done."

He squeezes my ankles before he divulges his second term. "This one might be harder for you to swallow then. I don't want the possibility of moving back to San Diego to be completely gone. But I'm also aware that there's no way we'd be able to afford a life this nice back home so we need to figure out some stipulations."

"Like what?"

"How much do you think we'd need to take home annually to afford the life we'd want in San Diego?"

That question catches me a little off guard. "I honestly don't know. We'd want to buy a house, at least a three bedroom and two bathroom so there's enough room for dogs, and anyone else that might come along. We'll both need cars, and I don't want to be house-poor. I want to live in a decent neighborhood but also be able to go out once a week for bowling, dinner, or whatever else we want to do for fun. That's just off the top of my head."

Will nods along with what I've said. "Naturally I've had a little longer to think about this than you have. I also guessed we'd need to be able to afford pets, you'll want to still be able to buy nice clothes. An average middle class income. Maybe even a fun vacation every other year?"

The thought of traveling with him again excites me. I wiggle with joy a little in his lap. "I like the picture of our future you're painting. So how much is this going to cost?"

"During some night shifts, I did a bit of research and crunched some numbers. Compared to what my sister and Thomas bring home, my parents, and your parents, I think we'd need a minimum of one hundred and fifty thousand take home a year."

I let out a low whistle. "Hate to break it to you Will, be we definitely don't make that much."

He chuckles and kisses me on the forehead. "You don't say? So here's my second condition, when we start taking home a hundred thousand annually I would like the conversation of the location of our home to be opened again."

I put my hands out to object but he doesn't let me speak yet. "I'm not saying that when we do make enough we *have* to move, I'm just asking that we talk and decide what's best for us, and possibly our family, at that point in time." As Will finishes his hands stop moving across my legs. He waits with bated breath while I mull over his points.

Will's conditions are incredibly logical and well thought out. I weigh his proposal with a quick pros and cons chart and come up thinking this is a sane thing to ask of your partner. When I finally answer him it's a resounding, "Yes."

Will pulls me to straddle his lap and wraps me in a bear hug. He yells happily into my hair, "Yes?"

I lean back and cup his cheeks in my hands. "Yes," and I capture his smile with a kiss.

We remain entwined with one another for a short lifetime. Will kisses me as if he's making up for lost time. Our tongues dance to the familiar rhythm of one another no trepidation to be found. My fingers twine through Will's hair as his hand grabs my ass possessively. He breaks our kiss and growls, "Mine."

My toes curl in response to his claim over me and I bite my bottom lip. I brace a hand against his chest and say a little breathlessly, "Before you go all domineering on me I need to know, why were you packing?"

His head tilts to the side like the adorable golden retriever he is on the inside. Well, with that blond hair maybe on the outside too.

He can't seem to remember so I clue him in, "Why is our bed covered in your clothing and a suitcase?"

I see the connection click in his mind. "Oh," he draws out. "We're going home in a few days babe. I wanted to see what I had clean and what laundry I need to do before we leave."

"Makes sense, but why are you home tonight? I thought you had a shift?"

He squeezes my ass one more time, reminding me that his hand still hasn't moved from its new favorite resting place. "Detective Welch came home tonight didn't she?" he teases me.

I squint my eyes at him, demanding an answer.

He rolls his eyes at my scrutiny. "If you must know, a coworker asked me to switch shifts with him. I figured it was a good idea since I'd finally figured out my feelings about staying in Oregon. Any other questions for me ma'am?"

I take a deep breath for what feels like the first time in weeks as all of Will's answers make sense. I shake my head as an idea sparks into my mind. "Only one, have we christened this room yet?"

Will's eyes darken with desire and his voice drops even lower, "I suddenly can't remember."

# Twenty-Two

# *Road Trip*

"Are you sure Toph is going to be okay while we're gone?" I ask Will as he pulls his car onto the I-5 South. Nine hundred and seventy-seven more miles to go.

He places a hand on my knee. "Babe, we haven't left her alone for ten days. Shona is going to come by and scoop her litter every other day. She'll be fine."

I sigh, "I guess. I just wish she could come with us, or that she had a friend. She must feel so lonely already."

I can feel Will roll his eyes at me. "We've been gone for four minutes. She may get a little sad, but we'll be back. You know taking her on the trip with us would be more stressful for her right?"

I cross my arms at his level-headed thinking. Who does he think he is knowing that our cat is going to be fine? I scoff, "Fine, but I blame all her cries of loneliness on you. You're the one who wouldn't let me pack her up and take her with us."

He forces one of my hands free of my annoyed pose and kisses the back of my hand. "If that helps you sleep at night I'll completely take the blame. But she'll be fine."

"Mr. Omniscient over here ladies and gentlemen."

"First off, I don't know what that means. Second, who are you talking to Nikki?" He asks while squeezing my knee.

I bat him off. "I'm talking to the ever present voices in my mind, they think I'm very entertaining." I deadpan.

Will looks at me quickly with bulging eyes. "How many voices are in there Nikki?"

"Shh, I won't tell him about all of you," I whisper to freak him out a bit more. "Just one or seventy-six. I usually lose count after chatting with Bethany, she *really* likes your hair."

"Nikki?"

I flick his bicep with my hand. "Oh calm down, would you? I always have an internal monologue going, like everybody else."

"Not like everybody else," he objects.

"Yes like everybody else. You know, how you think decisions through, or ask yourself if you're making the right choice? It's just me talking to myself, there aren't other personalities replying."

"I wish I could pull this car over and look at you straight on right now. Veronica, not everybody has conversations with themselves."

One of my eyebrows reaches for the sky as I ask him with a little concern, "You don't— You don't ask yourself questions?"

"Can't say that I do babe." He admits and pats my leg.

I stare off into the trees that line the side of the freeway and think about this. I could have sworn that everyone thought things through with themselves. How else would you make a decision? "Oh well," I break the silence. "I guess that's why I wanted a cat, so that you wouldn't learn how different I truly am."

Will laughs nervously at my joke and keeps his eyes on the road. A few minutes pass before he asks, "So what was that book you were listening to a few weeks ago?"

"I'm going to need more to go off of," I tell him as I tuck a strand of hair into my messy bun.

"All I really remember is that you were yelling at the book a lot. I think you said there were dragons too?"

I snap my fingers as that clue divulges the answer. "You mean *Fourth Wing*? Yeah, that was my book with dragons. It was fucking addictive."

"I guess if that's the one with dragons. Would you be willing to listen to it again?" He asks as he maneuvers our car down the road.

I pull out my phone and load it on my audio account. "Sure, but I'll probably end up falling asleep more since I've already heard it. I'm in the middle of listening to a vampire story called *The Serpent and the Wings of Night* right now."

Will suggests, "How about whoever is driving gets to decide what we listen to, and if the passenger needs to nap then the passenger gets to nap. We should be at my parents' by midnight so it's best to pace ourselves."

"Good thing I have a pillow and blanket close by then." I tease as I click on his book. Soon Will is learning about Basgiath War College and the rules of riders and dragons. I pay attention long enough to hear my favorite quote and then settle into a nice mid-morning nap as his passenger princess.

• ♥ • ♥ • ♥ • ♥ • ♥ •

"How was the drive yesterday sweetheart?" Marie asks me as I drag my feet to the dining room table at her house. I'm dressed in parent appropriate pajamas and I'm sure my hair is a disheveled mess. Will and I got here so late last night, really this morning, that his parents were already asleep. When I stirred from my sleep he was missing from the bed we were sharing.

I look past her in the kitchen and spy Will in front of a coffee maker. "It was better than I expected it to be actually. Can I have a cup please babe?"

He looks up at me and nods as his mother asks, "How so?"

I grin at her as I pull a chair out and sit down at the table. "Well, your son started reading a new book while he was driving and barely let me behind the wheel."

She pivots to Will and looks at him appraisingly. "What book was this? I don't remember you being an avid reader."

He scratches the back of his neck looking nervous under his mother's gaze. "Nikki's helped me realize that I like stories, my brain just doesn't do so well with words on paper. She's been letting me listen to her audiobooks when she's finished and I kind of love them."

"More than kind of Marie. He devours them. Out of a fifteen hour drive yesterday he only let me behind the wheel for three hours because he wanted to keep listening to his book but it got switched to mine if I was the one driving."

She closes the distance between her and Will with two strides and hugs him. "My baby boy learning to love reading. You'll have to tell me your favorite book the next time you're down and maybe I'll read it too."

That comment has me scratching my scalp nervously, I've been recommending faerie porn to her son. If he tells her about those books it could lead to an interesting conversation.

"If I read any that I think you'd like I'll text you the name, Mom," Will replies sweetly as he brings over a steaming cup of coffee to me. "Want to drink this on the patio? It's a bit chilly right now, but the coffee will probably be enough to warm us up."

I stand and follow him through the sliding glass door adjacent to his parents' kitchen. We walk past the wall that houses his childhood bedroom and round the corner to the rest of the patio. There's a large pool with a jacuzzi and a hill behind both that leads down to a small smattering of fruit trees Will's father tends to with pride. He calls out from beneath a Blood Orange tree when he sees us at a table next to the pool.

Will waves back to his dad as we sit down. "He'll probably come up when he's done taking care of the trees."

"Sounds good," I reply, too sleepy to care about anything more than coffee at this moment. I take a deep inhale of my medium roast and my eyes roll into the back of my head.

"Save that look for later when I get you to myself," Will taunts me with a wicked smirk over the brim of his cup.

I narrow my eyes at him and take a slurp of my nectar before deigning him with a response. "You won't be making my eyes do that until we're back in Oregon."

"But—"

"We are not having any funny business at your parents' house. Especially since we're staying in your sister's former bedroom." I scold him.

He looks out at the view from his parent's yard contemplatively.

Before he comes up with a retort, Paul makes his way over to us from his miniature grove. "Just getting the trees ready for the party tonight."

"Yes Dad, because when people come over here for a pool party and BBQ they also plan on checking out your trees." Will jabs at his dad.

"Do you hear the disrespect, Nikki? After I slave over his Blood Orange tree for months while you're up in Oregon he dares to tease me?"

I smile at him, not knowing how I should play this. Instead of coming up with a response, I take another swig of coffee and wait to see who has something to say first.

"I'm so sorry dear Father, can you ever please forgive me?" Will teases. "But really, are the trees looking good?"

"Come take a look for yourself, son." Paul motions for his son to follow and strolls back to the copse.

Will hops up and kisses me on the forehead before following after his dad. We spend most of the afternoon like that. I sneak away to the front room for a little and dive into the thick paperback that I brought with me.

"Did I leave you alone for too long?" Will's voice asks, pulling me from the European mafia romance world. When I draw my eyes from the page I see Will leaning against the wall with his legs crossed at the ankles and his arms folded over his chest. Either he looks good enough to eat, or the salacious Benny Butcher is getting into my head.

I shake those thoughts from my mind and clear my throat before replying. "Just long enough to get a decent way through this. I might need to run to the bookstore before we leave. I thought this one would be enough for the trip but I'm already a hundred pages into it."

Will saunters across the room and brackets his arms around me on the couch. "Is that so?" Then he nips at my bottom lip.

I crinkle my nose at him. "Well, you need to shower no matter what we're about to do next."

He doesn't leave my personal space. "I thought you liked this manly musk?" He waggles an eyebrow at me and flexes his arms.

I let out a disgusted giggle and try to push him back. "No, I like watching the activities it takes to create the manly musk, not actually smelling it."

He doesn't budge an inch.

I hide my nose in my book, hoping its scent will overpower his odor.

Will leans in a little closer, taunting me with the horror of his approaching armpits before drawing back and standing. "Well, guests will be here in about two hours, so we better shower and get ready." He holds out a hand to help me off the couch.

My nose is still scrunched up as I shake my head at him. "You go, I'll finish this chapter and then start getting ready."

"We both know you're going to get lost in that book until I come back to get you," he chides.

I pivot in my seat and lay down on the couch, propped up on my elbows looking up at him. "Then I guess it's a good thing it only takes me forty-five minutes to get ready isn't it? You can come back when you smell better."

Will shakes his head as he exits the room and leaves me to my reading.

Two hours later, we're both ready and waiting for the rest of the family to show up for the pool party and BBQ. Meghan and Thomas are the first to show up to help with the cooking and grilling. Stefan and Will's younger sister Kacey show up soon after that and we all settle into catching up. Within an hour, we're on the patio surrounded by Will's family. His Aunt Sherry and Uncle Richard are the natural life of the party, sharing stories of their past. Grandma Zukauskas is sitting quietly on the patio, taking in the surroundings and listening to the conversations floating around. In a group comprised of so many outgoing people, it's easy for me to follow her lead and sit back and enjoy the entertainment.

"So it's April Fool's Day and I get a call from my other sister, Carly!" Will's dad shouts from his station at the grill. "She tries telling me that she's been arrested! Jokes on her, I don't believe anything anyone says on April Fool's Day."

Aunt Sherry interrupts him, "You're leaving out the best part Paul! When she called to tell you she'd been arrested you hung up on her."

Paul flips one of the burger patties and turns to face us all. "I'm not leaving that out Sherry, I just hadn't gotten to it yet. Drink your wine and let me tell this story."

I snicker, watching Will's dad argue with his sister. It's good to know that even when we're fifty, sibling rivalries stand strong.

"As I was saying before my lovely sister tried to assist, I hung up on her. But then she called back!" Thomas takes the tongs out of Paul's hands and takes over grilling for him. Paul strolls across his backyard and keeps regaling his captive audience with his story. "This time when she called back she got all the other gals that were arrested to shout down the line with her, 'We're being held at Las Calinas.'"

I look to Grandma and ask her in hushed tones, "Did this actually happen?"

Will must have overheard me because he pats my knee and whispers, "Shhh, or you'll miss the best part."

"I just assumed she got a bunch of her girlfriends in on the prank so I hung up again!" Paul laughs at himself before continuing. "The next day Sherry calls me up all pissed that I didn't believe Carly when she called me the day before. I didn't believe her either until she showed me the receipt of paying our sister's bail."

"Was Carly upset with you?" I ask Paul.

He shrugs and takes a swig of his drink. "Doesn't matter. Everyone should know that I don't believe anything anybody says when it's April Fool's Day." Then he turns and walks back to his position at the helm of the grill.

Aunt Sherry looks at me seriously, "We probably damaged his sense of humor as kids. He would always fall for our pranks on April 1st, so now as an adult, he's as stubborn as a mule."

Will and I softly chuckle at his father's expense.

"What smack are you talking Sher? Don't go polluting Nikki's brain with your lies, she still likes me!" Paul calls from the grill.

I smile at Will and put his father at ease. "No worries Paul, Aunt Sherry is just providing depth to your personality."

Will pulls my hand into his and beckons me away from his family. We round the pool and stand with our back to the group as we look over the trees. I take in the view of the desert shrubbery lining the mountainside across from us. Everything is brown and sad here, even in the heart of winter.

Will's arm wraps around my lower back and he pulls me into a side hug. "Sorry about them, the Zukauskas side of the family can be a bit intense."

He kisses my temple gently before I reply. "I don't mind one bit. They're fun." I smile up at him, showing that I really am enjoying myself. "Your family is wonderful babe."

We pivot and face one another. "I'm glad you're enjoying being with them, hopefully we can do this every time we come back home."

I slide under his arms and hug his torso. "I'd like that."

We rejoin his family as they erupt into laughter at something Kacey said. I sit back down and enjoy the family dynamic that unfolds around me. It's like a well rehearsed routine, something they've been doing together for years. Thomas and Paul tag team the grill together as Meghan and Marie take care of all the other fixings in the kitchen. Aunt Sherry provides the bulk of the amusing stories and Uncle Richard is her steady copilot, providing punch lines and smaller details as needed. Kacey flutters around happily from one person to the next, talking with all of us in turn. Grandma is the matriarch, looking over a family that only exists because of her. They all dote upon her, making sure she has drinks, enough jackets, and anything else she might need.

I'm so engrossed in another story that I don't notice Paul and Thomas take the meat off the grill. Soon Meghan is calling through the kitchen window, "Dinner's ready!"

Stefan is the first in line followed closely by Kacey. Will and I join in after. There are burgers, hot dogs, vegetarian chili, and too many sides to list splayed out on the kitchen island. I grab a plate hungrily and have to remind my eyes about the size of my stomach so I don't take too much food.

Will grabs us two dirty Shirley's and we head back out to the patio. I dig into my plate happily and let Will field most of the questions his family directs at us. The smoky grilled Mushroom Swiss Burger melts in my mouth as soon as I take a bite. It's all I can do to hold back a moan. No wonder Will is a good cook, he comes from a whole family of cooks.

Aunt Sherry asks us how Oregon is going and we tell her all about the jobs we've been doing and how Will starts a new one as a lot porter at a car dealership when we get back from vacation. Stefan asks us about Toph and we show him pictures. All in all, it's a wonderful evening of revelry and laughter fueled by good food, and a bit of alcohol.

Sometime after our dinner has been devoured I hear Stefan shout, "Cannonball!" before sending a tidal wave splashing over the edge of the pool.

Aunt Sherry laughs and says, "I think that's our cue kids. Some of us have work tomorrow." She starts making her rounds of goodbyes with Uncle Richard and leaves Will and me for last. She bends down, hugs Will's shoulders, and pats one of mine. "Well kiddos, it was great seeing you. I bet the next time we catch up will be at your wedding. Don't be strangers!" With that, she and Uncle Richard depart for the evening.

Before I have too much time to think on her weird parting remark, Stefan decides to pull a Little Mermaid moment as he gets out of the pool. He slicks back his hair and balances on the concrete edge on his hips, making a spectacle of himself. Not that I'd expect anything less from the guy. I avert my eyes with a hand to my forehead and focus on Will.

He's rolling his eyes at his best friend and chuckling. "Man cover up, nobody wants to have their eyes poked out with your cold nipples."

I peek between two fingers and see Stefan clamber out of the pool. Will throws his towel at him. Instead of wrapping his towel around his waist, like every other guy I've ever seen wearing a towel, he tucks it under his armpits and covers up his nipples. "Better?" He cheekily sasses, popping a hand on his hip.

"Yes, thank you." Will deadpans.

"So am I the only one swimming tonight or is someone else going to join me?"

"I was just getting changed," Kacey says as she rounds the corner covered in a towel.

Will looks at me questioningly and I nod my head in agreement. We scurry away to our room for the trip and change into our suits. When we make it back to the patio, the true adults are inside socializing as they work together to clean up leftovers.

"Have fun, you remember how to work the jacuzzi right Will?" Paul asks as we walk past.

"Dad, I've been gone for six months. Even if it had been six years I think I'd still remember."

Paul raises his hands and bows his head in innocence. "Sorry kiddo, you go have fun with your friends."

"Thank you for such a wonderful dinner everybody," I offer to the room at large.

Meghan and Thomas give me a polite smile and Marie replies, "Glad you enjoyed it, sweetie. We're just glad to have you both back in town right now."

Will's hand finds my lower back and he guides us through the sliding glass door and back to the pool. He takes the towel I was using to cover up in front of his parents and drapes it over the back of a chair. "Pool or jacuzzi?" He asks.

"Jacuzzi, please. Not sure I want to fully submerge right now."

He jerks his head to the side, motioning toward Stefan, "Don't let him hear that. It will become his mission. Go wait by the hot tub while I get everything turned on for it."

"Sounds good." I grin up at him as he gives me a quick kiss and disappears behind the back of the house.

"So what time do you want to head out tomorrow?" Stefan calls from the shallow end of the pool.

I walk up the two stairs that lead to the hot tub and step in just to my knees as I reply, "I don't know. We don't really have plans. Are you working tomorrow?"

He ducks under the water and pushes off the side of the pool. I watch him swim underneath the surface to the edge of the jacuzzi. He pops up and returns to our conversation easily as he gets out of the pool and joins me. "Yeah, but I'm off at two. So any time after that works for me."

"How about just let us know when you're on your way over?" Will calls from behind the house. A few seconds after his appearance the lights to the pool turn on and bubbles start pumping around the jacuzzi. "It should heat up pretty quickly. I set it for one hundred, but if it gets too hot just let me know." He hops into the water and pushes the air bubbles from his trunks once he's submerged.

I slide onto the bench next to him and rest my head on his shoulder. Kacey joins in shortly after and sits on the same half as Stefan, but she keeps a healthy distance from him all the same. We spend the next hour or so catching up on life. As the evening sun fades into a starry night, I can't help but think how lucky I am to have a life like this.

Twenty-Three

# *Finding Forever*

"Shoot, I left my belt for this outfit in Oregon," I tell Will the next morning.

He quirks his lips to the side. "Would a regular belt work with it?"

I exhale loudly, "Yeah, it just won't be as cute." I trudge across the room to the belt that Will is holding out for me to borrow. Once I slide it through the loops I look at myself in the mirror. It's definitely bulkier than what I originally wanted, but that's what happens when you forget accessories I guess. I've got on a soft grey three quarter sleeve shirt paired with some dark burgundy capris. I finished off the look with some black Chucks. My hair is wavy and free, just how I like it. "Are you sure you don't want to come with us?"

"To get my nails done? Nah. You and Kacey go have some fun. I'll just help my Dad in the yard again probably." His words come out slightly mumbled as he pulls a shirt on. It's a shame that he has to constantly cover those muscles. I find myself biting my bottom lip as I ogle his body. *Damn, the Twisted Sister's writing is getting me secondhand horny again!* I need to remember the next time we go on vacation with family the only books allowed must be rated G!

I have to look away from this fabulous man's body to form a coherent sentence. "Okay, I'll call you when we're done?"

He opens the guest room door and waits for me to cross the threshold first. As I walk past he swats my ass. "Sounds good."

Kacey looks up from her phone at the dining room table. "Ready?" She greets me with a huge smile.

I adjust the strap of my purse on my shoulder nervously and do my best to plaster on a halfway genuine smile. "Do you have somewhere specific in mind?"

"Yeah, I just finished booking us spots online. Our appointment is for noon so I figure we can go get some coffee and then head over."

I let out a relieved breath. I am very capable of getting coffee. "Great, who's driving?"

She jingles her keys and stands from the table. "Let's go. Will, I'll have her back by two p.m." With that, she heads around the corner to the front door and I'm left alone with Will.

"What manicure takes two hours?" I ask him as he slowly walks me to the door, out of earshot of his sister.

He raises his shoulders in a noncommittal response. "It's San Diego, who knows. But I'll see you later and we can head to Balboa Park with Stefan."

I stop us and wrap my arms around his neck. "Why are we going there again?"

His hands naturally find their way to rest on my waist. "I guess there's some new science exhibit he wants to check out and asked if we wanted to join. Hope you don't mind that I agreed for the both of us."

"No, it's cool, if you two don't mind me tagging along. I'd only be sitting here reading. I can do that anywhere."

"True, if the exhibit bores you enough you can even download a book to your phone if you really want."

I perch on my tiptoes and kiss him. "Now you're talking."

Will wraps his arms tighter around me and he closes the gap between our bodies with a tight embrace. He says into my hair, "Have fun babe. I'll see you in a little bit. If you're not sure what to talk about with Kacey just ask her about her camera and what she's photographed most recently."

I separate from him and open the front door. "Thanks," I say as I pull it closed behind me and head out into the blinding Southern California sunshine.

I shouldn't have been worried about hanging out with Kacey. She's naturally chatty and is skilled at coming up with conversation topics. By the time we've gone to a coffee shop and arrived at the salon, she's completely updated about the new friends I've made at school and everything else going on with living in Eugene. We get out of her old school Beetle, trunk in the front and everything, and head into the nail salon. She checks us in at the counter and tells me that we should pick the color we want off the wall that's out here. I peruse the options, not feeling a need to talk while looking for a color that will work well with the outfits I've packed for the remainder of our trip. I scan the colors and find myself drawn to the darker shades of brick red, black, and dark grey.

"Ohhh, you should totally do a grey and black combo set," Kacey says over my shoulder.

"You think? Which nails which?" I ask as I pull both colors from the shelves.

Kacey pops her hip and tucks her thumb under her chin as she thinks. "How about black on the ring finger and middle finger?"

"I like that." I hold onto the two colors and watch as she picks out a dark purple.

"Never let them see your next move am I right?" She says as she makes her final choice.

"Kacey!" A manicurist walks out and calls. We both pivot and follow her to the back of the shop where two tables are set up side by side. The left side of the shop is lined with pedicure recliners and basins for people's feet to go into. On the right side, there is a row of manicure stations. There are probably eight of each in the entire salon. It's a long and narrow shop. Once we reach the back, the natural lighting from the front windows is left behind and our entire space is illuminated by fluorescent lighting. Kacey has me sit to the left of her and we both put our purses down next to the stations. My manicurist gestures for me to put my coffee on a coaster on the table and I follow her directions. Once seated, she informs me her name is Eva. I inform Eva of which nails I'd like which color and she starts soaking my fingers.

I relax and prepare for an hour of pampering. Kacey quickly interrupts these plans with a jarring question. "So what do you hope your wedding is like someday?"

My eyes pop open, I didn't realize they'd closed, and I stare at her with a gaping mouth.

She levels me with a single glare. "Oh calm down. I'm not saying you're getting married tomorrow. But you two did move across the country together, I assume someday you'll officially have the title of my sister-in-law. I'm just curious if you've thought much about it before?"

I roll my shoulders, trying to find the peace I was experiencing a matter of seconds ago. *Why is Kacey putting me on the spot like this right now?* "I don't know." My voice comes out a bit edgy. "I've never thought about it before."

"When you were a little girl you didn't dream of what your wedding would look like one day?" She pushes.

I shake my head. "No, when I was little I didn't even think about being married."

Kacey giggles, "Of course, you didn't think of being married. That's a mature daydream. You didn't think about a big poofy dress, or what color your friends would wear? What kind of flowers you'd want?"

"Not really no, I thought about when *Inspector Gadget* would be on again."

She cracks her neck, "No matter. Let's daydream now. What do you think you want at your wedding?"

I purse my lips as it sinks in that she's not going to let this topic drop. "I guess one thing I know for certain is I don't want to wear white."

Kacey's eyes almost fall from their sockets with how wide they go. "You what?"

I steel myself and flatten my face. "I don't wear white. You've never seen me in white. Why would I change that for a wedding dress? Besides finding a colorful dress will be a lot cheaper than a wedding dress."

She challenges me, "What about tradition?"

I scoff. "You mean the tradition of wealthy people spending money on a dress they'll only wear one day. And then how they added insult to injury by making it white because the working class could never afford white? Or the tradition of a bride being pure and chaste? Are my parents expected to have a dowry in exchange for Will taking on the burden of my existence?" I finish and look forward at the wall behind Eva. Out of my peripherals I see her and Kacey's nail tech exchange looks before they put their heads down and don't interject into the discussion.

Softly Kacey asks hesitantly, "This isn't some fleeting opinion. You've thought about it before haven't you?"

"Apparently yes, because the only white thing at my wedding will be our cake."

"Hey, no worries. I was just surprised is all. So what color are you thinking then?"

I look toward her and Kacey's half smile has me warming up to her a little bit. "I honestly don't care, just not white. My mom asked me not to choose black when I was in high school so I guess I can honor that wish too."

"Do you have any idea what silhouette you want?"

"One that looks good on my body? Look, I'm sorry but I really don't know." I say starting to feel exasperated.

She pauses and stares off into the blank wall. "Okay, how about this? Do you want a big or small wedding?"

That one I can finally answer. "I think it would be pretty big, I want all of my family and friends to be able to attend, and Will's people too of course."

"So four or five hundred probably?"

My jaw does hit the floor this time. "No, I don't even know that many people, let alone want them all at our wedding. I was thinking like between fifty and a hundred."

Kacey laughs lightly. "You really haven't looked into weddings then. That's considered a small wedding Nikki."

"Well, shit." I sigh.

"It's okay, how about this. Once Will proposes, tomorrow or a year from now, get on Pinterest and make a vision board. That way you can see what other people have done and Meghan, my mom, and I can help you plan everything. Does that work?"

I chew on my lip and think her idea over. "Yeah, I think so. I don't know the first thing about planning a big wedding."

She shakes her head at me. "That's what sister-in-laws are for! Now, how about babies? Have you thought about those?"

Oh no. Hell no. I mask my face with a smile and tell Kacey. "I like that we're talking and getting to know each other better. But if you don't get your head out of my uterus we will have a problem. How about this? How's that new camera you got working out for you? Get any good pics in L.A. recently?"

Thankfully Kacey picks up on my direct threat and changes to talking about her time in L.A. and how things are going at FIDM for her. It's a completely different college experience than Will and I are having so I'm enraptured easily. When our nails are done and we arrive back at her parents' house, I find myself a little bummed we won't be hanging out anymore today.

We head inside the house and when we round the corner to enter the living room I see Stefan has already arrived and is playing a video game with Will on the T.V.

"Hey Nikki!" Stefan calls out as we make noise to announce our arrival. "Just let me kick your man's butt and then we can head out. Shouldn't take more than a minute or two."

The two of them click furiously at the controllers with whatever game they're playing. It's got a lot of flashing lights, a fighting ring, and characters from the Mario Brothers I think.

"Nah, babe. I'm going to kick his ass and then we can go. I just..." his train of thought pauses as he pushes on more buttons. "One." A few more clicks happen. "Second."

"No!" Stefan wails as the screen freezes.

"Game set." Is announced from the T.V. speakers and the image changes to two characters clapping.

I glance at my boyfriend and ask, "Does that mean you just won then?"

He puts the controller down on the couch and strolls toward me. "Sure does babe." He dips me in an elaborate kiss.

"Gross, get a room you two." Kacey fake vomits in response to our public display of affection.

Will rights me but doesn't let go which is good because, with that sudden dip, I'm feeling a little light headed. "Did you have fun?" he asks.

I nod at him and hold up my perfectly manicured nails for him to swoon over.

"Ooh, ahh, very nice babe." He kisses my temple and keeps me tucked in close. "You driving man?"

"Yeah! Let me just turn the T.V. off."

The three of us head out the front door and walk to Stefan's car. "Nikki, you should take shotgun. I don't want you getting carsick with this one's crazy driving." Will offers as he opens the passenger door for me.

I hop on in and buckle up. As Will is about to close the door he pats down his pocket. "Shoot, forgot my wallet. I'll be right back." He clicks my door shut as Stefan gets in and turns on his car.

"Disney tunes?" Stefan asks me as he plugs his phone in.

"You know every song ever made by them don't you?" I tease him.

Stefan shines his knuckles on his shirt and blows on them with an arrogance that might be authentic as he retorts. "What can I say, only a true Disney fan does."

I roll my eyes at Will's ostentatious best friend. "So when do I get an invite to your fancy Club 33 then?"

Will returns and hops in the back seat behind me. Once he's buckled up he claps Stefan on the shoulder and we pull away from the curb.

"I don't know Nikki. Will, how long did I know you before you got to go to Club 33?" Stefan asks.

Will taps his fingers on the shoulder of my seat as he thinks. "Geeze, probably six years. You didn't let me join you until right before we moved I think."

"Alright, Nikki there's your answer."

I look at Stefan. "We have to be friends for six years before I get an invite?"

He laughs, "No. That would be too easy. Will is one of my best friends. If it took him six years then take that time, cut it in half, add those together and you get?"

"Nine?"

"Bingo!" Stefan exclaims with a finger pointed into the air. "Once you've been in Will's life for nine years I'll ask my mom if I can get you two in for a meal at The Club."

I fold my arms incredulously. "Is this a rule you and your family have?"

He merges us into freeway traffic before answering me. "Nope. Created it just now. Let me know when nine years have passed and we can all go have a good time."

"You're a dick dude," Will tells him.

This makes Stefan's face break into a huge smile. "Yeah, but you both love me." He cranks up the volume to "You're Welcome" from *Moana* and belts out every line as we near downtown San Diego.

As Stefan guides his car through the traffic he enters a parking lot that I don't recognize as the entrance for Balboa Park. "What are we doing here?"

"Oh, I parked on the West end of the park. This is where the locals know to go. The main lots are just tourist traps and asking to get into a fender bender." Stefan replies smugly.

"We just need to walk across Suicide Bridge to get to the park right?" Will asks from the backseat as Stefan pulls into a vacant spot.

We all unbuckle and get out before Stefan responds. "Yeah, we can walk through the park. It's technically the long way away from the science museum, but I figured your pasty Oregon skin could use some sun exposure."

Will moves to punch his best friend in the gut but Stefan blocks it. Will switches up his tactic and pulls Stefan under his arm. "Think you're funny do ya?" He asks as he steers them a little forcefully across the parking lot to the walking path.

I follow behind and watch as Will's grip lightens and the two walk ahead of me across the bridge. Will is on the inside closest to traffic and Stefan drags his hand along the ledge that separates us from a death fall to the freeway below. Stefan wasn't wrong, the feeling of the California sun on my skin is invigorating. I follow behind the boys with my head tilted back so that I can get maximum warmth across my face. It's a slightly cloudy day with a light breeze. We haven't seen the sun this much in Oregon since I had lunch with the girls. It's been storming non-stop since.

When the three of us clear the bridge, Will lets go of Stefan and falls back to walk hand in hand with me. We wander through the garden with Stefan and he takes a few pictures of us in front of a water feature. The park isn't very crowded, most likely due to it being a weekday, over a week before Christmas. We don't encounter many other people except for the locals who are using the ample space for their exercise routines. We walk past an art museum that's closed for construction according to its sign and then to our left I see it.

The most beautiful part of the park.

The lily pond, and beyond it, the nature conservatory. It's a gorgeous pond that's littered with gigantic lily pads. When you walk through here at night the frogs and crickets provide a natural melodic symphony. "Stefan, can you get a pic of Will and me in front of the pond?" I ask as I take my phone from my pocket and hand it to him.

"Sure thing Nikki." He takes it and takes back a few steps.

Will pulls us hip to hip and wraps his hand around my waist. We smile into the camera and Stefan takes the shot.

He gives us a thumbs up but doesn't lower the phone.

My brows furrow in confusion. I take a step away from Will to get my phone back when I feel his presence change.

Stefan's face has a huge grin plastered across it from ear to ear.

"Ugh, are you taking another selfie on my phone?" I demand of him.

"Shh, you'll ruin the moment." He teases me and then goes back to smiling and tapping on my phone.

I turn to Will to ask for assistance with his annoying best friend but when I look at him he's no longer standing.

He's kneeling.

He's down on one knee.

He's smiling up at me holding out a ring.

My hands fly to my mouth in shock. "What!" I squeal with disbelief.

Will reaches out a hand and takes one of mine. "Nikki, Veronica Welch. I know we haven't been together very long."

"Yeah babe, like only a year and a half!" I interrupt him.

He shakes his head and smiles up at me. "This wouldn't be a proposal between the two of us if you didn't interrupt me at least once. But babe, can you please let me get this out?"

I suck my lips between my teeth to hold onto all the words I want to shout, and nod for him to continue.

"Veronica, we haven't been together very long, but every moment of it has been wonderful. I knew when I chose to move to Oregon with you that I was going to ask you to marry me one day. I've known for a while now that you're it for me. I love you, I know you love me, even if you're afraid to say it aloud. You show me how much you love me when you buy salt and vinegar chips for me even though you hate them. You show me you love me when you tuck me in deeper into our bed when you think I'm still asleep. You show me how much you love me when you leave a light on in the living room so I don't come home to a dark apartment. You show me how much you love me with everything you do for us every day. So, babe, it's my turn to do the same. This ring is more than asking you to marry me, it's a physical representation of my dedication to us and our relationship. I'm here for you no matter what. I'm yours forever. I love you, Veronica Welch. Will you marry me?"

I stand there speechless.

Will is asking me to marry him.

My nails are done. I look cute. His friend is getting a picture. He did all the things and *he's asking me to marry him*.

He's holding a ring that's so much better than anything I'd dreamed up before. Some swirls allude to an infinity symbol without being too on the nose. Alternating emeralds and peridot, our two birthstones. In a silver band just like I prefer. It's absolutely perfect and glistening in the sunshine before me. Will looks up at me with a hopeful smile on his face as I find my words.

"Will, I—" I force myself to take a breath. This is it. I nod my head and smile down at my knight in a beige Camry as I tell him what he's waited so patiently to hear. "Will, I love you."

# Author's Note

Thank you to anyone who took a chance and read my second novel! The Pacific Coast Romance Trilogy began in 2023 when I had an undiagnosed, invisible, chronic illness. The creation of this love story gave me something to look forward to on the darkest of days. Nikki and Will spoke to me every day as I was writing their love story. Will has proposed, but is Nikki ready for that? Check out the final part of their love adventure in Delightful Deviations, coming September 2024.

To anyone out there dreaming of becoming an author. Do it. One day, one page, one word at a time. I took this insane dream I had and forced it to become a reality. Very little was easy. A lot of people told me I was crazy. I wanted to give up a thousand times but found a reason to keep going a thousand and one. Holy, fucking, shit... I did it, and so can you.

# Acknowledgements

To my readers. Wow, I can't believe I'm typing these sentences. Thank you for picking up my book and choosing to try out a new, independent author. Your purchase literally funds my future books and I sincerely hope that Nikki and Will provided whatever comfort, enjoyment, or escapism you were looking for.

Kendall and Wendy, thanks for listening to me drone on and on about my novels whenever we meet up. You two are gems, and I can't wait for you to read book three and get to know the characters inspired by you. Manny and Adrian, thanks for being cool with me showing your wives my unhinged smut and commissioned art. They're spicy!

Erica and Nancy, you saw me come to work and persevere through the hardest year. I don't know how we survived, there were days when our students seemed to literally be feral. You two are the best teaching partners a girl could ask for!

Nancy S. thank you for being willing to step in as my editor last minute! I appreciate all your insight and ideas for making my story stronger.

To the people who celebrated me in the sweetest way possible with *Logical Love*. Cynthia, Nancy, Erica, Erin, Callum, Alea, Kirsten, Kaitlin, Amy, JJ, Caiti (even though she had to stay home with the boys), Grace, Sarah, Mike, Jill, Tamie, Haley, Meghan, and Kaleigh, thank you so much for showing up to celebrate my debut novel. The support from all of your presence was amazing. It motivated me to keep going. Thank you.

Sarah, Tamie, Haley, Erica, Dawn, Becca, Olivia, and Summer. Your messages when you were reading my book are saved to my phone. Thank you for your words of kindness, support, and love for *Logical Love*. I hope you enjoyed *Finding Forever* just as much!

To one of my former best friends who will probably never read this. You inspired Tipp. Thank you for the laughs and memories. I'll forever wish the best for you in life.

All of my Beta readers Kendall, Wendy, Haley, and Dawn I'll never be able to thank you enough! Your commentary was hilarious. I save those pages, they bring me so much joy knowing exactly which parts you enjoyed, cheered, and laughed along with Nikki and Will. Dawn, you helped me with the Jambalaya scene. Haley, I learned wayyy too much about you, but thanks for critiquing my smut! Kendall, your attention to detail is fabulous. Wendy, is your red pen out of ink yet? Girl, thanks for all the edits! These books wouldn't be the same without your input and critiques.

My partner, Mike, I don't know how many times you came into my writing cave and had to feed me. Your memory of my body's needs on those 10,000 word days is what kept me alive. Will only scratches the surface of the multitude of ways you love me each and every day. Love you, thanks for filling my water.

Lastly, to the fur babies of our household. They kept me company as I would hide away and write, they stuck their butts on the keyboard causing way too many typos, and one is sitting between my arms as I type this. Love you Korra and Shadow, you'll forever be ridiculous.

# About the Author

Kate Pelczar is from a small town in Southern California, but now she lives in rural, central, Oregon. By day she is an elementary school teacher, by night she writes as much as she can. When she's not teaching or writing, Kate enjoys reading fantasy and romance novels, playing board games with her husband, and cuddling their fur babies. To find the latest news about upcoming books you can follow her on TikTok @katepelczar or Instagram @kate_pelczar.

Made in the USA
Middletown, DE
17 October 2024